What People Are Saying
About *The Last Fall*

"Jason Blevins has created a masterpiece of Christian fiction—**an exciting, suspenseful, and heartwarming story of redemption** that can't be put down before the amazing finish. This book should be at the top of every must-read list, for believers and skeptics alike!"
—**LARKIN SPIVEY**, Lt. Col. U. S. Marine Corps (ret), Military historian, speaker, and author of *God in the Trenches, Miracles of the American Revolution, Battlefields & Blessings: Stories of Faith and Courage from World War II* (2009 Silver Medal Winner-Military Writers Society of America /First Place 2009 Branson Stars & Flags Book Award)

"What **a delightful read!** I read the book in two sittings—I couldn't put it down and even forgot to eat supper."
—**PROFESSOR KEITH DRURY,** author and Associate Professor, Indiana Wesleyan University

"*The Last Fall* is a masterpiece. Jay Blevins' story of a successful but narcissistic trial attorney's response to terminal cancer **reveals the timeless truth that life is measured in the quality of our relationships and the gift of divine grace.** As a cancer survivor myself, I can attest to how a diagnosis with a life-threatening disease provides a mirror to the soul and reminds us that we are only guaranteed today, not tomorrow."
—**ROBERT CHRISTOPHER BROWN**, Licensed Professional Counselor and author *of Coming to Terms with the Potter*

"*The Last Fall* brought tears to my eyes. The story is **vivid, poignant, yet full of hope** when it appears all hope is lost. I thought about my own family and the importance of cherishing and nurturing relationships. I read it in one day!"
—**SHERILL SYLVERTOOTH**, Senior Consultant, McLean, VA

"In **a captivating true-to-life scenario,** Jay illustrates the deep, soul-wrenching self-examination every man and woman must face to find true peace and healing. *The Last Fall* captures the essence of the phrase, 'the ground is level at the foot of the cross.' Each page masterfully shows that God's grace is sufficient for the least among us—even lawyers!"

—**CALEB A. KERSHNER, ESQ,** Of Counsel with Simms Showers Law, LLP, Leesburg, VA; Former Assistant Commonwealth of Virginia Attorney; Former Director of Federal Relations and Lobbyist for Home School Legal Defense Association and the National Center for Home Education

"The Last Fall tells **one man's story of personal and spiritual redemption.** Through Eric Stratton's tale, author Jay Blevins suggests the importance of personal responsibility, empathy for others, and, most importantly, the forgiveness that exists for all of us sinners."

—**TRISH PERRY,** author of *The Perfect Blend, Sunset Beach*, and other inspirational novels

"I was drawn in and captivated from the very beginning and as the story unfolded revealing twists and turns along the way. Truly **a "feel-good" book that also challenges you to take a look at the importance of every decision.** Such a great confirmation of the goodness of God's Master Plan!

—**THERESA MILLS,** Motivational/Inspirational Speaker, On-Air Personality for Positive Hits 89.9 and 90.5 WPER

"I thoroughly enjoyed reading this gem of a book! Although I received a Catholic elementary and college education, **it wasn't until I read this book that I fully understood what God's grace is.** This book has given me a better understanding of God's unconditional love. In addition, I have made several attempts to reconnect with friends I grew up with and had not seen in over thirty-five years. We have a reunion planned at Cape Cod this summer. I hope others will enjoy this book as I have…and I hope these wonderful surprises continue!"

—**EILEEN CUTRONA,** Intel Analyst, Burke, VA

"The Last Fall was **hard to put down**, and I am looking forward to sharing it with my friends. I was entertained throughout. This story shows we're all here for a purpose,"
—**OFFICER CRAIG CAMPBELL,** Police Officer, Greer, South Carolina

"An interesting read that **beautifully summarized the brevity of life.**"
—**PASTOR GARY HAMRICK,** Senior Pastor of Cornerstone Chapel, Leesburg, VA

"It's nice to see a book come out that envelops 'free will' instead of blaming society for the wrongs one commits. The story is diverse, but **gets the point across that we are all here for a purpose.**"
—**JENN WALCHLI,** Analyst, Baltimore, MD

"Our Father's golden reassurance to work good things from bad things (Rom. 8:28) is fulfilled in **soul healing and redemption** for all His kids in *The Last Fall.* His gracious attentiveness and the loving encouragement of others lifts our hearts as we are riveted to this story of our Father at work. Read it and luxuriate in His love!"
—**SUE BULLARD,** Elementary School Teacher, Sterling, VA

The LAST FALL

The LAST FALL

JAY BLEVINS

Irv,
Please enjoy this
gift from Monica.
Best wishes, and
God bless you.

JBl

12/18/10

OAKTARA

WATERFORD, VIRGINIA

The Last Fall

Published in the U.S. by:
OakTara Publishers
P.O. Box 8
Waterford, VA 20197

Visit OakTara at
www.oaktara.com

Cover design by Muses9Design
Cover image © iStockphoto.com/inakiantonana

Scripture taken from the HOLY BIBLE, NEW INTERNATIONAL VERSION®. NIV®. Copyright © 1973, 1978, 1984 by International Bible Society. Used by permission of Zondervan. All rights reserved.

ISBN: 978-1-60290-240-4

The Last Fall is a work of fiction. References to real people, events, establishments, organizations, or locales are intended only to provide a sense of authenticity and are used fictitiously. All other characters, incidents, and dialogue are drawn from the author's imagination.

⌘ ⌘ ⌘

This book is dedicated
to Holly, with love.

As we continue this journey together,
I can't wait to see where the road takes us.

Acknowledgments

One of the important lessons I learned in this endeavor is that true success is a mix of faith, hard work, and a strong support system. My eternal thanks go to the following people, who made this book possible.

Holly, I'm blessed because you always believed in me and had the courage to tell me the truth. You're still the one.

Mom, thank you for strong examples of true love, sacrifice, faith, and hard work. Dad, you made up for lost time and introduced me to relic hunting, the outdoors, and oh yeah, our heavenly Father.

To Lee Blevins, for your undying support, your inspirational art, and for always having my back.

Danny Trevors, you were the first to finish. Thanks for your early encouragement and support. I knew if I could keep your attention, I was golden.

To my support team; Kevin Hancock, Travis Barber, Michael Perozich, and Craig Campbell—thanks for holding up my arms, dreaming with me, and for praying without ceasing.

Thanks to the following people—you read early copies of the manuscript and provided invaluable input and some unforgettable endorsements: Dr. Keith Drury, Rob Brown, Eileen "Shirley" Cutrona, Pastor Gary Hamrick, Jen Walchli, Barbara Blevins, Dr. Bud Bence, Sherill Sylvertooth, Katie Casey, Melissa Steinke, Kristin Chan, Sue Bullard, Tasha Kegel, Larkin Spivey, Trish Perry, Caleb Kershner, and Theresa Mills. Thanks, Kelly Sprague, for your input and early editing.

Thank you, Jerry Jenkins, for taking a few minutes to give guidance to a dreamer.

Deron Blevins, for your technical assistance.

Thanks to Ellie, Samuel, and Evie—you make it all worthwhile.

Thanks to Jeff Nesbit and Ramona Tucker—you've made a dream come true.

And last, but certainly not least, where would I have been without your friendship and guidance Chelsey Beyah…'nuff said!

Prologue

Twilight shimmered through windblown branches as Eric Stratton experienced his last few moments on Earth. For eight weeks he knew this moment would come, but the scene he envisioned was vastly different from the one that unfolded around him. Each breath became increasingly labored. He fought to inhale precious oxygen in a vain attempt to prolong the fleeting experience. The ground underneath him was cold except for a small area near the middle of his back where a warm sensation seemed to keep him insulated.

Eric's senses began to numb as he wondered which events were real and which were imagined. Dreamlike voices faded in and out of the background noise. Colorful lights reflected all around but never seemed to come into focus. But then something more striking and defined came into his line of sight. Eric turned his attention from the waning fall sunset to bright, angelic eyes that seemed to float above him. He became fixated on the eyes, which penetrated his soul from what seemed like a million miles away. As the face that held the cherubic orbs came closer to his, he realized it was somewhat familiar, but he wasn't sure why.

Just before crossing over the threshold separating this life and the next, Eric heard his name echo in the distance through the chaos around him. As he attempted to answer the God-like voice, all that came out was a faint jumble of unintelligible words. The twilight faded, and the tree-shaped silhouettes morphed into the darkness that surrounded him.

One

Nine weeks ago

Eric Stratton stepped out of his apartment and was engulfed by the crisp fall air on the morning after his thirty-fourth birthday. It was also one day before the most important day of the rest of his life. Eric squinted at the bright morning sun that exacerbated the pounding of his head. He fished through his overcoat for his sunglasses, and his weary eyes thanked him as he donned the expensive lenses.

As his eyes adjusted to the daylight, the change of seasons became evident even in the urban sprawl surrounding him. The wind picked up, and the brisk greeting refreshed Eric, further pushing away the grogginess that lingered from the previous night's overindulgent birthday celebration. The pungent cocktail of the aftertaste of alcohol, bile, and perfume from the stranger he met the night before still lingered. He hoped she'd be gone by the time he returned to his apartment later that day. He thought her name may have been Kristin, or Christina.

Eric ignored the good morning from the drug-store clerk as he hurried in search of his normal hangover remedies. Before getting back to the register, he had already guzzled most of his Gatorade, accompanied by several aspirin and chased by a strong mint gum. He hoped his recovery cocktail would kick in while he navigated the city streets to the next stop on his Sunday errands.

As annoying as the hangover was, it caused him to forget about the sporadic, sharp pains he'd had in his stomach for the last week or so…at least until his hunger pangs kicked in. They weren't strong enough to motivate him to eat, as they were still overshadowed by his recent loss of appetite. He knew he needed to eat, but he couldn't think of anything he could actually stomach. In fact, he had a hard time remembering the last time he'd eaten something substantial. Eric grabbed his stomach as it growled. He noticed he was thinner than any time in recent memory.

As Eric walked from the dry cleaner's to the barbershop, he practiced the opening statement he would deliver to the judge and jury the following day. His mental preparation morphed into a daydream as he impressed himself with the well-prepared defense he would present in circuit court at the nine o'clock docket. But Eric knew he would have to impress more than just himself if he wanted to fulfill his year-end goal of changing the name of his current law office from "Simms, Miller and Young" to "Simms, Miller, Young, and STRATTON."

If everything went according to plan, the goal would not be too farfetched. All Eric had to do was convince twelve simple-minded people that the corrupt police department had made a serious mistake; the chief operating officer of one of his firm's most important corporate clients was not guilty of solicitation of any kind (even if the chief operating officer really *was* guilty of solicitation of *every* kind). "After all, why would a successfully married businessman, philanthropist, and father of three risk his family and reputation to spend a night with a prostitute?" Eric would argue. The imaginary jurors would nod in agreement with his compelling points.

On top of his stellar argument, the Commonwealth's Attorney's star witness, who happened to be the arresting officer, had been tainted by another scandal several weeks prior. Still under investigation by the police department's internal affairs division, Eric was surprised when the Commonwealth's Attorney wanted to go forward to a jury trial instead of dropping the charges. But that would not matter, as the scandal with the officer would be the ace up Eric's sleeve for this highly publicized and pivotal trial. Regardless of the evidence presented by the prosecution, when faced with the brilliance of his defense and the card Eric had yet to play, the jury would be left with no choice but to deliver an acquittal for his client.

As Eric switched back and forth from preparation to daydreaming, he wondered if anyone was as lucky a man as he. He wasn't thrilled about the idea of being one year closer to forty. But at the same time, Eric knew he was in a much better place than most men he knew in their midthirties. How many other men could brag about the life he was able to lead? At *only* thirty-four, he worked for one of the premier law firms in the Washington, DC, metro area. He drove a brand-new Mercedes, was in excellent health (excluding the annoying hangover), and could easily hook up with just about any woman he wanted (including a short fling with the daughter of a prominent Senator). To top it all off, he had not made the mistake many of his peers had made by getting married and starting a family too early. He didn't have to worry about being tied down by a nagging wife or screaming children. Eric was content to maintain his reputation as "cool Uncle Eric" and indulge in all of the pleasures that came along with the freedom of his amazing setup.

Eric smiled as his daydream was about to conclude with a firm, congratulatory handshake from the aforementioned Mr. Simms following the pronouncement of an acquittal from the jury. But he was interrupted by a homeless man, who held out a cup and asked for some help or spare change.

"I'll give you some help, buddy," Eric said. "How about you get up off your lazy butt and get yourself a job? That way, I won't have to look at you or spend my hard-earned money to support your liquor habit. Now beat it before I have you arrested!"

Eric returned to his daydream, but just as he reached for the hand of Mr. Simms in the fantasy moment, a sharp, cramping pain struck his lower back, pulling him back to the real world. He barely had a chance to wonder what was happening when a second pain more severe than the first struck his stomach and caused him to double over and drop to one knee on the hard sidewalk. He released the grip on his meticulously packaged, pinstriped trial suit and attempted to right himself. But he only made it halfway back up and was forced to bend at the waist and support his weight with both hands on his knees. Two more pains struck from opposing sides and caused him to retch loudly. Now embarrassed and in pain, Eric attempted to catch his breath and return to normal. The episode was capped by a strong dry heave.

"Maybe if you didn't have a 'liquor habit,' you wouldn't be so mean—and so yellow!" the homeless man shouted as he walked away.

Eric was too preoccupied by his condition to shoot back a response.

After a few moments, the symptoms wore off, and he staggered to a nearby restroom. Relieved that the symptoms abated, Eric chuckled to himself over having been called "yellow" by the old man on the street. He'd been called many names in his life, but being labeled as a coward in that manner was a new one.

Eric splashed water on his face, then studied himself under the fluorescent lights. That's when he realized the old man hadn't called him a coward. He really did look yellow!

Eric leaned forward and closely studied his face. His eyes, skin, and tongue were two shades shy of his favorite yellow "Friday" shirt (which his coworkers constantly argued was somewhere between lemon and canary). It reminded him of his young nephew, Jack, who had to stay in the hospital for a few days after birth due to a serious case of jaundice. Eric was amused by the thought that it was Jack Daniels, not bilirubin, that caused his present condition.

Maybe I do need to lay off the booze, he thought.

Eric had never experienced anything quite like the combination of symptoms he'd been having over the last few weeks. He was generally in good health, and because of that fact he began to worry for the first time about what this strange ailment could possibly be. In addition to the other symptoms, what could cause a healthy person to be yellow? Food poisoning was the first thought that came to mind. The second was a fleeting thought of what Christine or Krista or Kristin or Crystal, or whatever her name was, could have passed on to him the night before. Then he remembered it was the beginning of flu season, so he hoped it was just a mild stomach bug. Whatever this odd affliction turned out to be, it could wait for his attention until after the important victory the next morning.

Sunday church bells rang through the walls and reminded Eric to move along. He wondered why they had to ring them so loud. Eric swore. "It's not like you're going to get mine or anyone else's positive attention with those blasted things. Go ahead. Ring them louder. I'm still not going to church," Eric mumbled.

Back at his apartment, Eric was glad to see that Crystal—or whomever she was—had left. The last thing he needed was to deal with her, while thinking about his ailment. When all attempts to self-cure the increasingly worsening symptoms failed, he gave in and called his doctor. The first available appointment was at two o'clock in the afternoon the following day. This would give him time to win a sweeping victory, impress his future partners, and get to his appointment.

⌘⌘⌘

The atmosphere of the courthouse never got old for Eric. This was *his* territory. Being an attorney by trade was part of the life he was destined to live. Although the setting never changed, every day that he stepped into the litigious world of modern practice, it was a new adventure. This day just happened to have an added bonus—making partner.

Eric smiled as he delivered his routine patronization of the overweight but friendly deputies who ran the magnetometers and checked him for weapons. Eric always wondered if they would be able to react effectively if a dangerous situation actually arose. After passing through the court security checkpoint, he yelled back his daily, "Don't have too much fun and stay safe" salutation.

After that, Eric beamed as the sound of his confident footsteps echoed off the marble floor and down the hallway, announcing his presence. As he worked his way down the long halls, he greeted every clerk, attorney, and janitor he passed.

Once he made it to the actual courtroom, the smile went away. At the doorway, he put his game face on and mentally prepared himself for the battles ahead. As he pushed open the heavy wooden doors of the courtroom, his favorite part of the day began. The slight breeze greeted him with the smell of aged wood, freshly waxed floors, and ultimate power.

Within the walls of his domain, Eric knew he would observe and participate in decisions that had a direct impact on the direction of people's lives. He was part of the system that determined the confinement or freedom of the weak and the strong, the guilty and the innocent, the poor and the rich. Although the rich were the ones Eric preferred, it was a matter of interpretation whether they were guilty or not. His power was godlike, and he cherished every second spent in court.

Eric knew all of the players by name. From the court reporters to the clerk, to the police officers and deputies, all the way up to the substitute judges that filled in on occasion. It was part of his trademark image. He was liked (or at least feared or respected) by his colleagues on both sides of the aisle. Although he loved the challenge of trial, Eric rarely had to take his cases that far. The Commonwealth's Attorney and her assistants knew of his reputation. They usually preferred to cut generous plea deals in order to avoid a battle in open court.

But when he did go to trial, Eric loved to make witnesses and opponents squirm with his eloquent and aggressive questions and arguments. He often humbled or humiliated police officers, so-called experts, and eyewitnesses. By the time he was finished with his brilliant cross examinations, once credible witnesses were left doubting their own testimonies.

Eric sat in confidence as he listened to the boring opening statement of the Assistant Commonwealth's Attorney. He glanced over at the Commonwealth's Attorney, who was sitting in on the case as well. He feigned a yawn and then covered his mouth with a fist as her subordinate continued. She returned his sentiments with a smile, raised her eyebrows, and nodded as if to say "we'll see."

Eric felt much better than the previous day, and he even considered canceling his doctor's appointment in case there was a celebration to attend. After getting through the routine motions, he stood to approach the jury with his opening statement. Eric buttoned his jacket, walked up to the jury box, and began another of his trademarks: the dramatic pause for effect. He took a deep breath and leaned in to look into the eyes of the twelve people who would deliver his desired verdict. Little did they know they would clear his client of the solicitation charges and usher him into a new phase of his career.

Eric turned one last time to smirk at the Assistant Commonwealth's Attorney and began his brilliant opening monologue. Then, as if on cue from some unseen script, his words were lost with the first jolt of pain that hit his side. He did his best to hide the grimace and wondered if either the jury or his client noticed. Severe nausea struck within a few seconds. He suddenly became aware of beads of sweat forming on his forehead. He took a few steps forward and tried to compose himself. After a deep breath, another sharp pain struck him. When his hand went down to the area where the pain was coming from, he noticed his stomach was no longer slender but seemed bloated. His dramatic pause turned into a growing uncomfortable silence.

Eric turned to the judge and said, "Your honor, I'd like to—" but before he could finish his statement and ask for a recess, the room began to spin, and he was struck with a massive head rush. His legs gave way underneath him, and he ended up curled in a fetal position on the floor. The last thing he heard before passing out was the bailiff, whose name Eric oddly could not recall, shouting a request into the radio for an ambulance.

⌘ ⌘ ⌘

Eric slowly regained consciousness to the echo of a PA announcement ringing in a distant hallway. He squinted as his eyes adjusted to the brightly lit room. It was one of the few times in life, outside of partying, that he had awakened not knowing his current location. Fortunately, he looked around before moving because he had an IV and other tubes attached to various parts of his body. His memory slowly returned, and he remembered the pain and loss of control he had experienced in the courtroom earlier that day. As he began to put the pieces together, he was embarrassed and shocked at what he must have looked like.

Searching for the nurse call button, Eric pressed it.

A pleasant female voice asked, "May I help you?"

"Yes, this is Eric Stratton. I'm not sure what room I'm in, but I'd like to talk to someone."

"Okay, Mr. Stratton; we'll be right with you."

As Eric waited for the nurse to come to his room, he was keenly aware of a now-constant ache in his stomach and lower back. Oddly enough, when he touched his midsection, he was still bloated. Other than those pains and the discomfort caused by the IV and catheter, Eric felt okay overall. He certainly didn't think his symptoms would cause him to pass out, let alone warrant admission to an emergency room. Whatever the ailment turned out to be, he already loathed it, as it had interrupted his important performance. It had also struck in a place where he was normally in control—in his territory.

Eric wanted someone to blame for the pain, the embarrassment, and the situation as a whole. If this was a case of food poisoning, he was going to own the restaurant he and Christine—or whomever—had eaten at the night before. Then he remembered he had barely picked at his food, so there couldn't have been enough to make him this sick. For the moment, there was no established scapegoat to attack, so he hit the nurse call button again.

Fifteen seconds later, a taller, older gentleman opened the curtain. "And how's our newest patient feeling?" he asked as he approached the bed and closed the curtain behind him.

"I've been better," Eric responded. "What in the world is going on with me, Doctor—"

"Reese," the tall man said. "I'm the resident for the emergency room on this shift, and I'll be in charge of your care while you're with us today. In case you didn't know, you're at Metro Regional Hospital center, and for now, you're in ER room 1009. As far as what's going on with you...well, we're not sure just yet. You've been unconscious for about three hours now. Other than the now obvious jaundice, there aren't any obvious or outward signs of injuries. This is a good thing, considering you took a header on a marble floor. You really should wait until there's water around, you know."

Eric smiled slightly.

Dr. Reese began to ask a series of questions that started with his medical history and continued through the most recent events. Eric advised him of the aches, bloating, jaundice, and loss of appetite and weight. The doctor, in turn, asked him about his lifestyle habits, including whether or not he smoked, drank, or was sexually active.

Eric laughed. "I smoke an occasional cigar and occasionally drink like a fish." He then bragged about his dating prowess until his answers led to more uncomfortable questions. He didn't really feel like discussing his bedroom activities with a total stranger. But he was honest, as he wanted a speedy diagnosis of his ailment so the doctor could prescribe the medicine and treatment that would get him discharged from the hospital as quickly as possible. In his world, time was money, and he certainly wasn't making any lying there in the emergency room.

Eric had always been a straight shooter, so he asked for the same courtesy from the doctor—good news or bad. In a poor attempt at humor, Dr. Reese said, "The bad news is you're a lawyer, but the good news is your condition is not fatal."

"Good, then I'll be well enough to sue for this atrocious care," Eric joked without skipping a beat.

"Touché!" Dr. Reese said. He then informed Eric that nurses had already taken blood and urine samples. "We'll have to run more tests before we can say for sure what's going on. But you asked me to shoot straight, so I will. Based on the symptoms you're experiencing, there are several things we're going to check for. They run the gambit from relatively benign to pretty serious.

"On the less serious end, this could merely be a gallstone. Although uncomfortable, it's easily treated. Based on both your symptoms and active sexual life, we could possibly be looking at acute hepatitis. This is more serious, but it's still treatable.

"On the more serious end of things, we could be dealing with cirrhosis of the liver. I don't mean to alarm you too early, but worst case scenario, some of the things you've experienced in the last few weeks are consistent with pancreatic cancer.

"Considering your age and everything I've seen so far, I'd lean towards one of the first two I mentioned. Just file away the latter as distant possibilities. Again, we'll have to get results back from the samples we've already taken, and we will have to run some more tests. But if I were a betting man, I'd definitely put your mortgage, and maybe even mine, on one of the first two."

When Dr. Reese's second attempt at humor only drew a slight courtesy smile, he returned to the business at hand. He informed Eric that he'd probably order an abdominal ultrasound next, and depending on the results, Eric could be released later in the day.

Being an attorney, it didn't surprise Eric that the next order of business was the business side of things. An administrator met him in his room with stacks of files and documents tucked neatly under her arm. It had been awhile since he had been in a hospital, and even he was amazed at how much paperwork there was to fill out. But the last thing Eric was thinking about was paperwork. His mind wandered to the things the doctor had said...at least until the administrator flipped to the form about personal/emergency contacts. Then Eric was somewhat embarrassed that it took him awhile to think of someone to list. Since he didn't have family in town (and didn't regularly keep in touch with those who were out of town), he listed his assistant, Angie Simpson, as the person to contact.

The thought of having to list Angie caught him off-guard. Was there no one else he could call in a time of need? Worse yet, he wondered if anyone (short of another client being caught on the wrong side of the law) would list *him* as a contact. These thoughts bothered Eric more than he wanted to admit.

When the administrator left the room, Eric was left alone with his thoughts.

Just the day before, Eric had been counting on his fortune and success to bring him continued fulfillment. Now he realized that, in his search for that contentment, he hadn't invested much time in anyone but himself. And that sad fact led to his current lack of people to list as emergency contacts. He was amazed that something as simple as this little ailment, and a stupid contact list, could jar him so much.

Eric turned on the TV and tried to suppress the nagging realities creeping into his head. But he soon lost track of *Fox News*. Instead he pondered his life and the people he should have been able to call upon in his time of need. *How pathetic is this,* Eric thought. He chalked it all up to one of those moments in life where he was supposed to learn to slow down a little and build meaningful relationships. *Oh brother, it must be the drugs. I'm already getting sentimental.*

He filed the thoughts away and promised himself he'd take the time to deal with these issues later and maybe change a few small things. But first he needed to take care of two more pressing matters. The first was whatever treatment would get him back to 100 percent the fastest. Second, he *had* to make partner....

Eric was quietly awakened by an obese orderly who was breathing heavily. The orderly advised him he was going to be taken away for an abdominal ultrasound. He was transported in his bed to another area that housed the ultrasound machine. A technician quickly walked him through the painless process. Eric was glad for the explanation, since he didn't like tight spaces, and he'd pictured something more like a CT scan in a closed chamber. The ultrasound was much simpler. The least comfortable part of the procedure was the cold gel slathered on his stomach; otherwise, it was quick and painless.

Back in the ER, Dr. Reese checked in on Eric and informed him that he wouldn't be discharged until the results returned. "Just be patient and take some time to relax. Maybe think about some things your busy schedule doesn't normally allow," Dr. Reese said. "Take a few minutes and call your family or friends to let them know that you're okay. Maybe they can bring you something a little better than the stuff our cafeteria offers."

"I'll try to relax, Dr. Reese, but I'll be honest. I'm not used to just sitting around and waiting. Would it be okay if I took a walk around?"

"I'd love to allow you to do that, but since we're not sure yet what we're dealing with and you already passed out once today, we can't take that chance."

"Okay, then. I'll be a patient patient and wait here until I hear from you," Eric promised.

But that was easier said than done. Waiting for the results of the ultrasound proved to be a long and grueling process. Eric had plenty of time to rest, but instead of doing that, he turned to worrying. He liked to think of himself as an optimist, but he didn't like the options Dr. Reese had presented earlier. Gallstones didn't sound too bad, but even if it wasn't cirrhosis or cancer, he could still be looking at hepatitis. He didn't know all the symptoms that came along with it, but he remembered it was one of those diseases they warned him about in high school and college. Still, if it was a plea deal, he'd take that over cancer any day. Eric didn't know anyone personally who had dealt with cancer, but he knew it was usually treatable as long as they caught it early. Nonetheless, the word continued to echo over and over in his head, and the only other word that bounced around with it was *death*.

More time to think. More time to ponder. Out of his element, out of his comfort zone, and way out of control, Eric felt helpless for the first time in his life. All he could do was wait on the test results, and although he knew the odds were in his favor, there was the small chance it was the worst-case scenario. And that small chance began to make him feel more closed in than the thought of the CT chamber he dreaded earlier. What would he do if it was cancer? Where would he go from here? What about cirrhosis? At thirty-four, this could not be a good sign for his health. He wished at the very least he had internet access so he could check to see what his options were. But more than the internet, he truly wished there was something else he had.

Interestingly, the thing he wanted most was to talk to someone and vent. At the very least, he wished he had someone to share his normally sarcastic and witty jokes with. Any time pressure built in his life, his humor kicked in to aid in relieving stress. Again, he was reminded that most of the people in his life consisted of those who occupied roles in the courtroom. He didn't want to call Simms, Miller, or Young for fear he would appear weak. Angie Simpson would answer his call, but that would not only be awkward but also inappropriate. Krista(?) was a no-go, although he still had her number in his wallet.

He hadn't spoken to his older brother in months. To call now would cause more stress than it would be helpful, as all the old familial arguments would just resurface. But in the end, he knew his brother was the best option, so Eric picked up the phone and dialed the number to his brother's house. It rang once, and he quickly hung up. *How pathetic.* He felt like he was back in elementary school; only now, instead of being afraid to call the girl he had a crush on, he was afraid to call his own flesh and blood.

Just when he didn't think he could take another minute of channel-surfing and worrying, Dr. Reese returned. Eric tried to read his face before the doctor delivered the news, but his expression did not *seem* to convey anything worse than it already had.

"Well, we've been able to rule out gallstones, but that's not necessarily good news. We saw some things on this test that are of some concern, but I'd rather not speculate on what we've found until we can confirm the results. At this point, we need to check more blood samples, and I've ordered a CT scan. Eric, you asked me to be straight with you, so I will be. We have found what appear to be rather large abnormalities that are most likely tumors on or near your pancreas. Although this does not mean it's definitively cancer, this is not good news, as it appears to be pretty advanced growth. This condition is well outside my area of expertise, so we're going to run the CT scan and then turn you over to someone who can walk you through the rest of this process. You'll be transferred out of the ER and admitted to the hospital since it looks like you'll be here overnight. I realize this is all coming at you very quickly, but let's just take this one step at a time and cross each bridge as we come to them. For now, I'd suggest you call your loved ones and let them know you'll be here a little longer."

His helplessness morphed into outright fear. He wished more than ever that he had someone to walk beside him through the uncertainty of the moment.

⌘ ⌘ ⌘

The time between waking up in the ER and hearing the results of the ultrasound had been long and grueling. But the next few hours and tests seemed to pass by too quickly. The CT scans confirmed the worst of the doctor's and Eric's fears.

The next day he was turned over to a surgeon for a biopsy, which eliminated any doubt about what they were dealing with. At thirty-four years and three days old, Eric Stratton was officially informed that he had pancreatic cancer of the worst kind.

Two

Six to twelve weeks

An oncologist named Dr. Sheila Redmond was assigned to Eric's case. He liked Dr. Redmond for several reasons, none the least of which were her looks. He found himself wishing she was not his doctor, but someone he could date. Although she didn't have model-like good looks, her long brown hair and dark eyes made her attractive in a girl-next-door kind of way. It definitely helped him take his mind off his disease when she was around. Aside from her looks, Eric was also impressed by her intelligence, professionalism, her frankness, and the fact she was surprisingly compassionate. She also had an uncanny ability to use the perfect words for every conversation they had. It was clear she had dealt with this type of difficult situation numerous times before.

Eric's diagnosis wasn't a good one. Dr. Redmond had told Eric his cancer was "metastatic," meaning it had spread well beyond the pancreas and was now affecting other organs. That explained the severity of his symptoms to include the collapse in court and the episode on the street several days prior.

Dr. Redmond compassionately explained that there were not many treatment options, and at this advanced stage, they would only prolong the inevitable by a few months at the most. They even discussed alternative treatments and clinical trials, but short of a miracle, Eric simply did not have much time. Based on all the test results, Dr. Redmond estimated Eric had anywhere from six to twelve weeks left to live.

Eric fell into an almost immediate depression with the news. Just to be sure that he had exhausted all options, Eric had his charts sent to several other oncologists in the area. One hundred percent of them responded back with the same prognosis and bad news that Dr. Redmond had given him. Because of the advanced nature of the disease, any treatment administered would only prolong his life by weeks or months at the most. And all of those weeks or months would have to be spent in the hospital. So the first question was not a matter of "if" but of "when."

The second question was more difficult. That one involved a decision on how Eric wanted to spend the remaining time he had. Dr. Redmond discussed the different options for hospice and palliative care in the area. No matter how nice or caring those options sounded, they didn't mask the inevitable. Dr. Redmond gave Eric some pamphlets and paperwork and left him alone to decide where to spend his final days.

⌘⌘⌘

The odd thing about being told he was rapidly dying was the fact that Eric did not yet feel like he was dealing with anything serious enough to take his life. Other than the constant aches and bloating, he felt pretty good physically. Emotionally, he was a train wreck.

Eric had always considered himself a "good" person. But that didn't mean he wasn't self-centered. Eric chose to live the life he wanted for a long time and didn't care if that choice negatively affected others. Until now. Now he was left to dwell on the ghosts from his past. He wondered if everyone in his situation did that. But his thoughts also reverted to the things he'd thought about early on in his hospital stay. Before he could have cared less about anything or anyone but himself. But now that he was staring down at the last few weeks of his life, he dreaded the thought that he hadn't taken the time to develop or maintain any meaningful relationships. And that choice meant he had to face cancer alone.

At first, Eric called his cancer everything but what it was. He used words like *disease, ailment, sickness, pc* (short for *pancreatic cancer*) and *malady*. But he didn't like any of those terms. He wanted to use a word that was true to the final outcome of his illness, so he began to refer to the cancer as his "death sentence." Legal terms always seemed to fit best for him. In his mind, he had been tried, judged, and sentenced. All that was left was the arrival of the executioner to carry out that sentence. Eric sat alone in his hospital room on death row and wondered what on earth he was supposed to accomplish with only six to twelve weeks.

⌘ ⌘ ⌘

Two days later, Eric was still in severe denial about what was actually happening. He still didn't feel very bad physically. Dr. Redmond continually reminded him of the need to make a decision. She stressed that although they couldn't prolong his life, they could make the process of dying a less painful one. Eric was thankful to Dr. Redmond for seeming to genuinely care for him. She became the first person he opened up to in a long time. And because she was the only person he really had, they built what, to him, seemed like a deep friendship (even though he'd only known her for a short time). Not wanting to let her leave each time she visited, Eric always came up with questions to make her stay longer.

"So how many times have you gone through this with your patients?" Eric asked.

"One time too many. I stopped counting when I reached the thirties. But I haven't forgotten the name or the face of any one of my patients who died from their disease. I have my own 'mental memorial,' if you will. I mean, there were also many survivors, and I'm grateful for each and every one of them. But an unfortunate part of my specialty is that I see a lot of deaths too. I have to say that, by far, you're the easiest to talk to about it."

"That's because I'm still in the denial stage," Eric said with a smile.

Dr. Redmond laughed, as they had talked about the different mental stages of coping with his cancer—stages like denial, anger, and finally, acceptance.

"I think I'm the easiest to talk to because I don't have anyone else. I don't want to tick you off so you won't see me anymore."

Dr. Redmond smiled again.

"Dr. Redmond, can I ask you a tougher question?"

"Sure. But only if you stop calling me Dr. Redmond and agree to call me Sheila from here on out."

"Fair enough, Doct—ah, I mean Sheila. I guess, I was just wondering...."

Eric swallowed the growing lump in his throat and quelled the flood of emotions that would have come with it. Sheila waited for Eric to gather himself. He realized that if this were a court case, he would have articulated some brilliant line of questioning long ago. But his "death sentence" was so far from anything he had ever dealt with mentally that it rendered him helpless or speechless at every turn. For the first time in many years, he was at a loss for words. And with that, Eric and Sheila sat in surprisingly comfortable silence for a few moments.

Finally, Eric's question pierced the quiet hum of the medical equipment in the room. "Have you ever thought about what you would do if you were in one of your patient's shoes? What would you do if you were living under this 'death sentence'? What if you only had a few months to live?"

"I'll answer you, not as your doctor, but as a friend. To tell you the truth, I've thought about it many times. I've seen the movies and heard the songs where the people with cancer go skydiving, drag racing, mountain climbing, or bull riding. All of those things sound fun, and maybe some people feel like they didn't really live unless they accomplished these goals. But I'm not sure they'd be meaningful for me. I've always tried to live my life in such a way that if I ever received the news that you've had to hear in the last few days, I'd have already done all of those things. I also consider myself a spiritual person, so I don't have to make peace with God or anything like that either. Of course, in my line of work if God wasn't close by, I think I would have gone insane a long time ago. So in the end, my perfect ending would be time spent with my loved ones. One final celebration, if you will. And speaking of God, if you don't mind my saying so, you should know that He has not forgotten about you."

Sheila's answer stunned Eric. On the one hand, the honesty and obvious depth of her answer resonated within his soul. But on the other, it frustrated him, as he could not yet fully understand the reasons behind his predicament.

"Wow. Sheila, I envy you. Up until a few days ago I loved my life. I had everything I ever wanted—or so I thought. But it's hard to know what to think in all this. I've never been a bad guy compared to some of my clients. I can't say I'm one of those people like Mother Teresa or the people on that show *Extreme Makeover,* where they build houses for the needy. But I'm also not like Jeffrey Dahmer or Osama Bin Laden."

He took a breath and plunged on. "I mean, is there really anything wrong with enjoying life, being happy with my job and success, having a few good times, and meeting some nice women every now and then? All I really wanted was to make partner at my firm and continue the awesome life I'd been living. So why is this happening to me? And as far as God not forgetting about me, I can't see where He might be involved at all. Sorry, but He never really did anything for me before. And if this is some kind of punishment for making the most of life and having a little fun, then forget Him, or her, or whatever He—it is."

Eric was surprised when Sheila didn't react more to his comments about God, which he'd chosen out of both frustration and an attempt to get a rise out of her. Deep down he knew he was looking for a debate, and since there wasn't anyone else to argue with, Sheila took the brunt of his outburst. But he got more than he bargained for in Sheila. Not only was he unable to get a rise out of her, she came right back with a compelling point that made him question his confidence.

"Eric, don't take this the wrong way, but if there was nothing wrong with the way you were living before, then why do you have so many questions? And why do you envy me? I can't tell you what you should do with your remaining time because, frankly, as much as I can imagine how hard it would be, I'm not *actually* in your shoes. You seem to have lived for the moment before, so maybe all you'll want to do is jump out of a plane and eat some exotic last meal or have a few more nights with some beautiful women. But if you have doubts, questions, or, most importantly, regrets, then maybe there is something more you need to do with the time you have left."

18

Exposed, Eric stared at the floor. "See, there you go again. You always have the exact words for the moment. Are you sure you weren't a lawyer in a past life?"

Sheila smiled as she gathered her things. "Please. I wouldn't even associate with lawyers."

By the end of the day, time spent on the spectrum of differing emotions left Eric drained. He still could not accept the truth that he only had weeks to live. He didn't have time to be angry with God, the devil, fate, genetics, or who or whatever else was responsible for his "death sentence." He didn't think it was fair, but pondering fairness, good and evil, fortune and luck were meaningless when the clock was ticking.

Eric drifted into a deep sleep, trying to come up with something meaningful to occupy his remaining time.

⌘⌘⌘

Eric awoke with one word resonating in his mind over and over again: *regret.* He was sure he'd dreamed something along that theme, but he couldn't remember the details. What could "Eric the Great" possibly regret about his short life on Earth? Suddenly, he thought of his life as a great wall of accomplishments. He pondered the cases he won, the money he'd made, the partnership that was almost his, and most importantly, the reputation as an exemplary attorney that he wore like a shiny Olympic medal.

Then he began to wonder what that wall of accomplishments really amounted to. One hundred years from now, would anyone know or care about who Eric Stratton was? Actually, he was beginning to doubt anyone would care about him in a hundred days (save Simms, Miller, and Young, who would now have to find someone else to step into the partnership). The wall of accomplishments really didn't matter much unless there was someone to share and celebrate them with.

But it was too late for that. He'd squandered his chances at a real relationship on a series of one-night stands and short-lived flings. How many hours had he spent partying with fair-weather acquaintances and fickle lovers? He kicked himself for not taking the time to come to these conclusions earlier and wondered what relationships could be meaningful now. A great emptiness accompanied his regrets.

Instinctively, Eric reached into the stand next to his bed to look for a pen and paper. The pen was easy to find. Ironically, the pad of paper was tucked beneath the Gideon's Bible that lay inside the drawer. The glimmer of light on the gold painted words of its cover reminded him of the one his grandmother left him when she passed away a few years earlier. It was the only meaningful thing she could afford to leave him, and she promised it would change his life one day.

Eric put the Bible back in the drawer, sighed, and stared at the blank sheet of paper in front of him. He wished he had more time. In fact, speaking of his grandmother, Eric wished he had spent more time with her, especially when he found out she was sick. That was impossible now. And that's when it hit him. Eric's regrets did not stem from things he never did, places he never visited, or goals he never accomplished. All of his regrets stemmed from relationships he had neglected or ruined.

He'd always been praised for being an extremely driven young man. In high school, he was encouraged to study hard and never sell himself short for the future. He'd claimed that future for himself, and as high school turned into college and then college into law school, Eric found himself determined to prove he was made for success. He worked hard enough to finish undergraduate studies in three years and was the youngest person from his class to take the bar exam after law school. But his scholastic and vocational success didn't come without a price tag.

The more time Eric spent preparing for his future, the more people he left behind. By the time he'd worked his way up the Washington, DC, metropolitan legal scene, Eric had all but abandoned his parents, his brother, his grandmother, his friends, and even one girl who could have been "the one." In order to reach his goals, Eric no longer placed value on his close relationships, like he had when he was younger. He had been more than willing to forsake them all. And he was more than willing to steamroll anyone he saw as an obstacle. For the person he'd become, the end always justified the means. And there was no line he wouldn't cross, including the one that separated right and wrong; anything he did was right in his own eyes.

Finally coming to that sad realization enabled Eric to have an epiphany. The past six to twelve years of his life had been spent on himself. Therefore, the last six to twelve weeks of his life would have to be spent making up for those regrets through reconciliation with others. The last days of his life would somehow be about relationships.

Eric began to write down a plan. He needed one that would cover both his need to end his life with meaningful relationships and a desire to erase the regrets that now weighed him down like a ball and chain. He began to brainstorm. The first three or four sheets seemed cliché and quickly went into the trash. This was serious business. Eric had at least a handful of people he owed a conversation, an apology, and in some cases much more. In order to make his last days meaningful ones, he'd have to uncover some ugly skeletons he'd hidden away for a very long time.

Eric started with a fresh sheet and wrote *"To do before I die"* at the top. As situations came to mind, he began to write the name of a person, what he had done to wrong them, or how he had ruined the relationship. It started with his brother and parents. It would be relatively easy to mend those relationships because he knew they all thought the world of him (even when he was unkind or uncaring).

Then there was his grandmother. That would be a little more difficult, as she had been dead for several years. But for some reason he left her on the list. There were a couple of friends he had forsaken, the kid he used to pick on in high school, and finally the one woman he had abandoned (and didn't ever want to face again).

Eric prioritized the list of names only, then rewrote it on a clean sheet. He changed the title to "Regrets and Reconciliation." When he was finished with the list, he felt a shimmer of happiness for the first time since his death sentence. He wasn't sure if it was the realization of a purpose or just something to take his mind off dwelling on the death sentence. Either way, he had a renewed sense of purpose and excitement and wanted to get a start on his list. The list would take him on a journey that would allow him to live out the rest of his days with a real and noble purpose. And he didn't want to waste any time before beginning that journey.

Eric depressed the nurse call button and buzzed the attendant on duty. "Hi, this is Eric Stratton. Is Sheila—er—Dr. Redmond available?"

"No, she won't be back until two o'clock," the nurse replied.

"Okay. Please have her stop in when she returns. It's very important."

"Can I help you with anything, Mr. Stratton?"

"Nope, I need to see her. Thanks, though!"

⌘⌘⌘

Eric's final list consisted of seven people he needed to visit with. He didn't include his brother and parents since they could be contacted via phone. He also had not wronged them in any way comparable to some of the other people he would reach out to. He didn't like the idea of having to drop such horrible news in any way other than in person, but he knew they would understand.

Placing a call to his brother was more difficult than he could have imagined. As Randy picked up the phone, Eric could hear his niece and nephew talking in the background. He hadn't seen either of them since they were toddlers, and to hear young voices, even if they were arguing, made him wish he had more time. Eric quickly apologized for his pride and lack of contact over the last few years and had to fight the urge to break down several times.

⌘⌘⌘

Randy knew Eric was not the type to admit when he was wrong, let alone apologize for anything. The sudden change of character piqued Randy's curiosity, and he listened carefully as Eric brought him up-to-date. Randy was speechless. Eric assured him there was nothing that he needed at the moment but excitedly told him about his plan. Although he couldn't understand the reasons behind the plan, Randy had learned to respect his driven brother and his space.

"Do me a favor," Randy said. "First off, you have to forgive me for the bitterness, too. We let too much time get by, and now it looks like we're running out. I know you have to do these things and finish off this list. But if you could find the time to make it home to see Mom and Dad and the kids…"

There was a long silence on the other end. "Randy, I'll do my best, and…" Eric took a deep breath as his voice trailed off into a quiver.

"I know, Eric. Now get going. I know you'll succeed. You always do."

⌘ ⌘ ⌘

Eric hung up the phone and shook his head. How could he have been so self-centered and stupid? He and Randy were very close when they were younger. They were only two years apart in age and were best friends all the way through high school. While Eric went on to pursue his career in law, Randy became a police officer, married an amazing young woman, and started a family. Eric attended the wedding and then disappeared save a sporadic Christmas here or birthday there. He was so involved with his pursuits in the legal field that he missed out on a lot of their lives. He blamed it on his commitments and their distance apart.

Several arguments had always arisen because Randy wanted his children to know their uncle. But Eric always defended himself as the innocent party. He claimed he was simply too busy to make more frequent trips, phone calls, or emails. Now, sitting in the quiet hospital bed, he realized he was wrong and was glad this was one of the first things he was able to make right.

The next call to his parents was difficult as well. Although Eric's mom and dad were now in their late sixties, they were in good health and state of mind. Having the same complaint as Randy through the years, they were still proud and supportive of Eric in all of his endeavors. It broke his heart to have to give first his mom, and later his dad, the bad news on the phone that day. Although they tried to feign strength on the line, Eric was certain his news devastated them. He couldn't yet sympathize with the idea, but he had always heard that one of the worst pains a human has to endure is the death of a child.

Eric's parents insisted he come home immediately, or at the very least allow them to drive up and take care of his needs. He spent the next half hour explaining the reasons he couldn't concede to their request. He informed them of the list, as well as the plan he intended to carry out over the next few weeks and months.

His parents finally let him get off the phone when he promised to yield to their wishes at some point soon. Of course, this was not an unreasonable request, as he owed them his time after neglecting the relationship for so long.

Towards the end of the conversation, Eric didn't want to hang up the phone. He chalked it up to a fear that it would be the last time he would talk to them. But he suppressed that notion and reluctantly put down the receiver in order to wait for Sheila to return.

⌘⌘⌘

Sheila stopped at a local coffee shop and picked Eric up a little something to break the monotony of the bland hospital meals he'd been enduring for the last few days. She was fond of her conversations with Eric and hoped she'd be able to have some impact, other than a medical one, on his life before his short time was up.

Truth be told, Sheila had developed a slight attraction to Eric. She knew it was futile at this point, but he was charming, attractive, and had a great sense of humor. Like Eric, she, too, had spent a lot of time pursuing the vocation she felt she was put on Earth to fulfill. She had not yet had time for a meaningful, romantic relationship. But she differed from Eric because, as busy and hectic as her life had become, she always made time to maintain her existing relationships with friends and family. She also differed from him on spiritual matters.

Sheila wasn't quite ready to share the depth of her faith with Eric but felt compelled to do so later in the day, as he'd be moving home or to another facility soon. After all, she, too, had once shunned spirituality and religion as superstition and old wives' tales…until someone came along to show her there was more to life than the world she could see around her. As she headed to his room, she whispered a quick prayer in hopes that God would prepare her with the right words.

⌘⌘⌘

Eric sat up in his bed and gratefully received the high caffeine and sugar treat provided by his only friend. As sad as it was to admit he only had one friend at this point, he needed to in order to motivate himself to action. While he sipped a drink that his old college roommate would call "the dew from the grass of heaven" (in a thick Southern accent), Eric began to discuss his plan with Sheila.

"I've had a lot of time to think about what to do," Eric said.

"Good," Sheila replied. "I know it's hard, but it's good that you've been able to make a decision. So are you going to chose in-home care, or would you rather go the hospice route?"

"Well, I had something a little different in mind. I've been thinking about some of the things you've said, as well as a few other things that have been on my mind recently. And I don't think I like either the home or hospice options.

"I've been thinking about my past and all of the regrets I have," Eric continued. "You were right in some of the aspects from our conversation the other day. Of course I've had plenty of time to sit here and ponder not only where I want to be, but what I want to do in the next however many weeks it turns out to be. What I've realized is that, justified or not, I've enjoyed my success and some of the pleasures of life to this point. But I've really been lacking when it comes to meaningful relationships. That's obvious by the lack of people visiting me in the last few days. I can't blame anyone but myself. I've focused so much on my career that I've forsaken the important relationships. And I've also done some pretty bad things over the last few years. So I'm left with the fact that I can lie somewhere and die with all of these regrets on my conscience, or I can do something about it.

"So I came up with a list of the seven people I've either wronged or forsaken relationships with in my adult life, and I plan to go to each and every one of them in order to reconcile if they'll allow it. At the very least, I owe them an apology. So, in answer to your question, hospice and palliative care are not options for me. If there's no reason for me to continue to be admitted here, I'd like to be discharged in order to get going on this list immediately."

To Eric's surprise, Sheila was not only supportive but also understanding. "I'm really happy with your decision, Eric. It's not an easy one to make, and it will be an increasingly difficult task as time goes on. But as you said, you're dying regardless, so why not do something meaningful with that time? Listen, before I discharge you, I really feel led to share something with you, especially in light of your decision."

"Of course, Sheila. Shoot."

"Well, first, I need you to understand that what I'm about to share with you doesn't in any way reflect the position of this hospital or its staff. I'm sharing with you today as your friend, not as your attending physician."

"Are you giving me a disclaimer?" Eric joked. "Don't worry, I won't sue you."

"Well, I figured I'd give you the fine print up front, given that you're an attorney and all," Sheila said. "Seriously, I just wanted to share with you from my heart, but I don't want you to think I'm speaking for anyone but myself. I wouldn't normally share this type of thing with someone I just met, but in your case, you don't have much time, and I'm not sure when I'll see you next, so this is something I need to tell you now. Besides, I already consider you a friend. Even though I've only known you for a few weeks, I feel like it's been longer. It's probably because I'm the only one who will put up with you for more than a day or so."

"Hey now!"

She grinned. "Just kidding. I don't expect you to make any decisions today—only hear me out, and then we'll get you on your way."

Eric listened intently as she continued.

"I won't sit here and tell you my entire life story, but the relevant stuff pretty much starts with my career. Not to toot my own horn of course, but I was a pretty bright but very much by-the-book medical student. I quickly earned a reputation for my aggressive research and ability to find new ways to treat different forms of cancer. After losing my father to lung cancer when I was a teenager, I was motivated to cure what I used to call 'the devil's scourge.' I spent countless hours in the office and hospital lab fighting what I deemed as my righteous battle. I was fascinated by modern medicine and technology, which assisted me in many ways. I was able to prolong some people's lives by many years. Others I was able to cure altogether. But as an oncologist, one truth I knew I would face and one that my professors and mentors never could have prepared me for was the fact that no matter how hard I tried, no matter how many hours I put in, no matter how much I didn't want to face it, there were always patients I could not save.

"No amount of scientific study or modern explanation could help me or the families deal with the inevitable loss of their loved ones. I began to see that there had to be more than science involved when it came to a profession like mine. But at the same time, I was always taught to treat all of my patients the same way. I was told to be professional, but to NEVER get involved on any personal or emotional level. In other words, I was pretty much a robot on the outside. But on the inside I was hurting so much due to seeing all of that pain and suffering and not really having a healthy way to process it all.

"Then my world as a doctor was turned upside down when I met an exceptionally gifted young patient. She taught me a lot of things, but the most important lesson was the ability to tap into a higher power in order to truly help both myself, from a mental standpoint, and then those who I could not save physically."

Sheila paused, as if trying to get a read from Eric. "I'm sorry. Am I boring you with all this?"

"No, quite the opposite," Eric replied. "I'm on a caffeine high. Just kidding. So far I'm captivated by your story. So cut out the small talk and get on with it."

She smiled. "So, as I said before, early in my career, I was always careful not to cross the line of professionalism governing the doctor/patient relationship. It was almost a safety mechanism for me because I never wanted to get involved personally or care too much. I think it's the same defense mechanism that police officers and soldiers try to employ when they come across traumatic situations involving suffering and death. You almost have to remove yourself altogether and compartmentalize the event, or otherwise go crazy. That worked for a while in theory. But in reality, living like that took its toll. Every time I saw a patient, I thought about my father. I began to regret that I couldn't save people, so I became cold and treated patients as mere cases and not people. Then all of my training, defenses, and methods became especially blurred a few years into my career, and I was forever changed because of it.

"Several years into my practice, I was assigned to a ten-year-old leukemia patient named Emily. Emily was the first child I ever treated, and I only became involved with her case because of some research I was working on at the time. There was something about Emily that made her stand out from most of the people I had ever met, both young and old. Even as the illness and treatments ravaged her young body, she always brightened the lives of those around her.

"Emily was an extremely gifted child. Had she not been sidetracked by her illness, experts in the school system predicted that she would have finished high school by her twelfth birthday. Prior to meeting her, my bedside manner was always professional but noticeably more distant and cold. Emily picked up on this early on and called me out on it. Believe me, I tried to resist, but Emily's infectious personality drew me in. It made me want to know her as a person rather than as a case, illness, or name on a chart.

"At only ten years old, Emily had the uncanny ability to use the perfect words for the moment, whether it was a short encounter or long conversation. It was a trait I was envious of and learned to hone later on."

"Yeah, so I've noticed. I'm glad you learned that one for my sake," Eric interjected.

"I connected with Emily on a level of understanding that I had not been able to with people twice her age and older. Insights from this 'child' changed the way I lived my life and caused me to look beyond the hard science of medicine.

28

"We quickly developed a mutually deep and trusting relationship. Because she was so in touch with who she was as a person, I asked Emily what it was that she believed made her so special. I also wanted to know how she could be so brave in the midst of such a terrible ordeal. Emily blushed and, in her humble but special mix of high intellect and ten-year-old mannerisms, explained she had been put on Earth to enrich the lives of those around her. This was not an arrogant statement but an honest assessment she was confident of. She believed God's plan for her did not include using her naturally high IQ to achieve some scholastic record. Instead, she was supposed to use it to learn how to interact with people and change them for the better."

Sheila shook her head. "How could she have known that as a ten-year-old? Even though I didn't believe in them, I sometimes wondered if I was conversing with an angel. At the very least, I began to wonder if she was getting insights from somewhere else. In the end, the 'treatment' Emily provided to my starving soul was much more than anything I could offer the little girl in the form of medicinal healing."

Eric was glued to Sheila's story. Here he was in the twilight of his own life, and Sheila was describing the exact opposite of everything that he had been as a person. But it was most certainly the kind of life he now wanted to lead. "So where is this little girl now? I'd love to meet someone like that who has been in my shoes, yet was able to gain the proper perspective through it."

Sheila paused, stared out the window, then swallowed hard before answering. "It wasn't just the way Emily lived that touched me so much. Equally impacting was the way she handled her own mortality, and eventually her death. It turned my scientific world upside down."

Eric frowned. "I was hoping this story had a happy ending."

"Trust me; it was sad for those of us who lost her. But for Emily, it was a happy ending, and one that touched my life forever. On a warm spring night, Emily succumbed to her illness with her family surrounding her. Although there was sadness at the impending loss, I was floored by the amount of love that permeated the room that night. In my mind's eye, it was almost a visible glow. I mean, there we were, trying to cope with the fact that such a precious gift was being taken away. Yet at the same time, instead of happening in what could have been a cold and impersonal hospital room, that place was transformed into, for a lack of a better word, a *sanctuary*.

"Emily refused drugs to ease the pain of dying because she wanted to be coherent until the end. It was a wish her parents honored. She quietly went around the room and told each person exactly what they needed to hear to endure her loss. It was the strangest thing; the experience was both heart-wrenching and, somehow, amazingly comforting. At one point she looked straight at me—her little eyes penetrating to the very depths of my soul—and said, 'Please don't feel guilty anymore. You did everything you were supposed to do, and now I have to fulfill my destiny. You will save others, but you have to learn to let go of some of us. And Dr. Redmond, your dad will always be proud of you.'"

Sheila's eyes misted over. "I no longer cared about my professional appearance and openly wept in front of everyone. Surprisingly, I felt more cleansed than sad that day. She delivered what I came to believe as a divine message. Then, as if on cue, Emily looked right past everyone in the room and asked, 'Are you here to carry me home to Jesus?' Then after a short pause, as if receiving an answer, she continued, 'Good, because there are a few things I need to talk to him about.'"

Chills went up Eric's spine as he listened to the story.

Sheila's eyes filled up, and tears gently rolled down her cheeks as she continued. "My scientific mind wanted to explain it away as a child's fantasy or a partial dream that were side effects of the fact that her brain was shutting down as she slipped out of consciousness. But in my heart, I knew the experience was very real and was not explainable by any experiment science had yet conceived. That experience served as the catalyst that led me on a spiritual journey. That journey enabled me to find answers that only faith, not science, could provide. When I found that faith, it affected my life in many ways.

"When it came to work, the line of professionalism was still there. But I was changed. The longer I practiced medicine after meeting Emily, the more I cared about the people I treated. And I noticed patients responded to my advice, guidance, and treatment more positively when they knew I cared about them as a person.

"And in my personal life, I became hungry to fill a void that I knew existed at the very core of my being. I knew I had been touched at the very least by a message and at the most by a presence I could only describe as divine in nature. Emily had just been the mouthpiece, but I was, and still am, convinced the message was from God. I know that all sounds crazy, but in my heart of hearts, I know it's the truth. In time I found out God was the only the thing...well, Person...able to fill that void I talked about earlier. Once I had that experience, I had to share it with others. It was just as important, if not more, than my service as a physician.

"In your case, I simply felt I needed to share this with you and somehow play a small part in your redemption story. I'm not sure what exactly that will mean for you, but now that you've told me about your plan, I'm convinced I'm not the only one who is trying to reach out to you. Knowing about your plan strengthens my resolve and belief that God is trying to get your attention."

Eric allowed the story to soak in. He didn't know what he was supposed to think. It was an amazing story and one that probably helped Sheila get through the tough days when she couldn't save the lives of some of her patients. But was Sheila actually expecting him to become some kind of "religious" person? He didn't have time to take away from his plan in order to worry about religion. Yet he was thankful and surprisingly moved by the story.

"Sheila, I—"

"Eric, I know you have doubts and questions right now. But please let me finish, and then I'll help you with anything you need for your journey. I know you don't believe in God, and I know you think He's a cosmic killjoy who's somehow getting pleasure out of what you call your 'death sentence.' Please, if you would just humor me, I want you to know that I think—"

For the first time since he met her, Sheila didn't have the right words for the moment. "Just remember that although it may not seem like it sometimes, God loves and has a purpose for every person on this Earth. That includes you. You just may not have found yours yet. Having said that, I think the thing you're setting out to do is nobler than anything I've yet encountered from anyone in your situation. I know this isn't about you getting what you want out of your final days. It's about redemption. It's about you giving back the greatest gift you have—are your last precious days on Earth."

Eric was speechless as Sheila fought her tears in vain. "It may not mean anything to you now, but I'll be praying for you. I know this has all been a lot to take in, but I need you to accept the fact that you are running out of time. This plan of yours is admirable, and I want to do whatever I can to help you. But the reason I told you all of this is because I need you to know that God has a plan for you. The question is, are you willing to acknowledge and accept that plan? I can't tell you what He has in store for you in the next few weeks, but I can tell you that you can't run from Him forever."

Sheila's story about Emily and the things she discovered piqued his curiosity. And the passion with which she spoke indicated she was either telling the truth or crazy. He knew it was more likely the former than the latter.

For most of his life, Eric had chalked up most religion as a crutch for weak-minded people. Some of them had good intentions (like his family, and of course, Sheila), but at the end of the day he felt that most people who were religious were either looking for personal gain or something to make them feel better about something bad they had done. Because of this belief he had to be honest.

"Sheila, I really appreciate you sharing with me. Again, I'm glad you found all of these answers for your life, as they have clearly made you a better doctor and person. I just know what I have to do right now and that is to work through this list of people I've wronged. Maybe along the way I will deal with God—if He'll deal with me."

Eric wiped the tear off Sheila's cheek, then pulled her in for a long embrace. Talk about crossing the line. For a second time in recent days, there was a part of him that wished he'd met Sheila under different circumstances. The other part, the one that reminded him of the urgency of his time, forced him to pull away and begin the most important journey of the rest of his life.

Sheila composed herself before giving Eric some guidance for the journey. "Eric, as the cancer progresses and affects more organs and systems, new and old symptoms will increase in intensity and frequency. You need to be prepared for anything—from sudden pain to incontinence to a loss of other motor functions. I'm going to give you some prescriptions for medications and a list of supplements that will boost your energy and immune system. As more symptoms appear, you can come in or call, and I'll do my best to find other treatments to help you cope as best you can and to keep you as comfortable as possible."

Sheila left the room to prepare his discharge orders. She returned with another stack of paperwork and all of his personal items.

"Thanks for everything, Sheila. I owe you big-time."

"I'll add it to your tab. Insurance doesn't cover this part."

Eric smiled and started down the hallway towards the automatic doors that would lead him out into the cold fall evening.

"Eric, wait!" Sheila yelled from the end of the hall. She rushed down to talk to him face-to-face. "One last thing. A few years ago, when I started my journey of faith, I was led to a local church. I met a pastor there who was able to help me through some really tough questions and turmoil. Just in case you need or want someone to call on, here's his number."

Eric looked at the name and number, and his eyes widened. "Now that's a funny coincidence."

He handed Sheila his regrets list, and the first name on it was the same as Sheila's pastor.

Three

In spite of the most recent developments in his life, Eric could not bring himself to believe his "death sentence" was somehow ordained by God or part of a larger cosmic plan. He was, however, at a loss for words to explain the fact that Sheila's pastor was, in fact, the same Mike Davenport that was the first person on his "R&R" list. For the time being, all he could tell Sheila was that "this is the mother of all coincidences."

The "R&R" list, as he had come to call it, was short for "Regrets and Reconciliation." As he'd told Sheila, this represented the seven people (other than his brother and parents) that he had somehow wronged over the course of the last half of his life. He vowed to spend his remaining time tracking down those seven people in order to "right" the wrongs he had committed against them. Eric had stashed a substantial amount of the money he had made as a successful attorney into savings and stocks, so financing his endeavor was not an issue. In addition to financing the journey, he also planned to use some of his money as financial compensation in some of the situations. Thinking ahead, Eric knew that, in several of the instances, it would be more than appropriate to provide some financial help along with an apology.

In most cases, Eric's bad choices and actions adversely affected the course of the lives of the people on the list. The more time he put into his preparations the more he wondered how each individual would react. As he sat in his apartment thinking about the possibilities, he realized he needed to be prepared for whatever outcome might take place. He could not be responsible for their reactions; he just needed to do what he thought was right at this point. Still, he worried that in a few of the cases, his actions were the catalyst to some really dark times. This moment of introspection and perspective was one that Eric had not been capable of grasping or even caring about before his death sentence.

Eric was relieved that it didn't take long to find the first person on his list. He had no idea how he would go about finding the rest, but through a search of court records, Google, Facebook, and the private investigator he employed from time to time, Eric figured he'd be able to track down all seven people.

Eric prepared for his encounter with Mike as if he were preparing for the trial of his life. *That's funny,* he thought. *Maybe this is the trial of my life. I've already been found guilty, and before my sentence is carried out, I have to do all that I can to pay my debt to society.* He had not seen Mike since law school and had no idea how Mike ended up in ministry.

The fact that Mike was a member of clergy added both a difficulty level and interesting twist to his situation. On the one hand, this would be more difficult because Eric was not the type of person who wanted to talk about religion with anyone, let alone with a former friend he had wronged. On the other, it was a chance to see how forgiving religious people really were.

⌘⌘⌘

"So what did you do to Mike that possibly could have been so horrible that you need to go back to him after all these years?" Sheila asked.

Eric switched the phone to his other ear and continued with the shameful story about how he wronged Mike Davenport so many years before. "Mike and I were students and one-time roommates at law school. I'm not trying to toot my own horn, but academics always came pretty easy for me. Everyone always told me how gifted and driven I was."

"Gosh, and so humble after all these years," Sheila interjected.

"Yes, I know. Anyway, Mike struggled to pass most of the classes we had together. But I have to hand it to him, even though it didn't come naturally, Mike worked hard and was determined to do his best in a difficult environment. I helped him out as much as I could, and Mike seemed to be thankful for it.

"Halfway through our third year, my grandmother passed away. That's a whole other story in and of itself. To make a long story longer, I had been close to my grandmother when I was younger. But as I focused on my own life and ambitions, I didn't keep in touch with her as much as I should have. This was especially true when she became ill. I only took one long weekend to go visit her, as she lay bedridden from her sickness. Once she died, I wasn't sure how to grieve over the loss. I turned to partying and sleeping around in order to drown out the pain I had been feeling.

"Instead of being studious and responsible, I switched roles with Mike. He tried to help me stay focused and listened when I needed to talk, even though we hadn't been the closest of friends before that time. I think that was the first time I felt that void you were talking about earlier—the one where no matter how hard you try to fill it, it's still there. Well for me, I partied long and hard in an attempt to cover that void up. And the more I tried, the easier it became to continually choose wrong instead of right.

"Things quickly fell apart for me. I put on a good façade and fooled almost everyone, except Mike, into thinking I was doing fine. In fact, that wasn't the first time in my life when I cracked under intense grief and pressure and was involved in destructive behavior. Most of those people I mentioned earlier, who said I was gifted and would be successful, well, those people just didn't know about the things I did when they weren't around. The truth is, whenever the pressure in my life was turned up, I tended to kick into survival mode and do anything I needed to in order to get out of a crunch. And that's what happened in the winter of that year just before classes were going to end for the semester."

Eric took a deep breath and sighed, knowing what came next.

"Eric, you don't have to share all of this with me if you're not comfortable," Sheila said.

"I know, but I need to get this out there. It's my practice run since Mike is the first person on the R&R list that I have to talk to. It will make it all easier when I see him in person having gone through it with you. Anyway, Mike and I were enrolled in a Constitutional Law class together. Each student was required to work on a randomly assigned case that was eventually overturned at the appellate or Supreme Court level. The cases were based on actual rulings, but the professor changed the details enough so the students had no way of researching the real case in order to cheat the assignment. Each student was required to study the case throughout the semester and then point out the possible weak points that could lead to a reversal of the original ruling in the appeals process.

"In spite of my grief over the loss of my grandmother, I somehow kept up with the rest of my classes, even though in some cases I was barely sliding by. But this was the one project that had to give way. By the time the semester came to an end, I had little to no research to even fudge some sort of half-hearted case study.

"Luckily for me, or so I thought at the time, I came home late one night to find that Mike had left his computer on. There, on the screen, open for me and the whole world to see, was the case study he'd been working so hard on all semester. I scanned his research and findings. It wasn't a stellar paper, but it was adequate for the situation. At worst, it was better than nothing. And nothing was all that I would have had to turn in. I couldn't afford to have any delay on my road to success, so I quickly weighed out the pros and cons of my situation.

"I knew the consequences on both sides of the coin. On the one side, I was taking Mike's hard work and ruining his future. On the other side, I knew I risked being caught in order to have something to turn in. Somehow in the end, desperation won out over wisdom and integrity. Once the decision was made, I had to move fast.

Eric hung his head. "So I attached Mike's work into an email and sent it to myself. Then I got online, downloaded a virus, and purposely crashed Mike's computer in order to cover up my tracks. Knowing I was putting mine and Mike's futures on the line, I went as far as paying a computer science student to hack into the professor's computer files. The student changed the professor's assignment spreadsheet to make it look like I was originally given Mike's assignment, and vice versa. This last devious step was all I needed to put the nail in Mike's coffin. At the time, it was well worth the six-pack and three hundred dollars I had to shell out to the computer genius to work his dark magic.

"Mike was blindsided by the whole thing. He was, however, diligent enough to have a professional recover a rough copy of his case study to turn in. Fortunately for me, I had already turned in my copy first. Since I had such a good reputation and had talked to the professor about helping Mike on many occasions, the professor sided with me from the start. I said nothing when Mike was accused of plagiarizing my work.

"The two of us were called into a hearing with the professor and the dean of students in order to resolve the situation. In front of everyone, the professor pulled up his doctored records for the semester. They were undisputable in the dean's eyes and supported my side of the story. I was allowed to go on and eventually graduate, whereas Mike's reputation was tarnished beyond repair. Mike was expelled from the program and ended his pursuit of a legal career. After all, he had experienced the ugly side of the twisted truth and technicalities of rules and law. Disgusted, he wanted nothing further to do with the legal system.

"The night Mike was packing up, he confronted me in the hallway. 'You know, Eric, I may not have been the brightest law student, but at least I didn't have to cheat my way to success. One day, you'll regret what you've done here, you rat!'

"I smiled and bragged, 'Maybe if you'd been smarter, you could have proved what I did. But then maybe that's the reason you weren't cut out for the practice anyway.' Mike drew back and punched me square in the jaw.

"'Prove that!' he said, as he stormed out of our room. That was the last time I saw Mike."

"Wow," Sheila said. "I can see why you might be nervous about seeing Mike after all these years. That's a pretty rough story."

"I know that now. And I know you're just being nice. What I did was so far beyond 'rough.' I ruined his life and took away the career he had worked so hard for over those first few years. At the time I was young and stupid, but I can't blame my actions on youth or immaturity. I was plain wrong. I'm definitely not proud of what I did to Mike. And

I'm not looking forward to meeting with him tomorrow. But it's something I have to do if I ever plan on getting through the rest of this list."

⌘ ⌘ ⌘

As Eric pulled into the parking lot of the New Hope Christian Church the next day, he continued to ponder the possible outcomes as he tried to get over his anxiousness over the task at hand. While he stared ahead, not willing to act just yet, he had a somewhat twisted thought of how the meeting would end. He imagined being able to use his skills as a debater and master position maker to somehow prove that Mike was wasting his life away as a minister instead of being an attorney. He could imagine Mike losing his temper and punching him square in the jaw like the last time he'd seen him. There was a cynical part of Eric that would be amused if that happened, as it would prove his long-running theory that most religious people are hypocrites. However, that's not what he intended to accomplish. On top of that, it was Eric's fault, not Mike's choice, which kept him from the legal profession.

Eric headed inside the church, and the receptionist directed him to Pastor Mike's office. The title struck him as odd, but he followed the receptionist's lead nonetheless. He had no idea how Mike was going to react to his unannounced visit. Eric didn't want the chance for Mike's emotions to cloud his opportunity to apologize to him, so he had used a pseudonym when he called to make the appointment the night before. Sheila had also promised not to let Mike know he was coming.

Eric stood outside the door for a few seconds until he gathered enough courage to knock quietly on the solid wooden door.

"Come in," Mike said.

"Thanks," Eric replied, as he walked into the room.

Mike looked up from his work and stood up to shake Eric's hand. As their gaze met, he immediately said, "Eric Stratton. Wow, you have no idea how odd it is to have you walk through that door. Would you believe me if I told you I was working on a sermon about forgiveness?"

Eric stood speechless for a second.

"You're not here to steal my sermon are you?" Mike asked.

Eric cracked a smile but still could not find the words.

"I'm kidding, Eric. This is obviously an awkward moment for us both. I'm sure there's a good reason why you lied to my assistant and gave a fake name and reason for this appointment. I'm not going to hit you, so why don't you pull up a chair and have a seat? So, what brings you to New Hope Church? I know you're not here to catch up on old times."

Eric nervously pulled up a chair and sat down on the opposite side of Pastor Mike's desk. He cleared his throat. "Mike, I've practiced what I was supposed to say to you about a hundred times over the last few days. But I had no idea that seeing you face-to-face would be this hard."

Eric looked down and noticed his hands were shaking. "Let me cut right to the chase and say that I can't use youthful indiscretion, my grief at the time, or anything else as an excuse for my past behavior. I'm sorry for what I did to you. I'm sorry for ruining your life. I don't blame you for hating me or hitting me, and I don't expect anything from you regardless of your job now. I just came to tell you that I now realize what I did was wrong on many levels, and I wanted to apologize face-to-face. I hope someday you'll be able to forgive me."

Eric felt like a broken man groveling in front of Mike. But when his eyes looked up from his trembling fingers and met Mike's gaze, he didn't see anger, resentment, or even frustration. He saw…compassion?

"Eric, you have some nerve coming in here and asking for my forgiveness after all these years."

The response caught Eric off guard until Mike cracked a smile. The pastor stood and reached across the desk to shake Eric's hand. "Just kidding again, man. You seem uptight, and I'm trying to break the ice!"

Relieved, Eric stood to shake Mike's hand.

Mike slapped him on the shoulder. "Let me make this easy for you. First off, I appreciate you coming here to see me. It does mean a lot to hear it. Yes, what you did was wrong. But you've shown a lot of guts and character coming here today after all of this time to see me. It was obviously important to you, and you clearly had to get this thing off your chest. Truth be told, I was angry and very bitter at first. I hated you for a while and even contemplated getting revenge somehow. But I need you to know that I forgave you years ago and could never rightfully call myself a pastor if I couldn't forgive you." He cocked his head. "This is obviously not a casual or quick conversation. Why don't we go get a cup of coffee or a sandwich or something and continue elsewhere before we get in too deep here?"

"I'd really like that, Mike."

Mike led Eric to a small café about three blocks from the church. As they walked, Mike said, "I've seen your picture in the papers a few times. I guess you fulfilled your dream of running with the big boys. Sounds like you were involved in some pretty important cases."

"Yeah, I've been lucky in that area, I guess. I sort of had to sell my soul to get there—as you know. But I have to be honest, I've enjoyed the success, and it's been a good ride."

"Until now?" Mike asked.

"What do you mean?"

"Well, something brought you here, and I doubt it's the celebration of the good life. Most people don't confront these kinds of skeletons when everything is fine and dandy. I'm your dirty little secret, and, if all was well, I don't think you'd have graced me with your presence."

After the two men were seated at the deli, Eric continued to bear his soul. "Mike, truth be told you're one of several dirty little secrets I have. And...I'm dying. I have cancer, and I've only got about two months to live. There's nothing I can do about it. So I'm dying, and I'm scared." Eric turned away as hot tears streaked down his face.

Mike was quiet for a minute, then said, "Eric, I'm sorry for your condition. I can't even begin to imagine what you might be going through. If you don't know of a good doctor, there's a lady in our congregation that's pretty amazing. Maybe you could get a second opinion."

"Sheila is an amazing doctor, but I've already seen her."

Mike was clearly shocked by the statement but allowed him to continue.

"I'm afraid I've exhausted all of my options. I'm not looking for someone to cure me now. I've gotten the second, third, and fourth opinions, and they're all saying it's only a matter of time. But I do have some unfinished business to take care of, starting with you. I appreciate you being so gracious, and I know you say I'm forgiven. But as I sit here across from you, it's like…a knife turning in my heart. I've never felt like this. I guess seeing you makes me realize how much I cost you, and I see how bad my actions really were. Here you are, stuck in this ministry, no offense, and you could have been a good lawyer. Worst of all, the thing I did to you was just the tip of the iceberg."

Mike laughed. "No offense taken. But that chain of events, my friend, is something you cannot take credit for."

What Eric thought was going to be a short conversation over coffee turned into a half-day event. Mike spared no details as he told Eric what happened between the last time they had seen each other and the present.

"I was devastated after I was expelled and had no idea what my next steps would be when it came to school, vocation, or life. I couldn't understand why I had worked so hard only to see that work stolen from me by someone I was trying to help. Not able to deal with the injustice of the situation, I descended into a deep despair.

"I would never have hurt myself, but there were definitely days when I no longer wanted to be alive. I resented the legal profession, the school, and most of all, you. I actually thought of tracking you down and doing something bad to you in order to get my revenge. I'm not comparing my situation then to what you're facing today, Eric, but I was at a place where I needed to find some answers. Those answers didn't come quickly, so I started working odd jobs to pay the bills and pass the time. Somehow I got hooked up with a company that sent people overseas to China to be English teachers and tutors. With nothing better on my plate, I signed up for a one-year tour.

"The decision to go overseas was one of the smartest things I ever did. The people there were amazing. I couldn't believe how happy they were with what little they had. They made the poor people in this country look wealthy. I was also amazed they could maintain such a good attitude with the government controlling so many aspects of their lives.

"I was there for about three months when I met a Chinese woman named Lin. Other than one other tutor, she was about the only person I knew who could speak English. She had spent a few years in the U.S. with her aunt and uncle, which is where she learned the language. After a while, we developed a close friendship. The more time I spent with her, the more I hoped it would develop into something more. I think she felt the same way, but for some reason, she wouldn't allow it to get to that point. That made me pursue her all the more. She was different from any woman I'd dated up to that point. I wanted so badly to get to know more about her. On top of her natural beauty, she was one of the most compassionate and kind people I've ever met. It didn't take long before I was madly in love with her.

"But there was a point at which she wouldn't allow me to get any closer. She became evasive when I started asking more details about how she spent her time when she wasn't tutoring. I began thinking she was part of a religious cult or something because she always wanted to talk about religion and how she wished the Chinese people had more freedom to worship. My curiosity got the best of me one night. I followed her and discovered the reasons she had been so secretive. It turned out she was involved in an underground Christian church, which is a big no-no over there. They are very intolerant of any religious practices except those sponsored by the state. I was surprised that a woman like her would be involved in something technically illegal.

"In time, I came to understand why those people were willing to risk everything for the underground church. I also found out it was the reason most of the people in that town were so happy. All their lives they suffered under the oppressive rule of communism. When they finally heard a message that taught something that could set them free, they accepted it and dedicated their lives to spreading the news. I admired them for their dedication and tenacity.

"But for me, the reasons I got involved were not quite as noble at first. I really didn't have the same appreciation for their faith-based freedom since I grew up in the U.S. and had experienced the freedom to worship already. So I don't know if it was the intrigue, the risk, or my attraction to Lin. But as soon as I gained their trust, I joined their cause. I started helping them smuggle Bibles into the town and neighboring cities from there. You'd be amazed how much those people would do to get their hands on something most of us take for granted here. They guarded and cared for those books like you and I do our cars or prized possessions.

"Anyway, things went sour one night when their version of the FBI raided our little operation. Eric, I was never so scared in all my life. It was like something out of a movie. In reality it happened so fast, but it seemed to play out in slow motion around me. The police started throwing people around and herding them off to God knows where. People were screaming, and kids were crying. There were a couple of gunshots, then mass chaos. You would have thought these people were drug dealers, gang members, or insurrectionists. All they wanted to do was worship in freedom and hand out some Bibles, and for these 'grave' crimes against the state, they were being rounded up and taken to prison.

"The police piled boxes of Bibles, papers, equipment, and anything related to the underground church and started a bonfire like the ones you used to hear about in Nazi Germany. One poor guy ran at one of the officers to try to stop him from throwing a box of the Bibles onto the inferno. Another officer hit the guy with a baton, and his momentum didn't stop until he landed in the fire. I broke free to try to help the guy and got smashed on the back of the head. There were two things that will haunt me forever from that night. The first was the indescribably horrible smell of burning human flesh. The second was Lin's screams. She struggled against the men who were trying to take her away. When I tried to get up again, it was lights out for good.

"I awoke several hours later and was questioned by this angry little man with a high-pitched yelling voice. His breath reeked of fish, and I had to smell it while enduring his squeals for what seemed like an eternity. They accused me of being a spy and insurrectionist. They didn't torture me or anything like that, but it was not the most pleasant vacation I've ever had.

"They held me for a few days until the consulate got wind of my situation and started asking questions. The government agreed to release me after declaring me persona non grata. I was free to leave but could never return to the People's Republic again. Before they turned me over to the consular officers, they warned me that if I ever talked about that night, they'd kill Lin. I've never seen or heard from her since then. I can't really pick up a phone and call anyone in the village there since they rounded up almost everyone. And I don't dare send a letter because I don't want to get anyone in trouble for being associated with me since I carry the title of an insurrectionist. I don't know her fate for sure, but if she survived the process that night, I imagine she's still rotting away in a horrible Chinese prison somewhere." Mike sipped his coffee and stared for several minutes past Eric through the window at the people walking past the small café.

"So I guess you could say after that I was grateful to be alive. In fact, I hadn't felt so alive in quite a long time. Don't get me wrong. I was hurt and depressed about not being able to see or help Lin or the others. Yet at the same time, I knew God was trying to speak to me through that situation and the one with you back in law school. I felt as if I was on the right path after being part of the wrong plan for so long. I was so motivated to find out more about the faith because I felt like I would dishonor Lin and those people if I did anything but spend the rest of my life doing what I could for God with the freedom I still had. So I dedicated my life to Him, enrolled in seminary, and have served in the ministry ever since. Luckily, no one stole my papers at seminary."

Eric smiled at the joke, then shook his head in disbelief. "And that story just made me feel a million times worse. If I hadn't stolen your paper, you wouldn't have had to endure all that horrible stuff."

"No, you still don't get it. If you hadn't stolen my paper, I would not have had the *privilege* of taking part in one of the most worthwhile causes in history. And I never would have found my life's calling. You see, Eric, I know beyond the shadow of a doubt that I'm right where I need to be. I was supposed to be there that night in China, as bad as it was, and I was supposed to go into ministry instead of legal practice. And I'm supposed to be here telling you this regardless of how crazy or cliché this all must sound to you."

"So God made me steal your paper and get you kicked out of school then?"

"No, it doesn't work that way. God doesn't put evil into our lives to make us do what He wants. But He does allow evil situations to take place in order to work through them and reach out to us to demonstrate

His love. We still have free choice in the path we follow with our lives, but He wants us to choose the right path."

Eric listened carefully to Mike's words but could not look him in the eye. Instead, he picked at the uneaten crust of his sandwich as he formulated his thoughts. "Okay, so then God gave me cancer so I would meet you and Sheila and hear all these wonderful things about Him? Come on. I have a really hard time with that thought process. Don't think I'm not grateful to you for making this whole apology thing easy. And I'm not saying that guy in China died in vain or that your friend was imprisoned for nothing. But I can't believe that God would give me this death sentence because it's part of some bigger plan. Is that what you're saying? Because instead of giving me cancer, God could have just showed up at my door and proved He was real. I would have listened then, too."

"I don't know why God allowed this to happen to you," Mike said softly. "What I can tell you is that from what I've experienced in my life, I know He's real. And from what I've seen so far, I'd say He's trying pretty hard to reach out to you. You need to open the eyes of your heart and step out in faith a little."

Eric slouched down into the café booth and sighed. He wouldn't admit it, but the things both Sheila and Mike had shared so far had really touched him. Furthermore, the fact they barely knew him, yet seemed to care so much, impacted him all the more. If this were a court case to prove somehow that God was trying to reach him, Eric would have to say the jury would probably rule in God's favor.

He finally said, "I'm trying to be open minded. You know that old saying about the fact that there are no atheists in foxholes? Although I'm not engaged in any type of combat, I'm pretty much staring death in the face right now, too. Everything has happened so fast, and I'm merely trying to catch up and let it all soak in. I'm trying to do the right thing."

Eric took out the "R&R" list and handed it to Mike. He explained what it was and what he planned to do with the time he had left. He also expressed his fear over not having enough time to complete the list due to complications from his death sentence.

Eric stared into his coffee cup while Mike read over the "R&R" list.

Mike couldn't think of a time in the last few years when he'd heard of a nobler cause. Being a minister was his life's calling, and he knew he was right where he was supposed to be as far as a vocation. But at the same time, as he pondered everything he'd heard in the last few hours, the gears started turning and he began to feel that he needed to assist Eric in any way possible. He could see this journey as another tangible way to serve God and the people Eric planned to reach, and he knew he was supposed to be a part of it.

Mike excused himself and placed a phone call back to the church. He spoke to his assistant and several of the other pastors at New Hope. Mike relayed the cliff notes' version of Eric's situation to the staff, and when he told them what he planned to do, they unanimously promised their assistance and blessing. Excited about the possibility of having an even bigger impact on Eric, Mike hurried back into the café to discuss some options with Eric.

❁❁❁

Eric held his head in his hands as Mike walked back inside. "Eric, are you okay?"

"I don't think so. I think—I dunno—I feel awful."

"Hold on, I'll get an ambulance."

"No, don't do that. Please. I can't go back to the hospital. I can't lose any more time. Just call Sheila and get me back to the church. Please."

Mike followed his wishes and helped him back to his office in the church. Eric slouched into a leather chair, trying to ignore the combination of pain, dizziness, and nausea that flooded his system.

❁❁❁

He never really fell asleep in the cool leather chair in Mike's office, but the combination of the discomfort he'd felt and the shot Sheila gave him made him numb to the world for a while. When his vision came into focus, he realized Sheila and Mike were standing over him and talking.

"How are you feeling?" Mike asked.

"Like I just swallowed roadkill. Actually, thanks, Sheila, I do feel better than before. I guess there's no getting used to all the weird sensations I'm going to encounter in the next few weeks. You know, I don't like it, but I don't mind the pain or discomfort of my illness so far. I just don't want it to get in the way of completing my task."

"Eric, we need to talk to you about that. I'm going to say this as your doctor first and then as your friend. Although you don't feel too bad now, as more time passes and the cancer spreads to more of your body, you're not going to be fit to conduct normal tasks like driving or walking from point A to point B. And you probably shouldn't be left alone for long periods of time either."

"Sorry to disappoint, Sheila, but I have to do this thing. You know how important it is to me, and I can't believe you're trying to stop me now."

"Oh, I'm not trying to stop you. I'm going to help you. I've notified the hospital that I'm taking an extended leave of absence. Between Mike and me, we think we can help you get to all seven people on your list."

"That's right, old friend. I, too, have worked out coverage for the church," Mike said. "I feel this thing you're doing is important, and I'd love to help you finish your journey. I can't promise I won't be nagging you for much of the way. But I can promise I'll stick by you and help you get to the other seven folks on your list. What do you say?"

Eric was stunned. "As much as I would love and need the help, I think this is something I need to do on my own. I'd feel too bad to take you all away from your patients and congregation."

Sheila crossed her arms. "We're not taking no for an answer. Besides, don't think I'm above getting you legally declared unfit to care for yourself. Because I will, and then Mike and I will truly be able to tell you what to do," she joked.

"Right," Mike added. "And we already know I could whip you in a fight back in college. Now in your weakened state, you'd definitely have no chance."

Eric smiled. "I don't even know where to begin. You guys truly are a godsen—well, you know. Thanks. As easy as things were with you, Mike, I have a feeling that might not be the case with the others. Especially the next one on my list. With this death sentence hanging over my head, my pride is gone. I'm not afraid to say that I've done some really bad things, and if you're both willing to look past them, knowing that my intentions here are good, I'd love the help.

"But there's one thing I want you both to know: I don't mean to look a gift horse in the mouth, but you both should understand that I have no intentions of converting or becoming a religious person or something. I want to be honest and forthcoming up front so we don't have any misunderstandings or disappointments. With that said, you never know when a doctor or a pastor might come in handy, especially for a heathen like me."

"Yeah. Even though we'll both suffer in the court of public opinion for assisting a lawyer, we're willing to do it just this once," Mike joked again.

"Fair enough. I do have one question, though, before we get this whole thing started," Eric said. "A minute ago you said 'the seven other people on the list.' I've already made amends with you, Mike, so by my count, that's six to go."

"Well, Eric, I did cross myself off. But there is one other person you're going to have to reconcile with before all is said and done. I don't have to tell you who it is now, but at some point, we'll have to stop and get that one done. For now, it'll be signified by the question mark at the bottom of the list. You'll just have to take my word for it for the time being."

"Fair enough. Where is the list now?" Eric asked.

"Right here," Sheila replied. "And it looks like Roland Hughes is the next lucky contestant. Roland Hughes. That sounds like a serial killer. Who is that, Eric?"

"The kid I picked on mercilessly in high school. The kid everyone joked would carry out the next school shooting. After the way I treated him, I'm surprised he didn't actually do it."

"Great," Mike said. "We're off to see Roland Hughes the serial killer. Based on my experience with the younger Eric Stratton, I think I'll grab my bulletproof vest."

Four

Six weeks ago
Reconciliation with Roland Hughes

An hour and a half into the three-hour drive to northern Pennsylvania, Eric gave in to the call of his bladder and asked for a pit stop. There seemed to be no end to the supply of supplements and medications Sheila force-fed him every half hour or so. The water he'd been guzzling along with the ginormous (as Eric liked to call them) horse pills had done their damage.

"Good, "Mike said. "I need to stretch my legs anyway."

On the way back to the car, Eric received a call from his private investigator, Robert Jenkins. Three days before, Eric had passed four of the names on the "R&R" list to Robert to track down for him. Information on Roland Hughes returned quickly. Roland was easy to track down since he'd been in the penal system for quite a while. There were many court records that contained his name and information. Although they didn't have a final confirmation on visitation, Eric didn't want to waste any time waiting for an official answer. They decided to get packed and started down the road with high hopes that the word would come shortly.

Robert called to confirm he did, in fact, receive approval from the warden at Cedarville State Penitentiary for an unscheduled visit. "I dunno who you know or what price you paid, but you must have friends in high places," Robert said. "Warden Williams was more than happy to accommodate your expedited request. He confirmed your 0900-1100 hours appointment with Roland Hughes. He said Pastor Mike Davenport is now on the visitor's list too. He did warn, however, that you'd have hell to pay if this guy isn't really clergy. For some reason they're real sticklers about any visit with more than one person at a time unless it's family, legal, or clergy. He also wanted me to let you know that Roland initially denied your request to see him. But then, when the warden told him you were a high school friend, Roland remembered you and said he wouldn't trade a face-to-face opportunity with you for a month of good credit. That sounded weird."

"Thanks, Rob. I'm sure you'll be more than happy with the compensation you'll get for your efforts on this one."

"Hey, Eric, no offense, but are you really rollin' with a priest?"

"Haha, not a priest. Yes, Mike is a pastor. It's a long story that I don't have time to tell. In fact, in case I don't get a chance to tell you this again, I appreciate all your help over the last few years."

"Whoa, he's hangin' with the holy rollers, and now he's sentimental. You ain't dyin' on me, are ya?"

"We all have to go sometime. Thanks again, Rob. Lemme know when you have some info on the other three people on your list."

"Okay, Boss, out."

Back on the road and refreshed from their pit stop, Eric decided it was time to tell Sheila and Mike the story about Roland Hughes and the reason he was on the R&R list.

"Roland Hughes was the kid in high school who would have been voted most likely to make 'America's Most Wanted.' No one ever gave him a chance to be anything other than the reject, loser, or outcast. You name the negative stereotype or label for an underdog like him, we affixed it to him and made it stick. We picked on and taunted that poor kid to no end. There were a few brave souls who tried to stand up for him, but they were few and far between. Most didn't instigate it but laughed when others taunted him. I was one of the kids who made life for Roland a living hell. I was the worst of them, and I'm probably a big reason he's in Cedarville Penitentiary today."

"Wait a minute," Mike chimed in. "Are you telling me you weren't always looking out for everyone's best interest, like the time you got me kicked out of law school?"

"Mike, not to minimize what I did to you, but some of the torment I afflicted on that poor kid would make that situation look like child's play. The sad thing about it is that Roland and I were actually friends in elementary and middle school. Back then, no one cared about what sports you played, who you hung out with, or what girls you dated. But that all changed in high school. Not only did I abandon Roland, but I turned on him. I probably made him wish he was never born.

"Roland was abandoned by his real parents at an early age. Raised by his biological grandparents, he was always physically smaller in grade school. It took him forever to get caught up to the rest of us, and that made him such an easy target. While everyone else got involved in sports and went to homecoming, pep rallies, and proms, Roland avoided all of those things. I don't know why it took something like this death sentence in my life to see things so clearly. That poor kid already had a rough life, and he didn't deserve the horrible things we did to him.

"If only I had known the things I know now, I might not have a longer life, but I definitely would not have all these regrets. I guess, at the time, it made me feel better to know that my life wasn't as bad as his, and it gave me a great sense of power knowing I could do whatever I wanted, and no one would ever stop me.

"Anyway, back to Roland. The stuff we did to him went way beyond innocent or normal high school pranks. The reaction of others really egged it on, so the bigger the audience, the worse the attack. Some of the smaller things were done in the hallways. We'd put 'Kick me' notes on his back, or flag him, or drop his books off the balconies. The locker room was never a safe place for him. We got inspiration from all the frat house and teen movies of the day and made Roland the test dummy for many of those pranks. Routine wedgies and locker stuffings were common. We'd steal his clothes or his bags and run them up the flagpole.

"Then there were a few times we took it too far. Aside from playing pranks on his grandparents' house with roadkill under his window or toilet paper when it rained, we set traps for him a few times. He'd come outside to things dumped on his head like buckets full of urine or rotten eggs. Once we even successfully rigged a Roland trap and got him strung up for ten minutes until his neighbor came over and cut him down. But the worst offense was committed our junior year of high school. I concocted this horrible plan to make all the other pranks pale in comparison. Unfortunately for him, he bought into it hook, line, and sinker.

"I recruited one of the cheerleaders and a few other friends to make him think we'd finally given up on the pranks and wanted to make up for it at the prom. We had this cheerleader pose as his date (although she had a real one of her own) and lure him into the gymnastics room prior to the dance. This cheerleader played it up and easily seduced him into the weight room. Ten of the football players were lying in wait for him when he entered the dark room.

"We jumped him, plastered his face with makeup, and put him in a dress. For the first half hour of the prom, Roland Hughes was tied up and on display for the entire school to see and laugh at. A faculty member finally found Roland and freed him from his misery. But the permanent damage was done. I never saw Roland again. He dropped out of school, and last I heard, he ended up spending some time in juvenile detention after a botched shoplifting attempt.

"We thought it was all just fun and games back then. I can't tell you how many times, until a few weeks ago, that I'd relive those pranks, laughing to myself about his reaction and the mockery of the others who would point and laugh. Although I can never justify in my mind why people snap and do terrible things to other people, I can at least understand why someone like Roland would want to get revenge on people like me for the horrible things I did. Again, it doesn't excuse their actions, but if I could ever have the chance to represent him at a trial, I'd have a field day with his past in order to get sympathy for him from a jury."

Eric shook his head and stared out the window at the passing scenery. Retelling the story of the horrors he'd inflicted on Roland squeezed his conscience like a vice. He couldn't explain why the death sentence made him see things so clearly now. But it was a clarity that carried so much pain, regrets, and guilt. Unlike the situation where he wronged Mike, part of the things that happened with Roland could be explained by poor decisions resulting from youthful indiscretions and immaturity. But they still could not serve as *excuses* for the horrible things he'd done to Roland.

Eric had been a mean, hateful young man. All the praise he had received from his parents, teachers, and coaches made him think he was on the road to a successful future. In the eyes of most of the world, that was the case. But in reality, that's when the rotting of his soul had begun. If he could inflict that type of pain on someone defenseless like Roland, it was no surprise Eric had turned out to be someone who was capable of even greater evil.

⌘⌘⌘

Sheila was a great listener, but she also stopped Eric at various points in the story in order to ask him questions that caused him to reflect on the things he said.

But Mike took a different route. He chose to remain silent when Eric finished his tale of the torment of Roland Hughes. He wanted to somehow reassure Eric that, in spite of the past, he was now making the right choices. Yet at the same time, he felt led to hold back, knowing that conviction was sometimes a healthy thing. Eric seemed to be reaching all of the right conclusions he needed to about the way he treated people in the past. Instead of coddling him or somehow excusing his past behavior, Mike allowed him to wrestle with his seared conscience. He hoped the time Eric spent reaching out to and reconciling with the other six people on his R&R list would allow him to see the necessity and ease with which he could reconcile with the one most important relationship in life.

But for Eric, that reconciliation only existed as a question mark at the bottom of his list.

⌘⌘⌘

In the early evening hours, the trio arrived in the small Pennsylvania town where Cedarville Penitentiary was located. There was barely enough daylight left for them to soak in the breathtaking surroundings. The small town rested in a valley surrounded on all sides by the rolling hills that led into the higher Allegheny Mountains. The deciduous trees stretched from the quaint northern town up to the lower ridges around them. Bright reds, pale yellows, shiny golds, and flat oranges adorned the tall trees for their fall spectacle. Beyond the colorful spectrum, at the higher elevations, the evergreens spread to the tops of the mountains. The trees blended in with the varying elevations for a celebration of the end of the season of life and the transition into the more skeletal landscape of winter. As beautiful as the scenery was, it reminded Eric that, as the year was coming to an end, so was his life. He sighed deeply, knowing this would be his last fall.

⌘ ⌘ ⌘

Eric checked everyone into the hotel, and he and Mike headed to their room to unpack. Across the hall, Sheila did the same. While organizing his belongings and gathering some notes, his cell phone rang again.

It was Rob with updated information. Eric had asked him to find out all he could about Roland's criminal past. Rob informed him the current sentence stemmed from six-year-old convictions for abduction and attempted sexual battery on a minor. Older charges included things like use of a firearm in the commission of a felony, larceny (several times), assault (several times), unauthorized use of a motor vehicle, and trespassing. Some of the more disturbing charges included statutory rape and contributing to the delinquency of a minor. Eric shook his head in disbelief. The anxiety he already felt increased tenfold. He had to fight hard in order to overcome it if he was going to get through this part of the list and on to some semblance of reconciliation.

After sunset, the trio headed out for dinner. Sheila handed out another round of medications and supplements. Eric started to call them his "life extension cocktails." As Mike read some of the labels and joked about the contents and possible side effects of the numerous medications, Eric marveled at how comfortable he was with Sheila and Mike. He felt closer to them than almost anyone in his entire life. He wondered if that was a natural consequence when approaching the end. Not having time to fool around with the normal facades or pleasantries of day-to-day life outside of the knowledge of impending death, authenticity now ruled his existence. It forced him to live life in fast-forward. Coming to this realization allowed him to be more authentic than he had been in years. And as that authenticity increased, so did his vulnerability.

Life literally seemed to be flying by, and every breath he took and every activity he engaged in had a purpose now. There was no longer room in his vocabulary for the term or practice of killing time. From his choices of food (which were much more healthy than ever before), to his phone calls, to time spent pecking away on his laptop, every thought and activity was spent on deepening his new relationships, working towards reconciling the old ones, or getting his affairs in order.

Munching on some fresh fruit, Eric changed the last subject of conversation at dinner and asked another deep question. "So, Mike, I already asked Sheila this question, but if you were in my shoes, what would you be doing with your last days?"

"That's an unfair question. If I say I have things I still need to do, you're going to ask me why I'm not doing them right now. And if I said I have no regrets and have accomplished everything I ever wanted to…well, I wouldn't be telling the whole truth."

Everyone laughed together.

Then Mike's face grew serious. "As a pastor, I have some answers, but I don't have them all. I do my best to serve God in the capacity I believe he's called me to. But I sometimes wonder if I'm doing enough. If I really had only six to twelve weeks to live, would I spend them in my office at church? Don't get me wrong, I know what I do is meaningful. But would I work one minute at a time instead of one day at a time? You know, somehow make everything I do more meaningful? Does that make sense?"

"More than you know," Eric replied.

Mike continued, "Maybe I'd be one of those crazy street preachers desperate to reach just one more soul. Or maybe I'd spend more than 10 percent of what I make to buy a few more coats for the homeless. Maybe I'd send a few more dollars to some children in India who need to eat more than I need a new DVD. I guess this trip has made me question a few things and wonder if I actually live every area of my life according to the things I say I believe.

"I hate to generalize, but I'd venture to say most people want their death to have some meaning or purpose. I've heard the generic answers people use when trying to rationalize the loss of people they know. They say things like, 'Their time was up' or, 'It was just their day,' and to be honest, that's not good enough for me. I'd like to think there is more to it than that. I'd like to think, just as God has a purpose for everyone in life, that although death is part of the process and it comes in many ways, God can use someone's death to reach other people too. I don't want to belittle or minimize a 'normal' death. But for me, I say who wants to die of a heart attack or in a car accident when you could sacrifice yourself pulling someone from a burning building, or saving your friends on the battlefield, or dying for something you truly believe in?"

Mike's eyes shone with passion. "Ever since I became a person of faith, I've had this one recurrent prayer. I don't pray it every day, or maybe even every week, but it pops up occasionally. It's usually when I'm thinking about the subject we're talking about now. In this prayer I ask God to take me when I'm serving him to the best of my ability. And then it hits me. That day should be today. Nothing is more important to me than standing before him one day and hearing the words 'Well done.' So I hope, if I heard the news you have, that's what I'd already be doing. I'm not there yet, but I'd like to be at that place soon."

"Wow, that was deep," Sheila said.

"I'd say it was perfect," Eric added. "It was even better than the good doctor's answer."

Mike and Sheila chuckled.

"Or maybe I'd just go sky diving," Mike said.

And with that, the laughter in the restaurant got louder between the three friends.

⌘⌘⌘

Several hours later, Mike and Eric talked as they began to fall asleep.

"Mike, you know I'm not a praying man. I have this image in my head that in order to talk to God, you have to be...well, a pastor or something. But I'm concerned about tomorrow. If I were in Roland's shoes, I'd probably spit in the other guy's face and call it a day.

Anyway, when you pray tonight, after you ask that one thing you talked about earlier, would you ask God to make things go smoothly tomorrow?"

"Well, it might not go smoothly, but I'll ask Him to allow you to do what you came here to do. But for the record, you could ask Him yourself."

"Nah, I wouldn't want to be insincere. Besides, you have much better rapport with Him than I do. Hey, how did that prayer go again? The one you said earlier about dying at the right time when you're doing something good?"

"I ask God to take me on the day that I'm serving with all that I am."

"So, to tie it in with the other things you said, you want to go out in a blaze of glory."

"Yes, that's another way of putting it."

"Thanks, Mike."

Just as the line between consciousness and sleep began to blur, Eric whispered a simple request, addressing it to whoever was listening: "Please let me go out in a blaze of glory."

⌘⌘⌘

Both from anxiousness and the physical effects of his death sentence, Eric's stomach was already in knots when he awoke on the morning of his visit with Roland Hughes. He was also weary since he hadn't slept very soundly the night before. He felt off, and although he was ready to talk to Roland, he wished it were already over. Mike and Eric planned to go straight from the hotel to Cedarville and then pick Sheila up on the way back through.

Eric crossed the hall and lightly tapped on Sheila's door. She peered through the peep hole in a half-sleeping daze, then opened the door. Even before putting any makeup on, Eric was amazed at how naturally beautiful she was.

She, on the other hand, appeared embarrassed to be caught in such a state. "How are you feeling today?" she asked. "Any new symptoms or complaints I need to know about?"

"Nothing new. Overall, the pain has subsided a little, but I still feel bloated and nauseated. And I'm thirsty all the time." Eric sat down at the small table and chair set in the corner of the room as Sheila grabbed her bag. She checked his blood pressure and his abdomen and gave him his first morning dose of meds and supplements. She also put together the next few doses, along with instructions.

"Any last-minute advice for someone who's going to visit the guy whose life he ruined?" Eric asked.

"Let's get the important stuff in first. Pay attention, as your comfort throughout the day will depend on how closely you follow my instructions. First off, you need to keep drinking water. Drink as often as you can even when you don't feel thirsty. Make sure your urine is clear when you go to the bathroom, and take everything I've given you on time. As far as advice for your meeting with Roland today, that's harder than giving medical instructions. I didn't know you back then, but you sounded like a pretty mean kid. Don't let that kid out. Be the person I've known for the last few weeks. Be the one who realizes he made some terrible mistakes and wants to apologize for them. No matter how he reacts, know that you tried to do the right thing. That's more than most people can say in your shoes. And last, don't lose heart."

Eric reached across and put his hand on Sheila's cheek. "Thank you. I don't know what I'd have done without you." He had to fight the urge to draw her in for a kiss.

She took a deep breath and broke the longing gaze they had locked into. "You're welcome, Eric."

"Thanks for the meds and the advice. We'll call you as soon as we're done. We can grab lunch afterwards, then hit the road."

⌘⌘⌘

The short ride to Cedarville left Eric feeling ill-prepared for his second attempt at reconciliation. He thought he was ready earlier in the day, but with the actual meeting quickly approaching, he grew less confident. Although things had gone better than expected with Mike, he didn't foresee the same outcome at the prison. Still, he knew what he had to do. After parking and going through a variety of security check points, Eric and Mike were led into a small room to await Roland's arrival. The room was bare, save a table and four chairs in the middle. Eric and Mike sat on the same side of the table and left the two on the other side for Roland to choose from.

As many times as Eric had been in prison to either visit with clients or teach classes to inmates, he never got used to the environment. Although he despised tight spaces, it wasn't the physical layout; it was the atmosphere. That atmosphere was ripe with the feeling of the broken human spirit. If the courtroom was the place that represented power for Eric, this place had an air of fear and captivity. The men and women locked behind concrete and steel were not only wards of the state but also servants of the strongest among inmates, and finally, prisoners of their consciences. It wasn't merely the walls that confined these people. It was their minds. They were reprogrammed to survive in a place where free choice was no longer an option. Eric knew the feeling. No matter how hard he wanted to fight it, he was a prisoner as well. So, in a way, he could relate to the men and women housed in this facility.

Eric and Mike sat without speaking as they continued to wait for Roland. Buzzers, slamming doors, latching locks, and distant shouts were the only things that broke the silence. Finally, another buzzer sounded, followed by the clank and squeak of a disengaging lock and then a door opening. It notified Eric he was about to see Roland for the first time in over fifteen years.

Eric's jaw almost hit the floor when Roland entered the room. Roland's formerly scrawny figure was replaced with a stocky build complete with broad shoulders and workout-swollen arms. He had a tough and scrappy look to him. Tattoos covered a good portion of his arms. Eric recognized the work of both professional and prison artists in the pictures etched into Roland's skin. His formerly thin face had filled out and was covered in a goatee. The mullet he had through most of high school was gone, and the fluorescent lights in the ceiling high above reflected off his freshly shaven bald head.

Eric took all of these details in quickly as he spent most of the time it took for Roland to walk from the door to the table staring straight in his maniacal eyes. He wasn't sure yet what lay behind them, but the squint and fixed glare sent a chill up Eric's spine. It made him wonder who the Roland he had known and victimized had truly become. He thought he detected anger in those eyes, then caught a flash of fear and maybe evil. Just before Roland sat, Eric had a far-off fantasy flash where he imagined Roland shaking hands and pulling him in for a "Hey, great to see you" hug. But that was far from the reality of this encounter.

At first Roland sat in silence while his harsh gaze alternated from Eric to Mike and back. Eric knew he was assessing the situation. He was sizing them up for potential weaknesses and threats, trying to surmise some logical reason for their visit. Roland let down his hardened façade for a second to allow Eric to make initial introductions. "Roland, thanks for agreeing to see us. If you don't remember my name, I'm—"

"Eric. Don't think I could forget you," Roland snapped back, eyes narrowed. "Who could forget you? Let's see...you were that guy who dated all the girls I wanted to, played all the sports I would have loved to, brown-nosed the faculty, and oh yeah, made my life a living hell. You tortured me because you used to be bigger. *Used to be* being the key term here."

Roland leaned across the table and whispered, "Somehow, looking at you now, I don't think you could stop me if I decided to rip your arms out of their sockets."

Roland's fists were balled up, and he was grinding his teeth together while staring at Eric. He stood to his feet and thrust his face over the table, until it was less than an inch from Eric's. "You're lucky I'm gettin' outta here in three weeks. Since I don't want to jeopardize that release, I'm goin' to be the model inmate for that much longer. But then, after that, it's goin' to be Roland's day all over again. I'll admit I'm a little curious as to why in the world you're here now. So let's just say I go ahead and let you live for a little while longer. Does that sound good, punk? Besides, you must be somebody important gettin' in here with no advance placement on my visitor's list. So I'll entertain your presence. If for nothin' else, it'll help to pass more of my time."

Eric's heart pounded. He had no defense and deserved whatever pummeling Roland could have delivered. But Roland sat back down and turned to Mike.

Eric cleared his throat, amazed that Mike didn't look the least bit intimidated or uncomfortable. "Roland, this is Pastor Mike Davenport. Mike is only here to help me with what I came to do…moral support, if you will. Roland, you're obviously still angry with me. And I don't blame you, even though it's been a long time since we last saw each other."

Roland began to pick the dirt from underneath his fingernails as if uninterested in anything Eric had to say.

"Look, I came a long way today to meet with you, and this is really important to me. I can never make up for the things I did to you when we were younger. I've been giving that and some other bad things I've done a lot of thought lately. I came to tell you I'm sorry. I'm sorry for the horrible things I did to you. I'm sorry I abandoned you as a friend in order to start picking on you. I'm sorry for laughing at you, for hurting you, and for all the pain I must have caused. I don't expect anything from you, but I'm hoping someday you'll be able to forgive me."

What started as a small "Heh" made a slow crescendo into a loud and boisterous laugh that originated somewhere deep in Roland's belly. "Now that is one of the funniest things I've heard in a long time. What a riot!"

Roland laughed loud and hard once more. "Boy, Eric, I hate to disappoint you, but you sure came a long way for nothin'. Lemme ask you somethin'. Do you expect me to say, 'It's okay' and shake hands and start singing 'Kum-ba-yah' or somethin' after all this time? No offense, Pastor Mike. You see, in my world, I live or die by protectin' what's mine. If I don't have somethin', I take it from people like you, Eric. If somebody tries to take somethin' from me, I stop them. If someone owes me somethin', they pay me back or get hurt. If someone hurts me or mine, then I get revenge. The way I see it, you owe me about three years of suffering or, at the very least, one long severe beating.

Whatever world you think you live in, where you can just say you're sorry and then everything is okay, that's a fantasy world. And as for you, Pastor, I'd keep your distance before lightning strikes this guy. His time is comin'...maybe sooner than he thinks."

Eric hesitated for a moment, not wanting to interrupt his rant. "Roland, I'm sorry you feel that way. Nothing I can say or do will make up for the things I did to you when I was younger. And you're right. My time has come. That's why I'm here. I'm dying of cancer. By the time you get out of here, you'll be done with your sentence. But I'll only have a few weeks left to live; my sentence is death. I was hoping this would have gone better, but again, I don't blame you for the way you feel. Maybe someday you'll be able to forgive me. If not, so be it. I can't change the past. So you're right—my time has come. Maybe it's because of all the bad things I did. Maybe that's why you ended up being someone who victimizes others—because I victimized you. Someday, Roland, you'll be in my shoes, and maybe then you'll understand."

"Well, boo-freakin' hoo. You came to the wrong place for sympathy. I've been in this godforsaken place for too long, and that's the only reason you're still in the chair and not crumpled up in a pile of pain on the floor. I won't take any chances on extendin' my stay even one day longer. I've been in here so long I don't remember what it's like to have any freedom at all. I can't think of the last time I smelled the air outside. Or felt the rain on my face. Or knew what it was like to have a woman by my side."

Roland sneered. "So like I said before, I'm gonna play the part of the nice and cooperative inmate who displays his best behavior until my time is up. And then I'm goin' to make up for many lost years of living. The world has yet to see what I'm capable of. If bein' in this place has taught me one thing, it's how to survive. So don't come in here and give me that psychobabble about victims. It's not about that. It's about survival of the fittest. You were the top of the food chain in high school, and I was the bottom. But now, I'm at the top. I take what I want, and if you're weaker, oh well. Laws were made to try to stop people like me—but they can't stop me all the time. I'll stay on my best behavior till those bars open for me. And then it's open season for Roland."

"I guess we're done then," Eric said, his heart sinking. "Thanks for your time. I hope you don't have to come back to a place like this."

"Oh, no problem. Thanks for lettin' me know what you look like now. I might have had trouble findin' you otherwise. And thanks for remindin' me about what you owe me. I think maybe you and I will see each other sooner than you think. I'd hate for you to go and kick the bucket and not have a chance to say 'good-bye' in a way that you deserve. And don't worry; this will be the last time I'm ever in a place like this. They'll have to bury me before they'll drag me back inside these walls."

⌘⌘⌘

On the way back to the hotel, Eric and Mike discussed the meeting with Roland. "Well, of course it was a threat, Mike. But I don't have any more time to deal with someone like Roland Hughes. I think I said what I needed to say, and I can't be responsible for how he responds. I have to focus on the four other people I still have to reach out to."

"Five, if you go by my count."

"I know, Mike. Wow, I have to admit…in the beginning there, I thought he was going to speed up the process and end things for me today. Did you see the size of his arms?"

"Yes, I did. All the more reason to take some steps to make sure you're protected. What do they feed them in there anyway?"

"Well, think about it. You put a bunch of convicted criminals together in a confined area. Give them weights, books, and more criminal connections, and what do you end up with?"

"Smarter and stronger criminals."

"Bingo, Mike, bingo."

"And all because of sue-happy attorneys."

"That's right! If my clients knew their rights…and maybe how to buck the system, then it made my old job a whole lot easier," Eric joked.

"Nice, Eric. Anyway, did you hear back from Rob about the other people he was checking into for you?"

"Not yet. But we can head back home and rest a few days. The next person I have to see is easy to find. Mike, on a serious note, you were right there. Was there something else I could have said or done to get through to him?"

"Eric, like you said, you did your part. It's up to him how he feels like he needs to respond at this point, and you can't feel responsible for that reaction, nor for anything that happens from here on out. Remember, in your case, you had to receive the worst news of your life in order to come back here and reach out to him. Think of all the people he's been prosecuted for hurting. I'm sure there are more that only he and God will ever know about. Imagine what it would take in his situation. That being said, there is no one out of God's reach. Hopefully he'll find that for himself before it's too late for him."

⌘⌘⌘

Back in his cell, Roland Hughes thought about all of the things Eric Stratton had done to him. He had to admit that it took some courage to track him down and apologize after all of this time. But that didn't change the fact Eric had wronged him so many times and in front of so many people. Roland took out a piece of paper and began to compile a list of his own—a list of all the people who had wronged him and deserved to have the score settled. It was the major players involved in his last conviction who would pay first, as they had wronged him most, in his eyes.

In his own mind, everyone in the system was mistaken about Roland. All of the judges, cops, lawyers, psychologists, and experts failed to realize that it was *their* system and laws, not *his* urges, which were wrong. So he had a fondness for young teenage girls. In his eyes, they had a fondness for him, too. Whether it was because he missed out on a normal life in high school, or because he knew he had power over them, Roland's appetite for them was insatiable.

Society had been given six years to cure him of his urges, and they had failed. If they were willing to release him back into society, it was them, not him, who would be responsible. If they were willing to let him out, he should not have been there in the first place. Therefore, his incarceration was an injustice. And this injustice would be avenged.

Roland's list would be his way of celebrating freedom by picking up right where he left off. It would also be a way for him to exact revenge on those who had wronged him along the way. So Eric Stratton was added to his list; it just wasn't the first name on it.

Five

Back home from the trip to central Pennsylvania, the trio took a day to rest and catch up on phone calls, emails, and other administrative items. Eric and Sheila needed to prepare for the next part of the journey, and Mike would stay behind to take care of church business for the next few days.

Eric had a particularly rough day dealing with the complications of his cancer and was emotionally drained from the experience with Roland. Taking a full day of rest helped to prepare him for the next part of the journey. It gave him the time he needed to process through the events from the previous day. He continued to tell himself he had done all he could to make amends with Roland. But the doubts and questions, combined with his physical discomfort, left him in bed for most of the day. Sheila stayed by his side and took care of him hour by hour.

Eric awoke from a troubled sleep around noon. He joined Sheila in the kitchen. She had already prepared a healthy meal of brown rice, fresh fruits, and vegetables. She also handed him a fresh smelling but horrible tasting green juice drink. He held his nose as he forced it down.

"Ugh, that better add three days to my life, or it was not worth it at all."

Sheila laughed. "I know it tastes like ground grass mixed with dirt, but it will do wonders for your immune system. No offense, Eric, but you look pretty rough today. Are you having any new symptoms or issues?"

"Thanks for reminding me of how good I look," he joked. "No, nothing new today. Same old process of dying stuff. You know, the usual for me these days. I feel pretty rough, and I'm sure some of that has to do with the 'death sentence.' But I think the last few days have been more draining emotionally than physically. I'm trying to stay focused and motivated. I can't keep from thinking that maybe all the others will react the same way Roland did. I couldn't take that kind of encounter four more times. I realize I was horrible to him then, but I wonder if that is the reason he has become this monster today. There was so much hatred in his eyes towards me." He shivered. "Sheila, I think he would have ripped my head off with his bare hands if there hadn't been a guard outside the room."

Sheila was making notes in her medical log while listening to Eric. She turned to him and said, "That has to be hard, especially as much as it took for you to swallow your pride and admit your mistakes. Who knows? Maybe one day Roland will come to the place where you are today. Maybe he'll realize at some point that the life he's living only ends in prison or death, and he'll be able to turn from it.

"You never know how far your actions, good or bad, will go. If nothing else, it shows that all of our choices have consequences for us and the lives of those intertwined with ours. So often we're self-centered and think our actions only affect ourselves. In reality, we're interconnected, and something we choose to do today may affect someone else we never even knew or intended to influence, whether positive or negative. Maybe your actions in the last few days really will cause him to pause before committing his next crime."

Eric pondered Sheila's wise statements as he continued to eat the rest of his meal. How true and far-reaching her sentiments were! But instead of thinking on the positive side of his latest actions, his mind envisioned the possible negative consequences of the ones he made when he was younger. The truth of his role in shaping at least some of Roland's criminal appetite was a burden he could hardly bear. Sure, Roland was ultimately responsible for his own actions. But Eric couldn't deny he was one of many people involved with the process of shaping Roland into the callous criminal he had become.

First, his parents abandoned him at an early age. Eric and his friends taunted Roland and caused him to be further alienated from a "normal" upbringing. Roland didn't have many friends at all when he was younger, and he became the butt of everyone's jokes. How lonely that must have been. Then the last prank they committed pushed him over the edge and caused him to drop out of school. With limited options for vocation and maybe thoughts that no one cared for him, Roland turned to a life of crime. Although Eric didn't know intimate details of the crimes he'd been prosecuted for, the pattern didn't point to a pretty picture. With convictions for crimes like abduction, attempted sexual battery, statutory rape, and contributing to the delinquency of a minor on his record, Roland was most likely a sexual predator who hadn't stepped over the line and killed anyone yet...or maybe he just hadn't been caught.

The reality and finality of this revelation hit Eric like a punch in the stomach. He put his fork down and stared past Sheila out the window and into the bleak, cold day outside. Could this mean Eric was responsible for some of Roland's victims? Could he, too, be blamed for their suffering? And if that was the case, what about the others Eric had wronged? Was he responsible for what they had become and the bad choices they made, at least in part? He wasn't even halfway through the list. How many more people would he find in worse shape who, in turn, negatively affected others? The guilt and remorse swept over him like a tidal wave until he was overcome.

"What have I done?" Eric put his head in his hands and fought off the urge to break into tears.

Sheila moved around to the bench where he sat and put her arms around him. Eric leaned into her embrace and let loose the flood of tears he'd been holding in for the few weeks that had passed since he received his death sentence. He cried first over his regrets. He cried over his family, knowing they would soon grieve over him. He cried over time he wouldn't have and the things he would not get to experience. And then he cried for himself.

Sheila sat in silence for a long time just holding him, allowing him to get it all out. But after a few minutes she, too, was overcome with emotion and cried with him.

"I'm sorry, I hope it wasn't something I said earlier," Sheila finally whispered, breaking the silence.

"No, it's not your fault. It's mine. Regardless of what I do now to make up for the past, the fact remains that I've made horrible choices in my life. I know I can't change them. But to know I had that much of a negative impact on people is too much to come to terms with. It's all hitting me now like a shot in the heart. I was thinking about what you said about the impact we have on people and how far reaching it is. Then I had a brief flash of one of Roland's victims, and I wanted to vomit, thinking I had an indirect part in that kind of suffering. What if some girl was victimized because of what I did to Roland?"

"Eric," she said firmly. "I know the person you are now. You are no longer the person who made those choices. Everyone is responsible for his or her own actions at the end of the day, which is why you've changed yours. Roland is no exception. Or take Mike, for instance. Admittedly, you did something awful to him. And look at all the people he's now reaching for good. So in the same line of logic, can't you take credit for that? But I don't think that's why you're in so much pain. I think the real issue here is a matter of grace.

She squeezed his shoulder. "Nothing you do can change the past. No matter how many people you go back to and reconcile with, no matter how many apologies you hand out, and no matter how much you grieve, you will not make up for lost time. Grace is the only thing that can cover you from the sins of the past. God's grace. There is nothing you can do to earn it. It's a free gift, and until you accept that gift, you'll be no better off at the end of this R&R list than you were in the hospital bed the day you found out you were dying."

"So what do I do? If I can't earn it or rectify the wrongs I committed in the past by apologizing, what am I supposed to do? Should I simply quit now? Or do I just say I want grace and leave it at that?"

"This ties in with the question mark Mike added to the end of your list. And it's what you're trying to figure out now. When looking at all these other people you need to reconcile with, you also need to reconcile with God and yourself. So in a way, that question mark represents two more people on your list; you'll have to deal with it at some point. You can't run forever, so eventually, you'll have to face God, and you'll have to face yourself. The question is, will you come to that realization in time, or is it going to be too late? Eric, there is no way to earn what you really need. Again, there is nothing you can do and nothing you can say, period. In order to experience true forgiveness, the only way is to accept his gift of grace. It's free, but you still have to accept it. Only then can you be reconciled to God. And after that, you'll fully understand and be able to finally reconcile with and forgive yourself."

"But what does that look like? How do I know I've accepted it? And what if I'm only doing it to get rid of the guilt and save my own skin? Does that mean it's still authentic?"

"God knows your heart. He knows why you're going through all of this, and He's not ignoring you. But if you don't think you're ready, don't force it. When the time is right and when you're ready, you'll know. Then it's simply a matter of telling Him."

"All I have to do is tell Him I want His grace?"

"Sort of. But you have to believe He has the power to save you. You have to believe God would do anything, including making the ultimate sacrifice, to get to you."

"And now you're talking about Jesus, I guess. That's one thing I can't grasp. I don't understand why someone would have to be willing or required to die for the things I've done. That's like making an innocent person go to jail for Roland Hughes."

She nodded. "That's exactly what it's like. You don't have to fully understand it. You don't necessarily have to agree with the reasons behind it. All you have to do is accept it, confess that you've done the horrible things you've already come to terms with, and then believe that what He did was enough to save you. And last, you have to follow Him. That's it, Eric. It's out of your hands."

"You say it as if it's easy. It's not easy for someone like me. None of this is. I realize that no matter what I do, I can't make people accept my remorse or apologies. And even when I do what I have to, I can't take away my own guilt. I want this to make sense to me, but I don't know about all this religion and faith and Jesus stuff."

"You don't have to have all the answers. All you have to do is take Him at His word and accept it by faith. I can't tell you how big a role faith has played in my life." Sheila reminded Eric about the story of how she met Emily, then began working her way to the present by filling in the gaps of how she came to a place where she accepted God's grace.

"After Emily's funeral I knew I had to find answers to the questions I had. I began my search by talking to Emily's family. I spent a lot of time with them both during her treatment and after Emily died. I found out they were deeply 'religious.'" Sheila lifted an eyebrow. "Well, that's what I called it back then. I've come to find out that it's much more about a relationship than about anything religious. Anyway, I was amazed at how much their faith sustained them as they dealt with the loss of their oldest child. They seemed to pray and seek God in everything they did. In some strange way, even though they were grieving, they had this incredible peace about them. They had the same perspective Emily had and knew her life had still held tremendous purpose even though, to the rest of us, it was seemingly cut short. Their faith was so strong that I asked them to share their views openly with me, which they did.

"Emily's family invited me to New Hope church. I began to attend the services there and was impressed with Mike and the ease with which he would deliver sermons. I was amazed that verses from the Bible, which were thousands of years old, had an application in my life today. I got more involved, started attending some home groups, and even bought myself a Bible. I still didn't understand everything that was happening, but in time, God revealed himself to me in ways I never could have imagined. I know it sounds crazy in this day and age, claiming that God was somehow communicating with me. But, as I said before, there was this void at the center of my being, and in time, I came to realize beyond any reasonable doubt that God was the only one who could fill it."

Sheila stared at Eric for a minute, as if she was trying to read his reaction to her words. When he didn't say anything, she continued. "I had many of the same questions you have today. But in time I came to a place where I was able to see that the things everyone was telling me about were the truth. And the truth was, I needed God's grace then just as much as you need it today. I was no better off as a straight-laced, by-the-book doctor than you were as a cutthroat law student who would do anything to anyone in order to gain success. All I can say is that you're going to continue to struggle with all of these issues until you come to that place where you can trust in Him. It's not about what we do or don't do. It's about accepting His grace on faith and believing in Him. It's that simple, and there are no strings attached, no fine print, and no catches."

Eric was moved again by Sheila's story and by the passion with which she told it. "You know," he said slowly, "Mike told me his story, too, about how he came to be a religious person. When I consider the things the two of you have said, combined with the crazy fact that Mike was the first person on my R & R list, it all seems a little too spectacular to be coincidence. But I still have too many doubts and questions. I don't know. It's a lot to take in and try to process on top of all the other changes I've experienced. I think I need to get a few more answers. There's still so much that doesn't make sense yet. Besides, it's not like I have to decide today. I mean, I have at least, what, four to ten weeks to think about it, right?" Eric shot her a grin.

Sheila smiled. "Whenever you're ready, God will already be there. And I'll be there, too."

"I know you will, Sheila. Thanks so much for being here for me. As discouraging as the encounter with Roland was, I have to look past that and just hope I'm doing the right thing with my time. Who knows? Maybe the rest of the list will go smoothly. And maybe all of this other stuff will fall into place as well."

⌘⌘⌘

While Sheila drove them farther from the Washington, DC, area, Eric gave her some of the background about the situation with his grandmother. "My grandma was born and raised in a small western Virginia town in the Shenandoah Valley. Although she spent a few years closer to my parents in southern Virginia, her dying wish was to be buried in the only place on earth she ever called home.

"I was in my second year of law school when my grandma became ill. She was in the hospital for quite a while before she passed on, but I always used the excuse that I was too busy to leave school to see her. She died in the middle of the semester, and there was no way I was going to leave at a crucial time of the scholastic year to go back for the funeral. But the guilt and grief got to me, and it ultimately led to my lack of judgment, subsequent partying, and the need to steal Mike's paper in order to graduate on schedule. Once I received my death sentence, I knew I had to come back and say good-bye the right way in order to make up for neglecting this responsibility the first time around."

As Sheila and Eric continued to talk, the two-and-a-half-hour drive passed quickly. When Sheila pulled into the cemetery, Eric surveyed the surrounding scenery. He couldn't think of a more beautiful scene to be buried next to. "I'm not sure where I want to be buried yet, but if I don't think of anywhere else, a plot in this cemetery near my grandma is as good a place as any."

Eric and Sheila stepped out into the crisp fall air and headed out to the row of headstones where his grandmother's body lay.

Elizabeth Anne Shelby was buried beside her husband in the middle of the Green Hill Cemetery. Eric's grandfather had died before Eric was born, and because there was some sort of falling out with his father's parents, this was the only one of his grandparents he'd ever known. As Eric approached he read the headstone, which was engraved with her name, the years she was born and died, and a poignant inscription, which read: *At home with her Savior after serving Him on Earth as a beloved wife, mother, and grandmother.* There was no better way to describe the person buried near the granite headstone that lay before them.

"My grandma spent her whole life serving others and never asked for anything in return," Eric whispered to Sheila.

It looked as if it had been awhile since anyone had been to either marker. Eric bent down to place the bouquet of flowers and small Bible he'd picked out at the Wal-Mart in town. Seeing her grave for the first time, Eric closed his eyes and began to relive very fond memories from his childhood. As he cleared some of the leaves and weeds away from the headstone, he conveyed these memories to Sheila.

"Up until my college years, there was never a Thanksgiving or Christmas that wasn't spent in Southern Virginia at my grandma's house. She was the glue that held my mother and four siblings together. Women of her era were cut from a different cloth. She never held a driver's license nor had a job outside the home. And it wasn't until much later in life that she even bought a loaf of sliced bread at the grocery store.

"She had some magical talent that allowed her to make even the simplest meals taste amazing. She actually ruined staple foods like eggs, bacon, soup, and cornbread for me because no one could ever make it quite like grandma. Her cakes, pies, and homemade bread were out of this world. And there was no such thing as not being hungry at her house. Even if you'd just eaten prior to your arrival, at Grandma's house, you were sitting down and eating something; that's just the way it was.

"For a short time when I was in elementary school, my mom and dad had some sort of difficulty, which to this day they have never discussed with us. My brother and I ended up living at our grandma's house for a while. It was a summer I'd never forget. There were open fields, deep woods, mountain streams, and the best trout fishing a young man could ask for. Combined with the friendship of my brother and many cousins our age, it may have been the highlight of my young life up to that point. My grandma took what was probably a difficult time for our family and made it into an enjoyable experience for me and my brother.

He sighed. "That's just the type of woman she was. Even going to church with her back then was not a chore. I have to be honest and say that I was prone to fall asleep during the simple country sermons, but the experience itself still was an enjoyable one. With such a solid example of a person of faith in my life early on, I can't really explain why, as an adult, I shied far away from anything that had to do with religion. I guess I got desensitized and cynical. I came to believe that religious people were either hypocrites or pushing some kind of agenda." Shaking his head, Eric stared across the field at the mountains in the distance. "I'm not sure how I forgot about such obvious positive examples in my life."

A cold breeze brought Eric from his fond memories back to the reality of the gravesite. A morbid thought crossed his mind as he realized that, a year from that moment, he'd be long in the grave. He suppressed the thought in order to accomplish his task. He knew his grandmother couldn't hear him, but he began to speak to her out loud anyway.

"Hey Grandma, it's Eric. That sounds silly; you know it's me. I'm sorry it took me so long to get here. Better late than never, I guess. I wanted to stop by and let you know that even though I had a lot going on, I should have come down here to see you more often. You meant a lot to me, and I'm sorry I didn't convey that enough while you were still around. Thanks for everything you did for us. Thanks for being such a solid anchor for me and Randy and Mom and Dad for so long. Thanks for all the Christmas memories, the birthdays, the Thanksgiving dinners, the home-cooked meals, and for all of the good times. Remember all the times we played baseball games in the yard? Or when I used to help out with the fall canning? Those times meant a lot to me, as did your sacrificial and loving spirit. You were always good to us.

"Sorry for missing so many holidays when I got older. I know you called and asked about me all the time. I wish I had taken just a little time to call back or visit. I'm sorry for not being there when you were sick. And most of all, I'm sorry for not being able to say good-bye at your funeral."

The strength of his remorse and regrets intensified, and Sheila pulled close.

"I know you always loved us and were always proud of us, Grandma. I love you, too. I love you so much." His voice trailed off into a whisper, and he concluded by saying, "I'm trying to do the right thing. God willing, maybe I'll see you soon if I can get my act together."

The wind picked up and blew across the quiet hill as if in answer to Eric's long overdue visit.

⌘⌘⌘

After visiting his grandmother's grave, Eric and Sheila headed over to his great aunt Mary's house. She still lived in the same small town and even the same house that both she and Eric's grandmother were born in. Now in her mid-eighties, Aunt Mary was still very alert mentally. Physically, it was tougher for her to get around. She was more than thrilled to have visitors, especially when she saw her "long lost" nephew had come back to see her. Assuming Sheila was a girlfriend or fiancée, Aunt Mary treated her to an introductory tour of the family home, complete with explanations of pictures, heirlooms, and other meaningful decorations.

"I don't know if Eric told you, but this is the very house that his grandmother and I grew up in. His great grandfather built it with his bare hands." She took Sheila to the wall of photos that charted the family history two generations back and three generations forward from where she was on the wall.

"My grandfather is right here. My great grandchildren are on this side. There are Eric, his brother, and his parents. I remember we used to try to pay Eric to get rid of that haircut," Aunt Mary said, pointing to the mullet that Eric had in his elementary school pictures.

"It's a family tradition to pick a picture each year and add it to this wall in order to keep track of our roots. When I'm gone, hopefully my children will move to this land and keep the family home alive. I believe everyone should have a heritage they can look back on—a strong foundation to remember when times get tough." Looking over her glasses, she peered at Eric. "We didn't think this one would ever have time to come back and visit. But here he is."

Embarrassed and somewhat ashamed, Eric gave her a half smile and started looking at the heirlooms again.

"Where are my manners?" Aunt Mary said suddenly. "Let me get some coffee going. I made some pumpkin bread yesterday, too. We can sit down and catch up a bit. It's good to see you, Eric. And you, too, Ms. Sheila."

As they drank coffee and partook of her scrumptious treat, Eric filled Aunt Mary in on his plan. He didn't tell her why he'd started on his journey, thinking it would cause her undue worry or stress. He figured she'd find out soon enough. But as soon as Aunt Mary heard about the plan and Eric's intentions to right some of his past wrongs, she quickly excused herself, leaving Eric and Sheila alone in the kitchen, both looking confused.

Eric shrugged. "There are a lot of memories in this house. We used to come here a lot for family reunions and Fourth of July and things like that. This place is old and has so much character. I hope it stays in the family for future generations."

"It's a lovely old place," Sheila replied. "Very homey. I'd be proud to have my roots here."

When Aunt Mary returned, it was obvious she'd been crying, but she seemed very excited. She sat down and reached across the table with her shaky hand and put an envelope in Eric's hand. Assuming it was money, Eric immediately turned it down.

"Oh, I don't think you want to turn this down, young man. Your grandma has been waiting almost ten years to give it to you. Before she passed on, my sister left me specific instructions to give this envelope to you if you ever returned to your senses and got away from that 'big city lawyer's life,' as she liked to call it. You know she was mighty proud of you, boy. But she also thought you'd lost your way and needed to find a way back. I was specifically instructed to give it to you when I thought the time was right or as a part of your inheritance when I passed on. I'm sure glad I'm here to see this day, and I think now is the right time. Especially since you already made it up to Green Hill to visit with her."

Eric took the worn and yellowed envelope and turned it over in his hands. It was addressed to "Bud" in his grandmother's handwriting. That's what she'd called him when he was younger. He put the envelope to his nose and could still smell faint traces of her perfume. Although it wasn't an expensive fragrance found at the fine stores he was used to shopping at, the aroma brought back so many memories. It was as if his grandma had handed him the letter herself and was waiting in the next room for him to read it.

Bud carefully opened the envelope, having no idea what was inside. There were several handwritten pages folded over in thirds to fit in the legal-sized envelope. Tucked inside the pages was a shiny silver dollar from the year 1975, his birth year. Behind that was a picture of Bud and his grandma standing in front of her house when he was about four or five years old. As Eric examined the old photo, it conjured up more sweet memories of good times long gone.

Eric unfolded the letter and slowly read the elegant cursive writing. He savored every word, not wanting the letter to ever end. The letter was dated *14 Sep 1999*. It read:

> *Dear Bud,*
>
> *Yes, I'm still calling you "Bud." I don't care if your big-shot attorney friends don't like it. Thought I didn't know? Well, as I write this, you're still in law school. But by the time you read it, I have a feeling you're already a big-shot attorney.*
>
> *Well, Bud, if you're reading this, it means I've gone to the only other place that I've ever considered "home." It also means you've either come to your senses, or your aunt Mary has now joined me. I hope the former is correct.*
>
> *I know you're a busy person now. I also know that things you're doing up there are very important, even if you do have to associate with all of those other lawyer types. In many ways, I'm very proud of the man that you have become. In others, though, I think you still have some growing up to do. But that's okay; we all find ourselves eventually. Now that I've passed on, you'll inherit my old Bible. I know it's worn, but that's because it has been used so much over the years. I'm not bragging, Bud. It just always bothered me when people would offer to buy me a new one because mine was so tattered. Until I responded by saying it was tattered because I actually read it. People hated it when I said that. I loved seeing the looks on their faces.*
>
> *Enough small talk, though; let's get to the impor-tant stuff. If by now you are still making excuses for your time constraints and busy schedule, don't bother. Life is too short for it all to be spent on work. You need to take time to be with the people you love. When facing death, no one ever says, "I wish I had*

spent more time at work." They always wish they'd spent more time with their family and friends. If you're reading this letter, maybe you feel like time is running out on you.

A shiver went down Eric's spine as he reread the previous line.

I'm not going to preach at you, Eric, but you know where I stand and what I believe. Although I know you think your time will last forever, someday somehow that time will come to an end. And after that, you'll stand before God and give an account of your life. When he asks you what you did to deserve heaven, what answer will you give him? Hopefully, if you've been doing your homework, you'll know to say "nothing." And I don't mean not speaking. I mean your answer should be "nothing." There is nothing you can ever do, and nothing I ever did to deserve God's grace. He just gives it to us, and that's all there is to it. Isn't it almost crazy to imagine He was thinking of you, me, and everyone else while he hung on that cursed cross?

Okay, so maybe I am going to preach at you a little bit. But that's what grandmas do. We spoil you and preach at you. I don't care if you're all grown up now. I used to change your diapers, so you'll just have to sit and listen to me now.

Bud, as my time, maybe Aunt Mary's time, and everyone else's time runs out, so will yours someday.

I don't know if you've opened it yet, but I underlined some verses for you to read in the Bible whenever you have time. You're a lawyer, so I assume you're used to finding passages in books. In the New Testament, the Book of Romans, chapter 10, verse 9 is the first one. And then I want you to find one more. It's in the book of Ephesians, chapter 2, verses 8 and 9. After you read these verses, if they don't make sense (which they should, they're a heck of a lot easier to understand than your law books), find yourself a good pastor to explain them to you. Those verses and many others in there carry answers to questions I'm sure you'll be seeking someday.

Lastly, Bud, I've missed you. I'm not trying to make you feel guilty now, but I've missed seeing you. But don't go kicking yourself for lost time. All is in the past, and all is forgiven. My hope and prayer is that you'll take this letter to heart. I know it'll be a while, but I'd love to see you again someday.

Bud, choose the narrow road. All the others lead to sadness and death. He is the only one that leads to life.

I love you, Bud. Keep that chin up.

Grandma

P.S. Don't spend all that money in one place.

Bud put down the letter and smiled. He dried the tears that had long since started flowing. He knew he was headed in the right direction now. But he still had a long way to go before he'd understand all of the things Sheila, Mike, and now his grandma were trying to tell him.

Energized by the letter and the numerous confirmations that he was at least headed in the right direction, Eric was ready to turn himself in to Police Officer Jon Jansen.

Six

Four weeks ago
Reconciliation with Officer Jon Jansen

The trio sat together in the conference room of the New Hope Church and discussed the best way to approach Officer Jon Jansen since the result of reconciliation in this case would have serious repercussions on Eric's personal and professional life. Not that his professional life was going to matter after six weeks or so. But Eric worried that criminal or civil charges could result from the situation, and he didn't want the possibility of incarceration to get in the way of completing his journey. No matter what the outcome, Eric had to put his fears aside and continue with his plans to talk to Officer Jansen. Delaying this reconciliation could mean an innocent man would continue to suffer due to Eric's actions, and Eric could not allow that to happen.

To complicate matters further, letters would have to be sent to the Commonwealth's Attorney's office and the police department. The revelations contained in said letters would instantly ruin his reputation as a licensed attorney. He would also be forced to deal with any negative media attention from this situation, which was the last thing he needed hindering his goal of reaching the rest of the people on the R&R list. Eric hoped that once justice was done, he'd be able to continue with his journey.

But he could no longer delay the inevitable and called Rob to get the information on the whereabouts of Officer Jansen. As difficult as this reconciliation would be, he knew he needed Mike and Sheila's support in order to continue. As he told the story of the horrible and illegal things he had done to Officer Jansen, Eric could only hope they would still be willing to help him with the remainder of the R&R list.

"Officer Jansen was one of the most aggressive cops I had ever met. I had the utmost professional respect for him as someone I had to face in trials. But I also respect him because he seemed to genuinely care about the integrity of justice. Unfortunately, he'd been too good. Approximately two months earlier, Officer Jansen and I crossed paths again. Only this time, I had no choice but to bend the rules in order to get an acquittal for my most important client. That client was the chief operating officer of a company that brought hundreds of thousands of dollars of annual revenue to our firm. If I lost that case, it could have cost my firm the entire company as a client. And that would also mean my road to partnership might have been put in jeopardy. Of course the partnership doesn't mean squat anymore. But back then, it was the world to me.

"Since the end justified the means, I knew the only way to get to a clean cop would be to set him up. I had been willing to break the rules during desperate times in the past, and this case would be no different. Because the case against my client was airtight, I had to discredit Officer Jansen as a witness, even if that meant bending the truth just a little.

"About a month before the case, I went into survival mode, much like I had when my grandmother passed away, and I ended up stealing Mike's paper. I began to brainstorm the things I'd have to do in order to get an acquittal. I couldn't think of any way to discredit a cop with a record that was pure as the driven snow.

I learned a long time ago that everyone has weaknesses that can be exploited. Rob gathered a folder full of information on Officer Jansen, but none of it led to anything promising for us. 'What we have here is a real life good guy. He's actually an honest cop,' Rob had said. 'Good guys don't go down easy. They have some internal moral code that drives them to always do the right thing.'

I remember telling Rob that everyone has a price or a weak point. I thought about trying to buy him off, but who knows how high I would have had to go. So I started thinking about pressure points. Everything back then was fair game, from his family to his job. Worst-case scenario, I knew I'd have to make it *look* like he was dirty, even if there was nothing there.

"Then Rob came up with an idea for a plan that could affect Officer Jansen's personal and professional life. Rob proposed that we try to use the very thing that our client had been accused of. We couldn't think of any better way to get our guy off scot-free than to show their guy was a hypocrite in the first place for arresting him for solicitation. The question was, how in the world were we going to do that?"

Eric could tell that both Sheila and Mike wanted to be supportive. But he could also tell they were sickened and disappointed in Eric's actions against Officer Jansen.

"Man, I don't like where this one is going," Mike said.

Eric nodded. They still had not heard the worst of the story, so he pressed on and hoped they would not pass judgment on him as he already realized what a wretched person he was.

"Over the next few weeks, I hired several escorts to try to seduce and entrap Officer Jansen into a compromising position. Knowing those attempts might not work, the escorts were instructed to at least make it look as if something was going on. Although the initial attempts at seduction didn't work, the staged pictures couldn't have been better.

"During a midnight shift, Jansen stopped near a diner and headed in for a meal. One of the escorts stopped him and said her purse had just been snatched. Without missing a beat, Jansen took out his notebook and began writing a description in order to broadcast a lookout on the radio. While he was writing, the escort crept right up beside him and propositioned him. 'Yeah right, lady. You got the wrong cop. I'll help you get your purse back, but I'm not in need of your services.'

"Jansen continued to write in his notebook, and when he wasn't looking, the escort scooted up close and kissed him on the mouth. Embarrassed and caught off guard, Jansen didn't give chase when she ran off into a back alley. He then went back to his cruiser to 'sanitize' himself. Jansen didn't report the incident probably more out of embarrassment than anything else.

"Rob told me the stories later on about how he laughed as he snapped numerous pictures from across the street in his car. The angles were perfect. Rob shot pictures of the initial encounter, the kiss, and even the aftermath. The ones of the kiss were classic. You couldn't see the notebook or anything else that made it look like he was taking a report of a crime. It was just the side of Jansen's face being smooched by a local escort. But we still needed something better.

"Several days later Rob and I found an escort who was willing to falsely accuse Jansen of roughing her up during a nighttime rendezvous. Rob put in a fake suspicious person call a block away from where Jansen's cruiser was parked one night. As he exited to check the area, the escort approached, carrying food and several drinks from a fast-food restaurant. Just as he was about to pass, she feigned as if she wasn't paying attention and bumped into him, soaking his uniform with super-sized sodas.

"She then played her part just right. She fell to the ground just as he started yelling at her. Then, when he went to help her up, she fell back to the ground, making it look like he had pushed her. She began to scream for help, and the few people on the street at the time started staring at the incident. She acted as if Jansen were attacking her until someone yelled from across the street. While Jansen was distracted, the escort took off. This time Jansen gave chase. As he rounded a corner, he stepped the wrong way off the curb and twisted his ankle. Once again embarrassed by the situation, Jansen walked off the injury by checking for and clearing the original suspicious person call. He then returned to duty in his soda-stained uniform. Jansen thought nothing of it until the next day when Internal Affairs (IA) called him in for questioning.

"That day, one of the shop owners who had seen the supposed altercation the night before called in to report a purse that was conveniently left near his shop. He told the police he saw a woman struggling with a cop and found the purse when they left. It didn't take long for IA to track down Samantha O'Brien."

Eric paused, then struggled to tell the rest of the story. "I coached Samantha for hours, and when the investigator showed up, she told them of the phony affair Jansen had paid her for. She said that when she went to collect her money for the last rendezvous, he got rough with her and threw her to the ground. She also told them the rumor on the street was that Jansen had numerous liaisons in his cruiser while on duty. Samantha's conveniently red and puffy eye helped sell her story to the investigator. Even though she refused to press charges, the damage was done. Jansen was placed on administrative suspension pending further investigation.

"The plan worked out perfectly, and it gave me the ace I needed to discredit the Commonwealth's star witness. Sure, it wasn't enough to show my client's innocence. But that wouldn't matter once it was presented to a sympathetic jury. I had been so proud of myself, knowing it only set me back about a thousand dollars in cash. A small price to pay knowing this was the case that was going to secure my partnership with the firm. I never even had to use the pictures because Samantha's story had been so convincing."

Eric cleared his throat and stared at the floor as he continued. "But the one thing I hadn't prepared for was my impending death sentence. I was in court, seconds away from delivering the opening statement that would introduce the situation with Jansen to everyone present when the symptoms of my cancer caused me to pass out and be taken to the hospital. I guess if I did believe in God, I'd say he stepped in just before I was about to cause further damage in someone else's life."

⌘ ⌘ ⌘

Eric was physically sickened after he relayed the story to Sheila and Mike. Realizing the depth of his depravity, he was ashamed of the person he'd become over the years. And he was truly embarrassed to convey this message to his new friends. They cared so much about him, and he almost felt as if he was disappointing them with yet another situation in the past where he had put himself above everyone else. He was, however, relieved when he didn't see judgment or condemnation on their faces. Clearly, they were disappointed in his past actions, but they were proud of him for realizing how wrong they were and for following a better path. They agreed that Eric could waste no time getting in contact with Officer Jansen in order to right this terrible wrong.

They all thought the best plan of action would be to reach him at his home first with copies of the prepared letters that would go to the police department's IA division and the CA's office. Eric had also typed out an official letter of resignation to his law firm, apologizing in advance for any negative attention his actions would bring for them.

This was one situation where no one knew how violent the reaction would be, so for safety reasons, Eric decided he wanted to go to Officer Jansen's house on his own. "You can go in on your own," Mike said. "But Sheila and I will be waiting in the car outside in case you need us. We know what we signed up for and can take care of ourselves." When Rob called back with the address and phone contacts for Jansen, they got into the car, entered the information into the GPS, and started towards his house.

The trio arrived at the Jansen's home around midday. He and his family lived in an upper-middle class suburb about forty minutes west of the city. It was surprisingly nice for someone on a police salary, so Eric guessed his wife also worked.

"Well, here goes nothing," Eric said as he headed towards the door.

As he approached, he could hear yelling inside, and, even in a few brief moments, could tell the argument centered on the false allegations that Eric was responsible for. Either Eric's timing was horrible and he'd have to come back, or it was amazing and he'd have a chance to save a marriage he'd caused to be on the rocks. Either way, he had to try to make contact. He knocked nervously several times and heard someone storming towards the door.

Jansen answered the door, looking older than Eric remembered.

Eric peered past his shoulder at someone he assumed was Mrs. Jansen, who was crying. "Hi, Jon. I know this might be a bad time, but I have some very important news I need to share with you. Would you mind if I come in?"

"Yes, Mr. Stratton, I do mind. Right now is not a good time. I'm sure you've heard I have too much on my plate to worry about your other cases right now. If you'll excuse me—"

"Again, I'm sorry to interrupt, but I think you should hear what I have to say. I have information that will allow you to clear your good name and be exonerated in the internal affairs investigation. Could I just talk to you and your wife for a few minutes?" Jansen opened the door and allowed Eric to step in.

"This better be legit, Counselor."

"Trust me. You won't be happy with the details of my information and how I obtained it. But by the end of the day, your department and the CA's office will know you're an innocent man."

⌘⌘⌘

Everything inside Jon Jansen made him want to choke the life out of Eric with his bare hands. The longer he listened to his tale of desperation and deceit, the stronger that urge grew. At first it seemed too convenient. He wondered if this could be some sort of sting or further setup to get information. He finally gave in when Eric told of his knowledge of the situation several weeks before his suspension, where the escort had called in the false report, kissed him, and ran off. Jon knew there was no other way Eric could have that information unless he was involved.

Slightly relieved, Jon was free to focus his rage. He wanted justice. He wanted revenge. And he wanted to exact it right then and there. His emotions were a mixture of seething righteous anger and extreme vindication and relief. And then he looked over at his wife, Lisa.

Before Eric showed up, Lisa had been ten minutes away from packing her bags and moving out. She didn't know what to believe about the whole situation, and although she trusted her husband on the one hand, it seemed too unbelievable that the department would suspend Jon based on some crazy setup. It sounded too much like a story that someone would make up when caught literally with their pants down. It was too much to handle, and her support for her husband had waned over time. Without solid proof of his innocence, she had almost decided she couldn't take the chance of him having blown their vows on cheap thrills and getting away with it.

But in came Eric...in the nick of time. He was all the proof she needed. As if Eric didn't exist, Lisa leaned over and embraced Jon, as if he had just walked back in from the grave.

"I'm so sorry...so...so sorry," she mumbled through grateful tears. Jon held her long enough to make Eric extremely uncomfortable. He then went to stand, and Jon turned back towards him.

"I'm not through with you, Counselor! So why are you doing this now? The trial has been rescheduled. Why not wait until your client walked? Now he has no leg to stand on. With nothing to get him out of his charges, he's going to be found guilty."

"If I said it was because it was the right thing to do, I'd be telling the truth, but not the whole story. I'm not the same person I was two months ago. As hard as that is to believe, I'm seeing things in a new light. I *had* to come here and make this thing right." Eric sat down again. "I know you two want to be alone. But if I could take two more minutes of your time, please let me say a few things that I need to. First, I'm sorry. I'm sorry for what I've done to you and yours. I'm sorry that I further tarnished the name of those in my profession.

"Second, Jon, I need you to know that you're cut from a different cloth. You're a good cop—probably the best I've ever seen. You stand for something I lost a long time ago. Please don't let this ruin your view of the system. There are guys like the one I used to be that exploit it. In fact, there are a lot of us out there. But every now and then someone comes along who can't be bought, bribed, or broken. You are the kind of person that makes the rest of us look good.

Eric felt his face burning in shame. "And you didn't need this or any other situation to make you realize it. You have something inside you that makes you choose good over evil and right over wrong. I want to be like that. But I have a long way to go. I'm just now getting started. Unfortunately, I'm running out of time. I'm dying, and I've taken too long to get to the place you found a long time ago. So in the six weeks I have left to live, I'm trying to right some terrible wrongs, including this one."

Eric began to feel lightheaded, but he pressed ahead. "I don't expect you not to come after me, and I deserve whatever criminal or civil punishment you see fit. I won't fight it. I owe a debt to you that I cannot repay, so when the time comes, you can have whatever you want. My career is over. My reputation is shot. All I ask is that you wait six weeks before you come after me. After that, do what you see is right. I just need six more weeks to make amends with a few others."

Eric stood up to hand Jon copies of the letters he planned to deliver to the department and the CA later that day. But as he reached out to

Jon, he felt a sensation come on similar to the one he'd had in court six weeks earlier. Pain, dizziness, and extreme discomfort set in as he pitched forward. Jon's quick reflexes enabled him to catch Eric just before his head would have smashed against the brick mantle in the living room.

⌘⌘⌘

Sheila couldn't wait any longer and decided to check on Eric. Against his better judgment, Mike agreed and walked to the door with her. As she went to ring the doorbell, she looked inside and saw someone pushing Eric onto his back while shouting, "Call 9-1-1!"

It was a good thing she heard that, as Sheila would have thought they hurt Eric. She banged on the door and yelled to come in. Lisa answered and allowed Mike to explain who they were as she leaned over Eric's motionless body.

"Mike, go get my bag. You, call 9-1-1!" Sheila yelled. Mike and Lisa obeyed as Jon stood there in shock. The one person on Earth who could give him his life back was now lying unconscious on his living room floor.

⌘⌘⌘

Mike waited until Eric and Sheila were loaded into the ambulance. He then went back to assure Jon that, no matter what happened, he knew the story and that original copies of the letters would go to the right places as soon as possible. He felt like he owed more of an explanation to the Jansens but didn't want to overstep his bounds. Mike introduced himself as a pastor and gave Jon and Lisa his word that his good name would be cleared no matter what happened.

"Six weeks, Pastor Mike. Tell your boy he has six weeks, and then after that, he's fair game. Maybe your boy really is sick, and maybe he is really dying. But if I find him alive and well after six weeks from now, then he belongs to me and the justice system."

"Fair enough, Jon. Six weeks is all he needs. If he survives the day."

⌘ ⌘ ⌘

Eric always hated tight spaces. On top of the small area he was confined to, the darkness inside was oppressive. The only sounds he heard were muted voices coming from what sounded like a few rooms away. At first he heard a normal conversation. Then it turned into an argument. He figured he was in the hospital again and started looking for a call button. When he couldn't find one, he lifted his hand to feel for a light switch or anything to cut through the darkness.

That's when his hand hit a fabric that felt like silk or linen. Behind that was a harder surface that enclosed him on the top and sides. He knocked, and it almost sounded like wood. He called out and no one answered. Feeling like the room (or container) was closing in on him, he reached up to loosen the collar of his gown, only to find he was wearing a tie. He felt around more and realized he had a dress shirt and jacket on as well. "What in the world?" he called out again and thought he heard Sheila answer him.

"Sheila! Help! What's going on?" Just then he heard the sound of splitting wood, and Sheila stood over what Eric quickly realized was his casket. She had a crow bar in one hand and seemed to be struggling to keep someone away with the other.

"He's not dead yet! See! He's alive!"

"NO, HE'S A DEAD MAN!" someone shouted.

Sheila was pushed aside, and Eric saw Roland. But he looked different. He looked like a zombie. "Oh, he's dead all right; let's get this thing closed!"

Eric tried to fight him but was overpowered when other zombies joined in. Zombie Jon Jansen, his grandmother, and the other three people that Eric hadn't yet reached were all helping Roland push the lid down again.

When they got it shut, Eric heard nails being hammered into the lid to keep it down. Eric screamed, pushed, and then clawed at the roof of the casket but couldn't get anywhere....

He woke up from his nightmare and sat bolt upright in the CT machine, hitting his head against the roof hard enough to knock himself unconscious again.

⌘ ⌘ ⌘

Eric awoke the second time in a hospital bed to a now-common experience—an IV in his arms and tubes in other places. Sheila was sitting at the foot of the bed.

When she saw he was awake, she stood and squeezed his foot. "Hey there, stranger. Having a better dream this time?"

"Ugh. Is the side effect of one of those medications you gave me crazy weird dreams? Because that last one was crazy weird. And very real."

"*Crazy weird.* Is that a legal term?" Sheila laughed. "How are you feeling overall?"

"Let's see…whoa, crazy sharp pain in my stomach. Head is throbbing like crazy. Kind of feel nauseated. Dizzy and very weak. I think that about covers all the crazy feelings."

"Well, do you want the good news, the bad news, or the really bad news?"

"Really bad first."

Sheila got serious. "I'm sorry, Eric. The cancer is spreading fast. It's affecting multiple systems. Your blood sugar is low, as is your blood pressure. Your white blood cell count is high, and it looks like your immune system is having trouble fighting off smaller infections. You're going to get weaker and feel more pain in the coming weeks. The more your systems shut down, the more uncomfortable it gets. We need to be careful with even the smallest things like cuts, sick people, etc."

"And the bad news?"

"Well, you split your forehead open in the CT scanner and had to get five stitches."

"And the good news?"

"You didn't break the CT scanner, so they aren't going to charge you for it."

"Amazing. How can you joke at a time like this? This is serious stuff. I'm so offended, and I'm suing the hospital."

"Go ahead. I'll tell them you're hallucinating. Hey, at least you're not having a heart attack."

⌘⌘⌘

Sheila thought it would be best for Eric to take a break from the R&R list for at least a week. To Eric, even a few days was precious time, but she warned if he continued to push himself he might be bedridden for the rest of his life. Not wanting that, Eric agreed to take some time off after he tied up the loose ends with Jon Jansen's situation. It would also give him a chance to go back home for a while and spend time with his family. It would be difficult to be home and not seek out several of the people on the list since they lived near his hometown, but he knew he needed to heed Sheila's advice. He was also waiting to find out from Rob where the last person lived in order to finish things up right. As he rested and waited for the information, Eric also decided he could get a few other administrative tasks done at home, so the break turned out to be a good thing for everyone.

The trio made the short trip around town to drop off letters for Jon Jansen's case. Their first stop was at his old law firm to turn in his resignation and say good-bye. Even with the negative situation that was sure to hit the press in the next few days, everyone was able to overlook it, considering the circumstances. Simms, Miller, and Young were disappointed in the way Eric ended his brilliant legal career. But they agreed he did the right thing in the end. It was tougher to say good-bye than he initially thought, but he was able to move on, as he was anxious to get home.

The trip to the Commonwealth's Attorney's office was more difficult. As Eric explained the situation with his solicitation case and what he had done, the Commonwealth's Attorney became smug. She pointed out all of the ramifications of his actions, which of course, Eric knew already. The Commonwealth's Attorney knew this also meant the highly publicized case was now leaning in her favor. Happy with that fact and not wanting to waste more time, she wished Eric luck and said she may see him soon regardless of the condition of his health. Eric informed her he was willing to face any charges and consequences of his actions. He also made it clear that he was the only person ultimately responsible for the setup and wanted to leave Rob and Samantha (whom he didn't name) out of it entirely.

The next stop was police headquarters, where Eric was led in to see the internal affairs investigator. He explained the entire story and handed over the official statement. The investigator promised Eric he'd be coming after him shortly as soon as he was able to clear more pressing cases. When asked what timeframe he was looking at in order to "get his affairs in order," the investigator told him it would be a few weeks. In Eric's mind a few weeks or a month would just about cover it, and he thanked the investigator for his time. As Eric was leaving, the investigator turned to him and said, "Hey, you realize you ruined your career and your life, right?"

"No, actually I'm doing all this to try to save my life. Sometimes you have to lose your life in order to find it." Eric smiled as he was buzzed out of the internal affairs division, wondering where he'd heard the "lose your life to find it" saying before.

On his way back home, Eric had one last stop to make. For one last time, he wanted to visit the courtroom and say good-bye. He approached the bailiffs working the magnetometers, only this time he didn't patronize them. He thanked Jim, Brad, and Thompson for keeping him safe all those years and handed them each $100 gift cards. "And don't tell me you can't take these 'cuz I know the rules. These are early Christmas presents, and I can give them to whomever I want."

"Thanks, Eric. We'll see you around, huh?" Deputy Thompson said.

Eric paused. "No, no, you won't. I'm stopping in one last time before I head out of town."

"Out of town, huh?"

"Yeah, something like that. Let's just say it's a permanent vacation. Anyway, guys, thanks again."

Eric slowly headed down the hall, breathing deeply with each step. He pushed open the heavy oak doors one last time and was glad to find the courtroom empty. Eric walked towards the front and stopped to lean on the rail separating the jury booth from the rest of the court. He turned around and took a mental picture of the place that had meant the most to him for most of his adult life. Some would say this was his church. He deeply regretted several choices he made along the road to and during his training and practice as an attorney. Aside from those decisions and the regrets from the relationships he had neglected, his time as an attorney was a wonderful ride. He would miss this place and hoped those who followed him treated it with the respect it deserved— something he had failed to do.

Eric walked over to the desk on the defense's side of the courtroom and took a seat as he had hundreds of times before. He began to think about his death sentence again. He still didn't have answers as to why this was all happening, but he somehow realized that it really didn't matter why. It was part of a bigger system of things that he didn't fully understand.

At that moment he felt smaller and even more vulnerable. Again he wondered what the consequences of his negative actions would be. Eric had done many horrible things in his time, and unlike his grandmother, Sheila, and Mike, he had nothing to show for his short life except for his success as an attorney and some wild nights indulging his own desires.

Eric let his mind wander, and he imagined what it would be like to be a defendant in God's court. What evidence would the prosecution present? What would he say to explain all of his actions? Who would attempt to defend him from the accusations? And lastly, what would his sentence be? He knew what many other people believed about life, death, heaven, hell, and judgment, but he still could not wrap his own mind around the idea that he really needed God to save him from some fiery torment. So if the last question mark, as Sheila had said before, represented reconciliation with God and himself, that one would truly have to wait. As much as he wanted to understand more, Eric was not yet ready to accept anything more than what he had experienced on his own. He quietly hoped he would have enough time to get to that point as he exited the courtroom for the last time.

⌘⌘⌘

Back at home Eric scanned the gloomy apartment and tried to relax his restless heart. He only needed to hear back from Rob about one other person on his list, and then he'd be able to plan out the last month or so of his life. As he waited to hear from Rob, who promised final information that afternoon, Eric called Jon Jansen to follow up.

"Jon, I just wanted you to know that all the statements, both in writing and in person, have been given. You'll be exonerated shortly. From what I understand, you'll be able to return to duty within the week. I'm sorry, again, for all the trouble and pain I've put you and your family through. Please stay strong and stay safe out there. We need guys like you around for a long time."

"Well, thanks for having the guts to come back and face all this like a man," Jon replied. "I'm sorry for the situation with your health too. That doesn't mean I'll soon forget this. And it doesn't mean you won't face legal ramifications."

"I hear everything you're saying. Believe me, legal consequences are the least of my worries right now. Nonetheless, you deserved better, and one day, I hope you'll be able to forgive me for all of this."

"We'll see, Counselor, we'll see."

⌘ ⌘ ⌘

Rob called just after sunset and gave full information on the remaining people on the R&R list, as well as a few others Eric had requested at the last minute. Thinking it was most likely the last time he'd speak to Rob, he explained the R&R list to him as part of the reason he needed all the information. "Stratton, why didn't you tell me sooner, man?" Rob asked. "I would have gotten this stuff to you more quickly and could have helped more, bro!"

"I know, Rob, and I appreciate it. You've always been a hard charger, and I appreciate all the times you stood by my side. Listen, I need to give you a heads-up on the Jansen situation. Before you get alarmed, know that I kept you out of the whole thing. But I gave my confession to the CA and IA about my involvement in the setup. I couldn't go to my grave knowing I ruined an innocent man's life. But your name will never be brought up. I'll literally take it to the grave. Rob, if this is the last time we speak—not to be overdramatic or anything—I'll keep to my word and not reveal the things we've spoken about. But I also know some of the decisions I've made in the past have now come back to haunt me. You have to do your thing and follow your own path. But some of the things we've conspired together on have led us down the wrong path. I'm trying to do the right things with the time I have, and I'm hoping you'll take the things I've learned and apply them even though you're not dying. I'm not trying to tell you what to do; just take some time to evaluate what's important and how you go about things in the future. Just a thought, man. Please, take care of yourself, friend."

"Please, Stratton"—Rob rolled his eyes—"I always take care of myself. And I know you're just going soft because you're rollin' with that pastor friend of yours. I'm kidding. Listen, thank you for everything. I would never turn down a dying man's wish, so I'll take what you're saying to heart. But you know I'm the type that's living for the minute, so I'll make sure to have a few cold ones in your honor tonight as well. Before I let you go, I have one last question though. This Emily Rutherford you asked me to track down. I see that she's only twelve years old. What could you possibly have done to wrong a twelve-year-old? You know she lives at the same address as the Renee Rutherford you're looking for, too, right?"

"Yes, I knew that, and the answer to your question about Emily is a long story, Rob. Let's just say I needed her information for the will. After all, aren't parents supposed to leave something to their children when they die?"

⌘⌘⌘

Roland Hughes was handed his personal clothes and belongings by the deputy working the discharge station. He changed out of his orange jumpsuit for the last time and stood by the outer door to the Cedarville Penitentiary.

"Open three!" A deputy shouted.

There was a buzz, a clank, and the squeaking of the door as it opened up to the world. Roland walked out into the windy fall morning and took a deep breath. As his eyes adjusted to the light of freedom, he lit a cigarette and scanned the parking lot that surrounded him. After enjoying his freedom for the first time in six years, Roland pulled out his list. A sadistic smile widened as he read the names of the people he needed to go see, starting with his former partner who, in his mind, was the person most responsible for the loss of six years of his life. And since Eric Stratton was later on the list, Roland hoped he would still be alive so he could say good-bye in a proper manner.

Seven

Three weeks ago
Homecoming

The last three people on Eric's R&R list still lived near his hometown in southwestern Virginia. This was a fact that would make the rest of his life a little less difficult. The trio agreed it didn't make sense for Eric to spend a few weeks down in his hometown and then come back to the Washington, DC, area for his final days. They decided it would be more beneficial to get his affairs in order in the DC area and then have him stay with his family for the remainder of his time.

Eric couldn't think of a better place to spend the last month or so of his life. The thought of being around his brother and parents warmed his heart. There was still some healing that needed to take place in those relationships, but Eric felt that healing could easily come if he was there. And in the end, his hometown was the place he felt he was supposed to be. To have the added benefit of his two new friends with him during the twilight of his life, that would make a very difficult situation much more bearable. But to have all of those things, and to be able to get in touch with and reconcile with the last three folks on his R&R list, that, would be perfection.

Since Eric was supposed to take it easy, Mike gathered half a dozen volunteers from the church, and along with Sheila, the eight of them were able to hold a fundraiser and sell off most of the items Eric no longer needed. The items that didn't sell went to Goodwill. The rest of the items were keepsakes and personal things Eric wanted to bring home for his family. After two days, he had only one suitcase, one backpack, and four boxes to take back home with him.

Eric was thankful for the gracious volunteers as his strength and health continued to deteriorate. They were an amazing blessing in a time when he really needed the help. He was impressed with both their willingness to serve and help him (a total stranger) and their ever positive attitudes. During the grueling and sometimes messy work, no one complained or argued even once. And they didn't treat Eric like a charity case or disease. They joked around with him as much as they did with each other while they worked. It gave him a glimpse of a brand of people he didn't know existed anymore. And it made him question things even more. Why did Sheila, Mike, and these people seem to be willing to give him so much when all he could really give back were his shortcomings, an apology, or maybe a "thank you"? Of course he knew the common denominator was their faith.

These people were an odd contrast to the televangelists, hypocrites, and self-righteous people he had known of or met through the years who called themselves "Christians." The ones he knew of prior to this recent group had misrepresented what Christianity was supposed to be. Up to this point, in his mind these poor examples gave Eric an excuse to stay away from the church.

As Eric thought about his past experiences, he wondered if these poor examples knew of the negative and detrimental image they portrayed to him. He turned to Mike, wanting someone to speak for the people he had encountered. "Hey, Mike, can I ask you a question?"

"Shoot," Mike replied.

"Well, I have to be honest with you. I'm a little perplexed about the stark contrast in some people I met before and you other Jesus freaks. No offense of course."

"None taken," Mike replied sarcastically.

"Well, I have to admit, I realize that you, Sheila, and these volunteers have common religious beliefs. And you've all given me more than I could ever have expected. Yet you seem to live by this unwritten code that I have experienced through other people in my life before but never really acknowledged—namely my family.

"In contrast to you fine people, there are these other people that I've known or heard about in my life who claimed to be Christians as well. When I think about their actions, I can't quite understand how two groups of people, both claiming to believe the same things, can act so different. Bear with me and let me tell you about some of them, and then you can decide whether I'm off base with my struggles to reconcile this or not."

"Please continue, Eric. You have definitely piqued my curiosity," Mike said.

"Okay, well, the first was a priest named—well, for the sake of attorney client privilege, we'll call him Father David. Father David was a clergyman I defended early in my career. He was accused of abusing several of the children in his parish. Although I was able to get an acquittal for him, due to the age of the offenses and the easily manipulated witnesses, I came to be convinced of the priest's guilt in the end. Here was a guy a lot of people trusted. I mean, they trusted their kids with this guy. And he turned out to be someone who claimed to be God's servant by day but was something purely evil by night. A true wolf in sheep's clothing if you will."

"That's a tough one for me to accept, too," Mike said.

"But hold on, there are more. There was this neighbor I lived a few doors down from while he was in law school. He was some sort of professor at a strict religious academy, and a local pastor. This guy Kevin rarely gave me the time of day even when I walked right up and said hello to him. I actually felt bad for Kevin's family, as they seemed to break their backs on house and yard work while Kevin sat inside doing God knows what.

"Not much for housework myself, I felt compelled to help with heavy items and other projects when Kevin's wife asked for it. What surprised me was that she would ask for help even when Kevin was around. One day, she was carrying some heavy tools and supplies into the house, and instead of him lifting a finger to help her, she had to come and get me because he was otherwise occupied. And by occupied, I mean he just didn't feel like helping—he knew I was helping her carry the stuff around the house. I mean, I'd be embarrassed if my wife or girlfriend ever did that. And some of the things she used to say led me to believe that, at the very least, there was some strong verbal abuse going on.

"Finally one day I couldn't take it anymore, and I tried to confront Kevin since it didn't seem like anyone else would stand up for the family. When I went over to speak with him, it was like talking to a brick wall. He had a million excuses for his bad behavior, and I ended up having to walk away because Kevin couldn't control himself enough to refrain from cursing me out. Now I was no stranger to bad language, but coming from a pastor and religious teacher, it was more than I could handle. I really wished Kevin's congregation and students could see his lack of control in order to expose the hypocrite he really was when no one from the church or school was looking. To this day, thinking about that situation still irks me.

"And then there are all of the televangelists that ask for people's money. They promise healing or blessings or riches in return for donations. I remember seeing one guy who would "bless" these handkerchiefs and then ask for money from people so they would be healed when they touched the stupid snot rags. I mean, come on, how could they get away with that for so many years?

"I have to be honest. I stayed away from the church and religious people because I was convinced these people only used God's name to get jobs or raise money or go after weaker people in order to fulfill some type of need. But I have to be fair. The people like my grandma, my parents, and the ones who now stand before me are giving me a completely different picture of true Christianity. All of you seem to live the faith you profess. I know you're not perfect, but you carry yourselves in such a way, that I have to admit, if there is a God, He'd be proud to call you His representatives. So how do I rationalize the difference?"

"Way to save a tough question for the end of the day," Mike said with a smile. "First off, I can't blame you for struggling to comprehend the actions of people like this Father David, Kevin the hypocrite, or the 'telecriminals,' as I used to call them. I've already told you my story, so you know I had doubts of my own, probably for similar reasons in the past. It's unfortunate that some people get to claim they are doing something for God or representing him when, in fact, they are only representing themselves. Or worse, they're really representing the other side. I'm not sure why God allows these types of people to do these horrible things.

"And you were also right in saying that none of the people, present company included, are perfect. We all make mistakes. I guess the main thing is that the Bible says you'll know people by the fruits they bear. If someone claims to be representing God but lives contrary to how His word says they should, then they may not be telling the truth. But in the same token, look across the room at these people. They will never get anything out of this time they're spending here. Neither Sheila nor I will ever reap some benefit to hanging out with a loser like you—" Mike winked. "But seriously, I think I can speak for all of us when we say we do this because we truly love God. And through that love, we are able to see past the horrible things you've done and love you for the person that we know God can make you. So in spite of your shortcomings, we still help you. So it's not we who are doing this but God. And we're either all crazy, or we know something you haven't been able to see yet."

Eric nodded and watched as the volunteers finished cleaning his apartment. He didn't admit it out loud, but everything Mike said made sense to him. He allowed it to soak in and reach him in parts of his soul that he had not bared in many years.

⌘ ⌘ ⌘

Before leaving for the day, one of the volunteers named Dan—a teenager from the church's youth group—asked if there was anything else that needed to be done. Jokingly, Eric said, "Let's see. You cleaned my bathrooms, vacuumed my floors, and did more work in two days than I could have done in two weeks. And you're asking me if there's anything else. No, I think that about covers it." Eric motioned for everyone to gather in the middle of the empty room and swallowed hard before addressing the sweaty workers who stood before him. "I'd like to thank you all for your hard work. You've helped me more than you will ever know. And you've truly touched me with your selflessness over the last few days."

"Well," Dan said, "I guess there's just one more thing left to do." He gathered everyone even closer and asked, "Mr. Stratton, do you mind if we pray for you before we take off?"

"Well, first off, young man, please call me 'Eric.' Second, I'd be honored if you'd pray for me. I think God will listen to you all much more than He will me."

So Dan began to pray for Eric. He prayed for his health, a smooth transition, the move, and safe travels back home. And then he prayed for something that had come to be known as "the legend of the R&R list" back at New Hope Church. Apparently, news of the mission that Mike and Eric were on had made it through to the congregation, and that fact touched Eric even further.

Dan finished by asking God to touch Eric's life through the good and bad. He also asked God to use him to reach others. Eric had no idea how God could ever reach anyone else with someone as messed up as he was. But in reference to the part where Dan asked God to touch his life, Eric hated to admit it, but that part of the prayer was already answered.

As Dan finished his moving prayer, Eric whispered one of his own: "God, if you're real, I need you to truly reveal yourself to me. Help me get past my pride, and see you in all this. And please, help me get to the last people on this list if it's the last thing I ever do."

⌘ ⌘ ⌘

As much work as they had accomplished over the last few days, Eric was surprisingly well-rested (thanks to the help of the volunteers) for the four-hour trip back home. He was surprised at how easy it was to part with almost everything he owned, including his late-model Mercedes (which he ended up giving to an ecstatic Dan). As Eric, Mike, and Sheila drove along Interstate 66 west to the merge with Interstate 81 south, the beautiful drive down the Shenandoah Valley reminded him that he was truly going home. He felt more like a real person than he had in years. Knowing this was the last time he would pass this way, he had asked to stop at a few places along the way. The very last stop before arriving in his hometown would be a final visit to his grandma's grave.

Wanting to go alone this time, Eric brought the Bible and letter from his grandma. He sat down under a cedar tree next to his grandparent's plot. The ground was cold, but strangely that did not bother him. Even stranger to him was the feeling of release and comfort in a place so full of sadness and death. It was almost as if that particular spot was ordained to represent something else to Eric. He wasn't sure if it was release from the guilt of the past or the thankfulness of the time he still had. Either way, he felt very much at home in the cold windy cemetery. As he sat there, Eric realized it was almost Thanksgiving. If his grandmother was still alive, he'd probably be heading to the family home for homemade bread and the juiciest turkey imaginable.

Eric opened the Bible and took out the letter his grandmother had left for him. He thumbed through the old leather bound Bible and began to look for the verses she had underlined. The first verse was found in the book of Romans. Eric read the words out loud again, as if speaking to his grandmother. "That if you confess with your mouth, 'Jesus is Lord,' and believe in your heart God raised Him from the dead, you will be saved." He then read the verse in Ephesians in the same manner. "For it is by grace you have been saved, through faith—and this not from yourselves, it is the gift of God—not by works, so that no one can boast." He tried to make sense out of how the two groups of verses fit together. It seemed straightforward enough, but Eric wondered what it was he needed to be saved from.

Eric remembered some of the points from his conversation with Sheila several weeks earlier. He wondered how it was possible that his grandmother, who had long passed on, was trying to tell him the same thing Sheila had said only a short time ago. Here, again, was another strange coincidence Eric could not just shrug off. Add that to all of the other things that happened since he received his "death sentence" and the odds of them coming together were virtually astronomical impossibilities. What were the odds that Sheila would be assigned as his doctor? That Mike would be her pastor and the first person on his list? How many more things had Eric missed over the years? How long had God been trying to reach him before he was actually willing to listen?

106

And how much longer was he going to run from something that in his heart, as impossible as it seemed, he now knew to be the truth?

As worthwhile as the R&R list had already been, in the back of his mind, he felt like there was still something left to do. Was that something the reconciliation with God that Sheila, Mike, and his grandmother had all talked about? Sheila had said that accepting the gift by believing and confessing could save him. And that was the same thing the Bible said in the verses he just read. He assumed that what he needed to be saved from was eternal separation from God. It all started to come together, and Eric was close. But he needed to make sure since he wasn't an expert. He called Mike on his cell phone and asked him and Sheila to join him at his grandma's grave.

⌘⌘⌘

Mike and Sheila stepped to either side of Eric as he stared past his grandmother's grave at the mountains in the distance. It was about ten minutes before sunset, and the day was spectacular...maybe even perfect. "I just wanted to be with the two people who have done more for me than anyone on Earth in this moment. And I want to make sure I understand this grace thing. I already feel like I'm a crazy person, so I guess there's no stopping it now. To make sure I have this all straight, here's where I'm at: I could never do anything, including finishing the R&R list, to get God's attention or favor. His grace is a free gift made possible through the sacrifice of His Son on the cross. All I have to do is believe that what He did was to save me from the consequence of the horrible things I've done, agree with Him that I'm a screw-up, which I already know, and accept His gift. And that's it?"

"That's pretty much it," Mike replied. "No strings attached, no hidden fees, no fine print. Just the acceptance of a gift you could never earn. He gave it to you because He loves you."

"And even though I still have doubts, I can still make a decision? I mean, I don't actually see God. I can't hear Him. I've tried talking to Him a little. But the only real evidence I have are witnesses. You guys, my family, the volunteers. Even if this was a case held in a court of law,

I'd have to call witnesses to make my case. So even though I have no physical evidence, all of the witnesses are testifying to the fact that God is real, He actually loves me, and that He is willing to accept me for the screw-up that I was and the imperfect wretch I continue to be.

And last, what I think I've learned from all of you is that even though I'm not a religious person, nor will I ever be, that doesn't matter. Because this belief in God and His Son is not about religion at all. It's about accepting a gift of grace through faith, which leads to a relationship and not a religion. A relationship with the true and living God. So all I have to do is believe it and receive it?"

"Yes, Eric," Sheila chimed in. "That's all you have to do. In fact, if you truly feel like you're ready to make a decision, Mike and I can pray and you can agree and repeat after us. That's all it takes."

"Well, why didn't you guys tell me sooner?" Eric exclaimed.

The trio laughed and bowed together on that holy hill where Eric finally reconciled with his heavenly Father in the same place he met with his grandma a few weeks earlier.

Eric looked heavenward and smiled. Before leaving, he took out the list and crossed off the question mark at the bottom. At the same moment he was able to reconcile with God, he was finally able to forgive himself as well.

⌘⌘⌘

Back on the road, Eric felt as if something had actually passed through him and relieved him of the guilt he'd been carrying around with him. He knew he still had a death sentence and still had work left to do on Earth. But for now, an inexplicable and almost indescribable joy washed over him. The old cliché about having a weight lifted off his shoulders was as close as he could come to verbalizing how he felt.

Most notably, the burden of the horrible things he had hidden for so long was gone, and Eric finally felt forgiven. He didn't really understand all of the changes that were taking place so quickly, but he accepted it all on *faith* (a word new to his vocabulary). Knowing there were more challenges that lay ahead, he felt even more prepared and motivated to face them than he had before.

"So what happens now?" Eric asked. "I mean, this is incredible. I feel like I'm a new person. And that has to be something from God. How else could I be so full of joy, knowing I'm going to be dead in a few weeks?"

"Actually, Eric, your body will be dead in a few weeks," Sheila said. "But almost instantaneously, you're going to be in the presence of God. No longer will you have to worry about pain or fear or suffering or guilt or heartache. For you, your job will be done, and you'll get to bask in His glory for all of eternity."

"What about my grandmother? Will I be able to see her?"

"Sure."

"Well, I have to say I'm really glad you all, your friends, and my family have been so persistent. Otherwise, who knows where I'd be right now. Worse yet, I don't want to imagine where I'd be a few weeks from now." A chill went down Eric's spine as he finished speaking the words. The thought gave him even more motivation to get moving on his list, for there were some people that he desperately needed to reach. But it wasn't just the old message of regret, forgiveness, and attempted reconciliation. Now he needed to deliver two messages: one from himself and one from God. But he couldn't shake the feeling that he was quickly running out of time.

⌘⌘⌘

When Eric pulled into the driveway of his childhood home, a flood of emotions overcame him almost immediately. The rare trips he made back to his hometown over the last few years usually ended abruptly in an argument or conflict. Eric used to think his brother and parents tried to guilt him into seeing them more often. He felt the blame was always placed on his shoulders when his family pointed out the fact that he was too distant and didn't keep them in the loop about his life, loves, or law career. In reality, he now realized they simply wanted a closer relationship with their brother and son. Still, because of his foolish pride and the constant strife, he was rarely able to enjoy those trips.

Now there was nothing left to argue about. There was no longer any reason to fight over matters trivial or serious, as there wasn't enough time. Anything not already settled on the phone would have to be set aside for the sake of enjoying the time he had left. He took a deep breath, and, for the first time in many years, felt like he was truly home again.

Eric planned to use his parents' home as a base to complete both the R&R list and the last leg of his life's journey. It would also be a place to say good-bye to his loved ones—a place to make final peace before heading into the next life.

Stepping out of the car, Eric was greeted with the fresh crispness of the late fall air mixed with the warming and comforting aroma of the wood fire. He stretched his arms and legs and turned towards the house. The door burst open, unleashing childhood energy and excitement as his niece and nephew ran out to greet them.

Eric picked them both up and hugged them for a long time. "What are you guys doing out here? It's way too cold, and you're gonna freeze to death. Let's go get some coats on!" Eric laughed as he carried them back into the house. He was surprised he had the strength to move both of the children with relative ease.

Randy greeted Eric at the door and led them into the kitchen, where hugs were shared and introductions were made.

"Now, pay attention," Eric said. "I'm only doing this once, and then there's gonna be a short test later."

Everyone laughed.

"Everyone, this is Sheila Redmond, my doctor, and Mike Davenport, my pastor. Both are friends, too, of course. Sheila, Mike, this is my dad, Jarvis; my mom, Diane; my brother, Randy; and his wife, Elaine. The knuckleheads running around are Lucy and Jack." Eric bent down to one knee and said, "And this old mutt is Lady. I have no idea how in the world she's still alive." Eric embraced Lady, and she began to lick his face and wag her tail in celebration of his homecoming.

After a few minutes, the kitchen was filled with the conversation and laughter of strangers who quickly morphed into a close-knit group that seemed like they'd known each other for years. Eric was amazed how everything could be put aside for his sake.

After a while, Eric got everyone's attention again in order to make an announcement. "As you all know, I'm home for good. So there will be no more arguing or telling me I don't visit enough. On a serious note, you all know about my health—my eight-year old condition of being a lawyer has been cured."

Everyone laughed again.

"Seriously, you all know what's going on. I don't want any of you to be too distracted by the things that are going to happen so as not to be able to enjoy the time that we have. Please don't act weird or timid, thinking you're going to hurt my feelings or say something that you shouldn't. Please don't think you can't use words like *dying* or *cancer* or anything like that. For my sake, I ask that you don't ignore what I have. But look past it and enjoy this time with me. I'll need help some of the time and patience at others. But I don't want us all to dwell on it. We only have a little time, and I need us all to make the most of it. So could you please do that for me?"

Randy was the first to chime in. "I'll speak for us all and say I think we can handle that. On a related note, I have an ingrown toenail that's coming out next week. If we could all ignore that and get on with our lives I'd appreciate it, too."

Everyone laughed again.

"Now can we please get on with dinner?" Randy asked. "Thanksgiving is two days away, and I need to stretch my stomach out!"

As the kitchen livened up to a dull roar again, Eric smiled, happy to be home again. It only quieted down again long enough for Jarvis to say grace. The stern Vietnam War veteran rarely showed emotion. But as he asked God to bless the food and thanked Him for family, new friends and strength for his dying son, even he got a little choked up. In his thirty-four years, Eric had never seen his father even come close to showing that kind of emotion.

Jarvis' prayer was interrupted by an uncomfortably quiet time, as everyone knew he was looking for the right words at that moment. Eric left his seat and walked over to his father's side and gently rested his hand on the old man's shoulder.

Jarvis quietly finished by saying, "And God, thanks for bringing my lost son home. Amen."

No one said a word as they all sat down to eat. One by one the dishes began to get passed around the table. Diane's Southern home-cooked meal was the medicine they all needed to get through the moment.

⌘⌘⌘

The Stratton's old farmhouse was more than cozy and large enough to accommodate Eric, Mike, and Sheila for the next month or so. Eric and Sheila took the two guest bedrooms on the second floor while Mike got the den on the first. Randy and his family only lived five miles away, so they promised to be there at the farm house as often as they could be. After dinner, everyone got their luggage into the house and settled into their prospective living quarters. Then they gathered back in the living room near the fireplace for coffee, dessert, and fellowship.

Wanting to get all of the official business out of the way first, Randy allowed Elaine to take the kids home and stayed behind with the other five to talk about Eric's wishes and preparations. There were a few tears and awkward silences throughout the conversation. But for the most part, everyone was able to get through the administrative items in an hour. Eric would have his funeral at the family church, and both their family pastor and Mike would conduct the service. Eric had already prepared a list of people who should be notified. He also wanted a notification/obituary published in several of the major papers in the Washington, DC, area in case there was anyone who wanted to attend from there. He advised he wanted Sheila to be the executor of his will, which was in a rough draft form but could be used at any time if he should pass. He didn't read the will and requested it remain sealed until after his funeral and interment. Lastly, Eric decided that he, indeed, wanted to be buried near his grandparents in the lot at the Green Hill Cemetery.

After all of the arrangements were in place, Eric sat with his family and new friends and simply enjoyed their company. His family didn't tire listening to the highlights of the R&R journey, especially when they found out what had happened earlier that day at his grandmother's grave. For his family, it was a day that was long overdue. Knowing Eric had made his peace with God, the family was able to bear the situation that night. It took enough of the edge off and removed some of the sting of his impending death. Diane made eye contact with her son several times, and Eric could see the grief welling up behind them. But mixed with that grief was the relief and pride of knowing he was finally on the right path after thirty-four years.

When Eric was finished telling his tale of the journey, Sheila and Mike listened with Eric while his parents caught them up on some of the more important things that happened within the family over the past few years. Randy chimed in every now and then with the children's accomplishments, as well as the challenge of being a full-time cop and father. Eric was amazed at how grown up Randy sounded, yet how much he still maintained a child-like joy about his family, his job, and life in general. He was a natural father and clearly cared deeply for his children.

"So what is your favorite part of being a father, Randy?" Eric asked. "Those of us without children are curious."

"That's a tough one. Between changing poopy diapers and the occasional vomiting, I'd say it's a toss-up."

Everyone laughed quietly.

"Seriously, just seeing them grow and learn is an amazing thing," Randy said. "It's like one day all they do is cry, sleep, and go to the bathroom. I mean, they can't even hold their heads up, for goodness' sake. Then it seems like a few days go by, and they start getting into everything. A few more days seemingly pass, and they want to say 'no' fifteen thousand times a day. Then one day you call home, and your little baby answers the phone and has a conversation with you. Everything 'they', whoever 'they' are, say about kids growing up in the blink of an eye, well it's true. So I guess in light of that, for me, it's all about having the privilege of being a part of it all. Just to have the chance to partake in their lives and watch them develop into their own little people is an amazing privilege. They're so full of curiosity and wonder and joy. Like knowledge sponges, they want to experience life to the fullest in this world. To love them, be loved, and experience a relationship with them—that's the best part. I don't know…. does that count as an answer? That was more like twenty-four of my favorite things."

"No, that works," Sheila said. "Something about the innocence of children and the way they live…they inspire us to become something greater."

"I don't have children of my own," Mike said. "I'd like to someday. But just sitting here listening to all of your insights makes me realize what I've missed out on and what I have to look forward to. The thing I think is so amazing is the insight they seem to have in serious situations. Sometimes, I'll visit a family in the hospital who is facing a dire situation. All it takes is one word or question from a child, and it's almost like everyone gets an injection of joy."

"Out of the mouth of babes," Jarvis said.

Eric continued to listen to the conversation and made smart remarks every now and then. But most of his thoughts turned to the deep longing he felt. It may have been there before his death sentence, but he'd covered it with his desire to live life as he saw fit. But over the course of the last month, that longing was dredged more and more. With the events at the gravesite and now this conversation, that void was fully exposed and ready to be filled with the only thing it could be: a relationship with his own child. He'd neglected it for too long and making amends was long overdue.

Eric pondered his situation and wondered how much longer it would take him to tell his friends and family that he, too, was a father.

⌘⌘⌘

Around midnight the fire and conversation were finally allowed to die down. Most of them could have gone all night catching up and laughing together. But the day had been an eventful one, and Eric needed to rest and recover. When the newness and excitement that had carried him to that point in the evening finally wore off, Eric was ready to pass out. He said good night to everyone and climbed the stairs to his old bedroom, which now served as a guestroom. On the way up, he wondered how many nights he had dreamt of getting away from this place. Not sure why he'd chosen to run from something that was so safe and familiar, he felt safe and protected from the uncertainty each new day would bring.

Before dozing off, Eric thought about the things still left undone. With all of the people on the R&R list nearby, he knew it wouldn't be difficult to see them all in a relatively short period of time. Still, one encounter every few days was about all he could handle physically and emotionally. Sheila made Eric promise that he'd take it easy until after Thanksgiving weekend. In order to give his body a break, he complied since Thanksgiving was only a day and a half away now. He also owed his family the time together. He couldn't let much more of it slip by since he was living on borrowed time. But the R&R list would be put on hold while Eric enjoyed the company of his friends and family at Thanksgiving.

Eric closed his eyes and thought of how wonderful the day had been. To cap it off, laughing and talking down by the fire was a more perfect ending to a day than any he could remember having in a long time. What a stark contrast to the parties, hook-ups, and fickle lifestyle he'd lived for so long. Interestingly, he didn't miss it much. He did, however, miss having close female companionship. Eric knew it wouldn't be fair to anyone to pursue any type of relationship now. Still, it would have been nice if he could have had a chance at a meaningful relationship for a season of his adult life.

Eric fell asleep, imagining what it would be like to marry Sheila and raise a family with her. But once he was actually asleep, his dreams and the characters were different. He was taken back to his college days.

Instead of making the choice to live out his own life and follow his own dream, he stayed with Renee. Together they raised the child he didn't want to have in the first place. Eric smiled in his sleep at the possibility of following the right path when they had diverged all those years ago.

⌘ ⌘ ⌘

On the second day the trio was back at Eric's childhood home, everyone was treated to an amazing home-cooked breakfast and more meaningful conversation. After cleaning up, Mike excused himself to attend a teleconference with his church staff. Sheila and Diane busied themselves with Thanksgiving preparations. Sheila had asked the night before if she could help Diane. She had always wanted to learn how to make a traditional Southern Thanksgiving meal. With all the other adults busy, Eric had the chance to spend some time alone with his father.

"Hey, Dad, wanna go for a walk and show me some of the updates you guys have made to the farm since I was here last?"

"That sounds like a setup, but okay, I'll bite."

Eric and his dad slowly walked around the fifty-acre property, checking on fences and enjoying the occasional wildlife. Eric was amazed at how much the landscape had changed. Many small saplings and bushes were now full-grown trees. The fields were more overgrown now that his father didn't farm as much as he did when they were younger. Eric also noticed his father wasn't getting around quite as quickly as he used to.

After walking for a few more minutes, they found themselves on the banks of the river that ran through the Stratton's property. The quiet trickle of the current flowing past the rocks soothed both Eric and his father's spirits. It reminded them of the countless hours they had spent near that river in years past.

"You know, Dad, I wish it hadn't taken all this stuff for me to realize what a self- centered jerk I've been over the years. I can't change the past. But I sure hope we can try to make up for some lost time before—"

"Son," his dad interrupted, "there are a lot of things we all regret about the last few years. I'm sorry for being stubborn at times, too— although it was mostly your fault." He grinned at his son. "I've tried to live my life in such a way that I wouldn't have regrets when my time was up. And there are some things I've tried to leave in the past where they belong—things from the war that don't need to be dredged up."

Jarvis winced and brushed the stubble on his cheek. "But that time affected me more than I ever let you kids know. There are things I did there that, although justified, would still haunt me if I didn't leave them buried where God put them to rest. So it's all in His hands now. Just like the lost time we'd all like to have back. So let's leave it at that." Jarvis scooted closer and laid his hand on his son's back. "I can't tell you how much it means to your mom, your brother, and me that you've finally come to this place. And you don't know how much it would have meant to your grandmother."

"Well, actually, I think I have an idea there." Eric went on to tell him in detail about that part of his journey to include the letter and the Bible.

"Dad, all of this has been an amazing journey so far. But there are a few things I need to tell you. I want you to know that, growing up, even though I probably didn't say it or show it enough, I really appreciate everything you did for Randy and me. We know you busted your butt not only to make ends meet but also to make sure we had some of the things we wanted. But you also took the time to spend with us, and that meant the world to us. I'm not dwelling on the last few years, but I wanted you to know that, in spite of the decisions I made for myself, those should not reflect on the way I was raised. You taught me well and gave me a strong heritage. Anything I did that was good or noble is because of what you taught me. Thanks for that, and thanks for always being there."

Jarvis stared ahead at the creek and nodded, as if to say you're welcome.

"And there's something else I need to tell you about," Eric continued. "In a few weeks, I'm going to get back in touch with Renee Rutherford. You remember the girl I was friends with in high school and then eventually dated in college?"

"Yeah, the one whose heart you broke. Yeah, I remember her. I hear she got herself knocked up quite a few years back. I guess she disappeared for a while. But someone told me she was back in the area as of about a year ago."

117

"Yeah, Dad. She did get herself knocked up. I needed to bring this up with you because, when I'm gone, I'll need someone to welcome your granddaughter into the family…if Renee will allow it."

"My what?"

"Yeah, Dad. Renee had a little girl. And she's mine. Her name is Emily, and, in a few weeks, I'm going to see Renee and meet my little girl for the first time."

Jarvis' jaw dropped. "Well, aren't you full of all kinds of surprises?"

"I need to rest for a few more days. Then I have two other people to track down. But after that, I plan to contact Renee. I did some bad things to her back in college. I was really selfish then, and I think maybe that period in my life is what I regret more than anything else. I won't blame her if she decides she doesn't want our daughter to have anything to do with me.

"But I've been making some recordings and writings for Emily. I've been doing them daily since I found out about my death sentence. I've tried to pass on everything I could think of—all of the good stuff anyway—to my daughter. I've learned some important lessons in these last few weeks, and I need her to hear them as well. I also want her to know who I am since I'm not going to be there to tell her about myself. So if Renee won't allow me to see her in a few weeks, it's going to be up to you and Randy to track her down when she gets older and can make that choice on her own. Will you do that for me, Dad?"

"Of course, Eric. Wow, I have another grandchild. I wonder what she looks like."

Eric's eyes welled with tears. "Me too, Dad, me too. It's not time yet. But in a few weeks, hopefully you'll know. I need to stay alive long enough to get these few things done. Thanks, Dad. Oh, and for now, please don't tell Mom. I wouldn't want to get her excited, only to be disappointed if things don't work out as planned."

"I'll try to keep it to myself. But you know how your mother is. By the way, Eric, there is something I wanted to tell you, too. While you were growing up, I know I had a difficult time always being transparent. It's a defense mechanism I've used over the years to deal with some of the things that happened in the war. But sometimes that defense mechanism keeps me from saying or expressing other things I

118

should. I never had a chance to tell you how proud I am of what you've become. And I wanted to say I'm sorry for anything I did or allowed to come between us over the last few years. Sometimes pride is a powerful thing. But I have no pride left save the pride I have for you as my son. I just wanted you to know that."

Eric and his father began chucking rocks into the creek like they did when he was a little boy. They couldn't look at each other for a long time for fear they'd both break down.

Neither of them thought something as simple as throwing rocks into water could bring two people so close together. But as the heavy stones splashed into the cold creek, years of healing and regrets were washed away with the current. Eric accomplished another important portion of the reconciliation he so desperately needed.

⌘⌘⌘

"So Eric was eight years old on a trip to Virginia Beach when he lost his swimming trunks in the waves. He didn't realize what had happened until he was out of the water and standing in his birthday suit in front of a packed beach full of total strangers. And then he stole someone's beach towel and ran to the bathrooms!" Diane finished.

Eric was amazed that his timing brought him back to the house in time to be embarrassed by that story. "Yeah, ha ha, Mom. That story is funnier every time you tell it."

"I thought it was! Especially since you ran into the *ladies'* room!" Diane said.

After the laughter died down, Diane asked, "You boys have fun?"

"Of course. Something smells good in here. Is this for lunch?" Eric asked, while reaching for a snack.

"Don't you touch any of that. It's for tomorrow. If you want lunch, you're going to have to go into the basement and get me a few things."

"Yes ma'am! I'm starving," Eric replied.

"Oh no," Sheila chimed in. "You can't eat until you take your next round of meds. I'll get them for you while you help your mom."

"Wow, I guess he finally found someone who can keep him in line," Diane jibed.

"Yep," Sheila replied. "All I have to do is threaten him with bed rest, and he'll do anything I ask. It's nice having all the power and control."

Later that evening, Eric was able to spend some time alone with his mother. Like the time spent earlier in the day with his dad, he and his mom were able to say things they hadn't had a chance to in years. It was a little easier than talking to his dad because there was no macho façade to have to fight through. It was simply a mother and her son trying to make the most of the precious time left.

Of course, when Eric told her the details of the envelope and the time he'd spent at his grandma's gravesite, Diane was no longer able to control her tears. He moved beside her and hugged her for a long time. He knew she was happy but also dreading the time she'd have to lay her youngest son to rest. Eric held her and wished with all his strength that he could take that knowledge and pain away from her. There were no more words to say. No time for regrets. So Eric and his mom merely stood in silence, arms clasped around each other—together for what would be one of the last times possible on this side of heaven.

⌘ ⌘ ⌘

Thanksgiving turned out to be a full day of eating and making memories.

The next day was more of the same as there were enough leftovers to feed a small army.

That Saturday and Sunday were spent relaxing more, getting started on the Christmas decorations, and going to church. After the service Eric decided to get baptized. His family pastor agreed to do it, and without advanced notice, he was immersed in the baptismal, dressed in the clothes on his back.

Eric didn't think he'd feel any different after the ceremony. But when he came out of the water that day, he was hit by a flood of emotions. He didn't quite know how to articulate the feeling, but there was something about the symbolism and the activity itself that made Eric feel he was connected to the history and people of the church worldwide. Once again in recent days he felt refreshed and touched by the hand of God Himself. By Sunday afternoon, Eric was well rested, recharged, and ready to move on to the rest of the list.

After dinner, Eric and Mike made their way out to the back porch to get some fresh air. Each of them sat in a rocking chair wrapped in warm clothes and blankets. They drank hot coffee and watched the sun as it finished its arch towards the Western horizon. "This week was almost perfect, Mike."

"Yeah, I was just thinking that. God seems to have a way of allowing us to have the moments we need on what I call 'the mountaintops' in order to continue through the valleys in life. Tomorrow is another valley we'll have to go through together. On a lighter note, I can't wait to see what wonderful thing you've done to someone else in your past and what angry person I'll have to protect you from again."

Just as Eric was about to tell Mike about the next person on the list, his cell phone rang.

"This is Eric."

"Yo, Eric, it's Rob. Listen, thanks for the final payment. You went way beyond what you needed to, but I'll put it to good use. I wanted you to know that your boy Roland Hughes was released a few days early in order to make it out in time for Thanksgiving. That wouldn't normally be a big deal, but he's already violated his parole and skipped town. No one knows where he is. I'm not sure why he'd risk going back to your hometown, but I wanted to give you the heads-up. Watch your back in case that moron tries to do something stupid. Do you want me to come down there and help you out? You know, have an extra pair of eyes around...in case?"

"No thanks, Rob. I do appreciate it. Actually, my brother is a deputy sheriff down here, so he'll be able to help us keep an eye out. Unfortunately, I can almost guarantee Roland will do something stupid. He told me when we were at the prison that he had no intentions of ever going back. Oh well. I had to have one piece of bad news, or otherwise this would have been a perfect week. Thanks again for the heads-up. Stay safe, and don't forget about the things I said to you last time we spoke."

"No problem, Eric, anytime. I'll call you if I hear anything further."

Eric hung up and shook his head. He filled Mike in on the information Rob had passed on.

Mike pursed his lips and shook his head.

"Oh well," Eric said. "What's the worst he can do? Kill me again?"

Eight

Two weeks ago
Reconciliation with Eddie Crowley

Well rested and reenergized, Eric took Sheila and Mike on a walk through the woods at the Stratton's property. As the trio slowly made their way through the crunchy leaves and dead branches, Eric noticed it was cold enough for them to see their breath. The woods were eerily quiet that day, save the sound of their footsteps and the wind that occasionally rustled a pile of leaves. They ended up on the old stone bridge that traversed the creek on the west side of the Stratton property.

There he told them the story of Eddie Crowley and the reason he needed reconciliation with him. "Eddie Crowley was one of my best friends in high school. In fact, Eddie was the guy who looked up to me, and wanted to be like me."

"Sounds like a classic case of the blind leading the blind," Mike added sarcastically as he leaned over the railing of the bridge.

"And such a humble view of himself," Sheila added.

"Tell me about it. Eddie was a good enough guy. He was as loyal as a friend at that age could be. If there was a fight, he had my back. If we were going to the swimming hole, he's the guy who would check the water to make sure there was no debris you'd crack your head on before diving in. He's also the guy who would egg your ex-girlfriend's car if she broke your heart. There wasn't a whole lot Eddie wouldn't do for me. The problem was, he was too much of a follower. If there was one person on Earth who gave Roland Hughes a harder time than I did, it was Eddie. But he wasn't a bad guy. He was merely following my lead and thought of it all as harmless fun.

"We drank and partied a lot in high school. Back then, we thought we were the kings of the world. We also thought we were indestructible. One night at a field party, we ended up getting together with some kids from a rival high school. Along with their group, there were also a couple of guys in their early twenties. We didn't know who they were, but since they were friends of friends, it seemed okay.

"As the crowd died down, Eddie, our girlfriends, and I were the only ones left from our school. There were four other guys sitting with us at the fire ring. As the night went on and the alcohol wore off, one of the guys pulled out a deck of cards. We started playing one and five-dollar hands of poker. My money went fast, and I didn't want to walk away having lost anything. So they started giving me IOUs and allowed me to try to win my money back. When it was all said and done, Eddie was only out $50, but I somehow managed to work up a $500 poker debt. It sounds crazy, but it happened really fast. Back then, it might as well have been a million dollars.

"Since I obviously didn't have the money to pay them, I thought I was going to get the beating of my life. But instead one of the older guys called me over to his truck and made a proposition. Holding a knife in one hand and feigning its use to clean the dirt from under his fingernails, he asked me how scared I was. Then he asked what I would be willing to do to work off my debt in order to keep my friends and me safe.

"At that point, I told him I was willing to do anything. He then handed me a ziplock bag with a bunch of joints in it. He told me that if I sold them for five to ten dollars each, I'd make my money back in no time. He took my driver's license and told me if I didn't have the money in a month, he'd come after me.

"I was scared. I asked him who I was supposed to sell it to, and he pointed over to Eddie and the girls. 'Start with your buddy and your girlfriends. This is the good stuff, and after one joint, they're gonna want more. Give them the first one or two for free, then charge them after that. These aren't just weed, friend. We added a few drops of something a little more powerful to spice it up.'

"I didn't know what to do. Back around the campfire we all sat around until the man with the knife pulled out one of the joints. He lit it up and offered it around. The two guys from the rival school took hits. Both girls hesitated, then declined them. I was hoping it wouldn't come to me, since I knew they were laced with God knows what. The two guys from the other school already looked dazed and confused by the time it was passed to Eddie.

"Eddie looked at me, wondering what he should do, and held the joint up as if he was asking for my approval or denial. Knife man gave me a look that told me I'd better convince Eddie to take the joint. He wiped the blade on his jeans to remind me he was willing to take it all the way.

"I looked back to Eddie, who still waited like a faithful dog. I knew he would do whatever I told him to. I should have warned him. I should have told him not to take the hit. At that moment, I knew it was wrong. But I was too scared of what the consequence might have been if I didn't tell him to take it. 'Go ahead, Eddie,' I told him. 'I'll take one after you.'

"Eddie took two long slow drags. By the time he passed it along, he was already on his way to another plane of existence. I never took my promised hits with him and threw the joint into the fire when knife man wasn't looking.

"Up to that point I'd always heard those rumors saying if you take one hit of some drugs, you're immediately hooked. Well, I wouldn't know because I didn't try them. But after that night, Eddie lived for getting high. To this day, I don't know if it was PCP, heroin, or some other potent combination on those joints. But Eddie ended up buying every single one from me over the next few weeks. I don't know where he got the money for them, and, frankly, I didn't care. Eddie seemed happy, and I was able to pay off my debt.

"I called knife man one day and gave him his money. He returned my license and asked if I was interested in making more money. Infuriated, I yelled, 'Never again!' He laughed, called me a loser, and I never saw him again.

"Eddie wasn't much of a follower of mine after that. He chased his high wherever it took him. His addiction became his new leader. He got involved with a crowd that was all about the drugs, and I only saw him in passing in the halls or at the mall. We hung out every now and then, but it was never the same. He started getting weird ideas about conspiracies involving the school, the government, and anything that had to do with authority. He became extremely paranoid and stopped talking to most people.

"It only took about six months for his parents to take him out of school and place him in rehab for the first time. By the time I left for college, Eddie had been in and out of rehab three more times.

"Once again, my poor choices led to a person's life getting ruined. And once again, I have no idea what I'm going to find when I see him today. Maybe he was able to kick the lifestyle and make something of himself. Maybe he's happily married with kids and a good job. Who knows what we'll find.

"Rob gave me an address that's only about twenty miles from here, so maybe we can make it back before noon. But before we leave, I'd like you to pray for us please, Mike. Pray we'll be prepared for whatever we find. Pray that things will go better today than they did with Roland Hughes. And pray that Roland Hughes will be stopped from whatever it is he's trying to do since he's on the loose again.

⌘⌘⌘

The address Rob provided for Eddie Crowley turned out to be a quaint country property on the east side of Interstate 81 not far from Roanoke, Virginia. The short driveway led to a well-manicured estate that spoke of meticulous attention. Almost all the leaves were off of the trees and only a few blew across the yard in front of the house. Eric asked both Mike and Sheila to accompany him inside. The presence of a few balls and toys outside the house was probably a sign he had a family, and Eric suspected he might need a little assistance once they got inside.

The Crowley family was home, but they weren't exactly what Eric expected at first. An elderly woman opened the door, and after squinting for a few seconds, Eric finally said, "Mrs. Crowley?"

She stared back at him and finally said, "Yes, and you are?"

"Mrs. Crowley, it's me, Eric Stratton."

126

"Eric Stratton!" She pulled him in for a firm hug. "Oh my goodness' sakes! I haven't seen you since you boys were in high school. Please come on in. Excuse the mess. Mr. Crowley and I don't get around as easily as we used to."

"Please, Mrs. Crowley. Your home is as spotless as I remember your other one was. I guess some things never change. These are my friends—Sheila and Mike."

"Nice to meet you both."

"Mrs. Crowley, I'm looking for Eddie. I know it's been a long time and, well, we sort of lost track towards the end of high school. I went my way, as Eddie did, and I was wondering if you could steer me in his direction by passing along his contact information."

"Oh, Eric." Mrs. Crowley's denture-filled grin quickly turned to a frown. Before she spoke, Eric had a flash of a gravesite in his mind. Grieved, he thought this was yet another person he'd waited too long to contact. "Eddie is here, honey. He loves having visitors and doesn't get them much anymore. But before I let you go up and see him, I need to prepare you for what you'll find. He's a lot different than you remember."

Mrs. Crowley told the story about the sad decline of the promising young man Eddie had been in high school. She shared his accolades for the benefit of Sheila and Mike, as Eric already knew them.

"Before getting involved in drugs, Eddie had been an up-and-coming receiver on the football team. He also did well academically. But once he started on the path that led to his addiction, he never really wanted anything else. At first, he kept it out of the house and used his money from work to pay for the habit. When that ran out, he started selling some of his old baseball cards and comic books. Then he moved to other personal belongings. Finally, he started to steal from us.

Mrs. Crowley's chin quivered. "We tried to get him help, but the more we tried, the more distant he became. He grew increasingly unpredictable and was rarely in control. His addiction was the master that drove his life. Not wanting to expose his younger siblings to his dangerous state or the things he was bringing into the house, we had to make some difficult choices out of tough love for him. We also had to protect the rest of the family. We were forced to kick him out of the house when he turned nineteen. We couldn't do any more for him, and our family could no longer watch while he destroyed himself."

Tears began to well up in Mrs. Crowley's eyes. "But you can never abandon your own. We bailed him out of jail a couple of times. We even hired an expensive attorney who was able to work out a deal that got him placed in a strict involuntary treatment program in lieu of going to jail on some distribution charges. He was clean for almost a year but fell back into the habit when some of his old drug buddies came around. After that, the last few remnants of the old Eddie disappeared. High on a mixture of several drugs one night, Eddie tried to hang himself.

"His brother found him and was able to get him down before he died. But, unfortunately, the damage was done. Along with the high amount of drugs in his system, he had hung there long enough for his brain to suffer from a lack of oxygen. The restriction caused extensive and irreversible brain damage."

Eric blinked in shock. It seemed impossible for his brain to grasp what she was saying.

Mrs. Crowley took a deep breath and continued. "When he woke from a six-week coma, he was never the same. Eddie had to relearn some basic things like talking, walking, and going to the bathroom on his own. He's pretty functional these days, but is only comparable to a person who operates at about the level of a four or five-year old. The doctors say he'll pretty much be that way for the rest of his life."

As she finished her story, tears began to roll down her cheeks. "Oh, Eric, I wish he'd stayed on the right path like you. You know he always used to talk about the two of you going off to college together and then conquering the world. Don't get me wrong; we're so glad to still have him. And actually, he's probably better off now than he was for the years he spent living as a slave to his addiction. But he had so much potential. You both did."

As Mrs. Crowley gathered herself, Eric sat in silence, dumbfounded. The story was so surreal. On one hand, he couldn't believe what he had heard. On the other, the reality of the moment seized him, and it was almost too much to bear. More than ever, he had the urge to go see his old friend and to finish the task he'd come to accomplish.

Eric, Sheila, Mike, and Mrs. Crowley walked slowly up the stairs. A loft one level above the bedrooms served as Eddie's "play" area. They had to pass his bedroom on the way, and Eric peeked in to see if he might recognize any of the pictures on the walls. The décor of the bedroom was an odd mix of a dorm room and a toy store. There were old rock posters on one wall and superhero comics, toys, and games scattered on the floor. He noticed a corkboard on the far side of the room that had pictures of Eddie and all of his old friends. Even a quick glance brought back a flood of memories and emotions for Eric. He swallowed hard and continued towards the room where Eddie was playing.

After cresting the stairs, Eric looked across the loft and saw the head and back of a medium-framed adult silhouetted against the TV. The three of them stood for a minute watching Eddie, who was glued to an old episode of *Scooby-Doo.*

Then his mom chimed in. "Eddie, you have some friends here to see you."

Eddie motioned for them to come in but was fixated on the screen.

Eric made his way over some balls and games and sat down next to Eddie. "Eddie Crowley. Hey, buddy, it's me, your old buddy Eric Stratton. Do you remember me?"

"Ewic Stwatton from Manhattan," Eddie replied.

Eric smiled in a sad way, fully realizing how limited Eddie's capacity was. Looking at the child trapped in a grown man's body, he quickly got past his discomfort and began talking to Eddie. "That's right, Eddie. It's really good to see you. Your mom tells me you like cartoons and playing ball. You want to go play catch after the show?"

"YEAHYEAHYEAHYEAHYEAH—ROOBY ROO!" Eddie said imitating the show.

"Okay, buddy. Can I watch the rest of your show with you?"

"Okay. But if we pway lataw, you hafta be Shaggy!"

"Okay. I'm Shaggy." Eric sat patiently as Scooby-Doo and his "meddling" friends solved the mystery. Once it was over, Eddie turned to Eric for a brief second, yelled "Catch," and ran down the stairs.

Before following along, Eric asked Mike to sit with Mrs. Crowley and explain the reason for the visit. Mike obliged, and Sheila and Eric headed outside.

For someone who had lost so many basic mental and physical faculties, Eddie could still throw and catch a football pretty well. In fact, after passing the ball back and forth a few times in the cold air, Eric was winded. But Eddie wanted to keep going. Eric held the ball for a minute and asked Eddie if he could talk to him. Knowing Eddie hardly understood any of their conversation, Eric talked to him as if he was still able to comprehend his every word.

"Eddie, you know we used to play football together on a team in high school."

"We did?" Eddie asked.

"Yeah. We used to do a lot of things together. We were best friends a long time ago. Do you remember any of that?" Eddie looked at Eric for a second, and then his eyes seemed to roam, as if searching for a memory or an answer for Eric.

"Hmmmm," was all Eddie said in reply.

"Eddie, I know you won't remember what we used to be like. But I want you to know that I look back on those times and have really good memories. We used to play sports together. We used to go fishing and camping."

"CAMPING!"

"Yes, Eddie, camping," Eric answered, worried that he sounded a little patronizing. But he didn't want to. He simply wanted to say what he needed to. "We used to hang out together all day and all night. You and I went to school together and had a lot of friends. We even dated some of the same girls. Anyway, Eddie, I have to say that you were a good friend. You were probably my best friend."

"Wike Shaggy and Scooby?"

"Yes, a lot like that."

Eddie smiled.

"Eddie— " Eric paused before proceeding with his next sentence, wondering, if like a child, there were things you weren't supposed to say to him for fear he wouldn't understand or take them the wrong way. Before continuing, Eric began to fashion the words in his mind prior to saying something he would regret later.

As he pondered his thoughts, he noticed it was getting colder outside. Eric started to cough and was still short of breath due to the cold and the physical activity in the yard. Eric began to panic as his breathing became more labored. The feeling was reminiscent of the times he'd had an allergic reaction to cats. "Tell you what, Eddie. Let's go on the porch and warm up, and I'll continue my story in there."

"Okay, Shaggy!"

As they walked to the porch, Sheila must have sensed his weakness, for she asked if Eric felt okay. Eric told her of the shortness of breath but assured her he was fine and could continue.

Back on the enclosed porch, the effects of the bone-chilling wind weren't as bad. Sheila, Eric, and Eddie sat down on a porch swing and continued their conversation.

"So yeah, Eddie, we were like Shaggy and Scooby. We had a lot of fun adventures. We did some things that were sort of mean to other people sometimes, too. But that was just a part of us being young and foolish. Anyway, I wanted to come back and thank you for being such a good friend to me."

"Yer wecome!"

Eric smiled. "You were a good friend. But I got in over my head with something one night and I forsook—er, took that friendship for granted. You won't remember this, buddy, but one night when we were out having some fun, we sort of got into some trouble. Well, *I* got into some trouble."

Eric tried to take a deep breath but was interrupted by another coughing fit. When he gathered himself again, he continued. "We were at a party and played a game that ended up costing us all a lot more than we could have ever imagined, Eddie. That night, to save my own skin, I talked you into doing something that I knew was bad."

"Bad? Uh-oh, I'm tellin' Mommy."

Eric felt Sheila put her arm around him to comfort and strengthen him to be able to continue. "By now she knows, Eddie. Please just let me finish. Then you can tell her whatever you want. Like I was saying, I sacrificed our friendship and your health for my benefit. And I'm sorry. I'm sorry I let that guy scare me back then. I'm sorry I didn't stand up for you. I shouldn't have let you take the hit from that joint. And I'm sorry for where you are now. I wish I could go back in time and change things that night. If I could go back and stop you from smoking that stupid thing or even have done it myself, things would be really different. Eddie, I hope you can forgive me for the horrible things I did to you. Shaggy would never do to Scooby what I've done to you. I'm sorry, buddy. So sorry."

Eddie stared out at the dead leaves blowing across the yard and focused on a group of them that swirled around like a mini tornado. Eric imagined for a minute that Eddie could comprehend everything he'd told him. He had a quick daydream of Eddie turning towards him in his right mind and saying, "It's okay, buddy, I forgive you." But he knew that wouldn't happen.

"Eddie, I won't be able to come back and visit anymore. I have to go soon. But I want you to be good to your parents. And take care of yourself, okay, buddy—I mean Scooby."

"Okay, Shaggy," Eddie replied, seemingly unfazed by anything Eric had told him.

⌘⌘⌘

Back inside, Mrs. Crowley made hot chocolate for everyone. Eddie dipped graham crackers into his mug and licked and slurped the sticky liquid off his fingers. When they were finished, Eric helped Mrs. Crowley carry the dishes into the kitchen. "I know Mike filled you in on everything that's going on. My condition now doesn't excuse me from any anger you have towards me. I'm really sorry things turned out the way they did. But I'm even more sorry for my part in starting this horrible chain of events. I could never make up for the pain I've caused you and your family."

Mrs. Crowley turned to Eric and grabbed his face with both hands. "Eric, what you did was something any stupid young man may have done in your shoes. I could spend the rest of my life angry with you or blaming you for the place Eddie's at now. But you didn't mean him harm back then. You simply couldn't see what the consequences of your actions might be. Besides, we're all responsible for our own actions. So please don't feel any more guilt over this situation. What's done is done, and we don't hold this thing against you. We're just happy to still have our boy with us. Even if he isn't at the place in life we would have wanted him to be. I know you didn't have to come back here to face all of this today. But I'm glad you did. I wish the best for you as you continue with your journey. I hope you find the peace you're looking for with the time you have left, son."

Mrs. Crowley pulled Eric into an embrace, then kissed him on the cheek. "Now you go on and take care of all of the things you need to. And don't worry about us at all. We'll all be fine."

"Thanks, Mrs. Crowley. May God bless you all," Eric said.

He went back into the living room to say good-bye to Eddie. Eddie didn't turn from his hot chocolate but waved good-bye and said, "Bye bye, Shaggy," as he chomped on more graham crackers.

The trio headed back out to the car, and as soon as the cold air hit him again, Eric started to cough.

⌘ ⌘ ⌘

Although Sheila became Eric's walking hospital, he had still spent more time in medical facilities since receiving his death sentence than the rest of his life combined. He had traded his daily visits to the courtroom for frequent trips to various doctor's offices and hospital rooms. Beds, tests, charts, machines, and worst of all, waiting, all became part of his routine. But it was a part of his routine he was never able to fully get used to.

A day after leaving Eddie Crowley's house, Eric's cough grew worse, and his respiration became increasingly labored until it got to the point where he could get no relief. Sheila had listened to his chest, and after confirming her worst fear, she and Mike brought him to the hospital shortly thereafter.

Not able to handle even simple colds or infections that a normal healthy person could recover from quickly, Eric could not afford to take any chances. What started as an annoying respiratory ailment morphed into a full-blown case of pneumonia. The side effects of the pneumonia left Eric feeling the most discomfort he had experienced since receiving his death sentence. His spirit was still willing, and he wanted to be home with his family to finish the R&R list.

But his body was getting significantly weaker. For the first time, Eric actually felt like something was seriously wrong; that this thing he'd labeled as a death sentence might actually be that. His mild claustrophobia got worse as the hours turned into days, and his air intake became increasingly difficult. He began to feel confined, imprisoned, and had way too much time to dwell on the things he still had to do.

Eric did what he could to deal with the pain and pass the time. He felt most comfortable when elevated to a position where he was sitting almost straight up. As bad as things had become, the time in the hospital and his inability to get a good night's rest had one small benefit. It allowed him to check off a few things he'd meant to do for a while. He spent hours on his laptop working on his will, sending emails, and journaling. When he wasn't working on those projects, there was always someone there to keep him company. Sheila and Mike spent the most time by his side, and his family rotated through as often as possible. His mother was there every day, saving him from hospital food with her home cooking. He was convinced her food was actually helping him heal faster both emotionally and physically.

He also continued to journal using his digital recorder. He felt silly speaking into the device when no one else around, but it was the only way he could think of to finish the project. No matter how silly it felt, this digital journal might be the only thing his family would have to pass on when he was gone. He wanted to make sure it was there since he wouldn't be to give his daughter advice and guidance as he saw fit.

So many thoughts raced through Eric's mind as he continued to record life lessons for the daughter he still had not met. He knew that Renee was probably a good mother and had surely passed on many of these things already. But Eric wanted Emily to have an identity and perspective from her father as well. He wanted her to know where he came from, what he was like, and who he was. But more importantly than all of that, he needed to make sure she knew about the man he had become and the faith he had only recently embraced. Eric had already covered most of his life up through college. He had apologized for abandoning Emily's mother and for being selfish for so many years. But now was the time on the recording where he needed to cover the most important life lesson he'd have to pass on. He started and stopped more times than he could count. Finally he swallowed hard and began to speak in a friendly but serious tone into the recorder.

Hey, Emily, it's me, your dad again. I hope you've gotten to this point in the tape and that I haven't bored you out of your mind. Actually, I hope you cherish these recordings and can see past the man that I used to be and the brand-new person I am now. I'm not asking you to forgive me right away. But I'm hoping that, with time, these recordings and the writings I've left will help you get to a place of understanding.

I'm also hoping you can take some of the guidance and lessons to heart. When you think of the person I used to be, think of those lessons as a way to avoid the horrible path I took. Then when you learn of the person I've become, think of those as the most important lessons; they are the ones that will be like a light to you in the darkness. They will be like a good map that can lead you down the narrow road, to the place where God wants you to be.

I know I'm going to sound like your great-grandma now, so Emily, I don't want to preach at you. But I do need you to know about the most important lesson I've learned in life so you can hear about it early on, and hopefully, by following that way, you'll be able to live the life that is truly life.

So let me explain what I meant when I said I was going to sound like your great-grandma now. One of the things I'm going to leave you is a Bible that my grandma, who is your great-grandma, gave to me. In it, she had underlined some verses that she wanted me to read.

Two months ago I would have laughed it off and read those words only in a passing moment to honor her memory.

But with this death sentence and all, I owed it to myself to do some soul-searching. I needed to find out if there was anything more to the success and self-driven life that I used to live, to see if there was a higher purpose or calling in life. Emily, what I found is that apart from God, we have nothing. We only have passing moments of temporary happiness, pleasure, and success. But with Him and in Him, there is everlasting joy, peace, redemption, and most importantly, love.

In the last few weeks I've learned that it's not about what you do in life, but about what HE did that enables us to truly live. Once we hear about that story, once we research the claims, and once we embrace the truth, we become changed.

On one hand, I still haven't found a really good reason for the fact that I have to die this way. I've tried to think of a good explanation, but at the end of the day, all I know is that it has happened, and I simply have to deal with it.

But on the other hand, if this was the only way for me to have found my faith and then, in turn, to pass it on to you, then I'm honored to have had things turn out this way. Because in death I'll be able to give you the one thing I chose not to in life. And that is myself.

Eric pressed the pause button, and felt a strong coughing spell coming on. After regaining his composure, he cleared his throat and continued.

Now that I have the perspective from this bed, I realize my biggest regret in life was not being able to spend more time with you. But since I can't do that now, I need you to know how important it is to understand who you are in God's eyes. In His eyes, you are His child, and no matter what you've done to this point, or what misconceptions you have about Him, you need to know He loves you more than anything and was willing to give His Son in order to be with you.

I realize that when I say He loves you as His child, it's a little hard to hear coming from the man who abandoned you all those years ago. But imagine the perfect father, one that is all loving, all accepting, and always there. And that is what God is to you.

I don't have time to mince words and water down this message, so what I need you to know is that the only way to partake of this relationship is to believe in what Jesus did for you on the cross and accept His gift. By doing this you inherit not only eternal life but a relationship that is far better than any you will know of in this life. Don't put it off too long. I was fortunate enough to have time to do this before my death sentence was carried out, but not everyone does. So please take the time to think about these things and don't wait too long to make a decision.

I know this is a lot to take in right now. I've been in the exact same spot where you are today. I want you to know that I have two friends who will talk to you about this any time if you wish. The first is a Doctor named Sheila Redmond. She is an oncologist at Fairfax Hospital in Northern Virginia, and her cell phone number is 703-555-1718. The second is a pastor named Mike Davenport. He's the senior pastor at the New Hope Church in McLean, Virginia. He can be reached at 571-555-6792. Please contact them at any time, day or night, if you want to talk about this or if you want to know more about me. They were a very important part of my life in the end of it, and they will treat you like family.

Speaking of family, of course you can always go to your uncle Randy or your grandparents on my side. Hopefully you'll have a chance to meet them one day. They don't live far from you, and if your mom will allow them to see you, they too know all about the things I've been talking about.

Eric tried in vain to take a deep breath, then finished his thought.

I'm not ready to say good-bye just yet. But I'm really having trouble breathing right now. Lemme get some rest, and I'll talk to you more later, sweetheart.

Eric put down the recorder and stared out the window at the trees blowing in the distance. He tried to relax and took a slow breath until another coughing spell came on.

⌘⌘⌘

On his third day in the hospital, the outlook became bleak, and no one was really sure if Eric was going to survive. Sheila was busy as his attending doctor doing what she could to work with the hospital staff and fight the pneumonia. But it got to a point where it was truly out of their hands and in the hands of the Almighty.

His family spent the afternoon saying good-bye and then began the grieving process. Even Mike, who was normally optimistic, stayed by his bedside in almost constant prayer, fearing the worst for his friend. He was convinced Eric's time had come.

Mike looked out the window as the sun began to disappear over the horizon and thought to himself, when it was his time, no matter how bad it was, he'd rather die at home than in the hospital.

Mike had been at the bedside of many people in the same position Eric was in that night. It was usually the family member of someone in his congregation. But on two other occasions, it was people he cared deeply about. In this instance, he felt he was playing a dual role. He was there to comfort and provide spiritual guidance to Eric's family and Sheila. But he'd grown close to and fond of Eric. In his heart and mind, Mike knew Eric's death would affect him more deeply than he would admit to anyone. He wasn't ready to say good-bye to Eric, as he felt he still had a thing or two left to learn from Eric's life.

Mike maintained the unofficial role of spiritual mentor to Eric. Although he always tried to provide good answers, there were times when silence and an ear were all that Eric needed. And as much as Eric benefited from Mike's presence on the journey, Mike also gleaned wisdom and lessons, in turn, from Eric.

Some of the insights Eric had gained in the time they'd reconnected changed Mike forever. It was like learning through Eric's spiritual growth. He was a man who was changed and touched by the hand of God in a very short period of time. In that sense, they had reversed roles, and Eric had become the mentor and he, the student. There was something about Eric that now seemed very much in touch with his Creator. Maybe it was merely a natural by-product of the process of dying. Eric displayed a level of peace and assurance that was almost indescribable. And he was so incredibly determined. Through disappointment, setback, pain, and hardship, thus far, Eric had persevered in order to finish the task he'd set out to accomplish in the first week he was diagnosed.

Mike knew it was important to Eric to reach the others on his R&R list. But how would that happen once Eric was gone? Mike couldn't allow the list to be incomplete, so he came up with an idea. At that moment, Mike promised himself that if Eric didn't make it through the night, he would do everything in his power to finish the list before returning to New Hope.

By ten o'clock that night, Eric was still fighting for his life. He had a high fever, and his breathing, although heavily assisted, sounded more and more like snarls and grunts as time passed.

His family was scattered throughout the hospital. Randy had taken Elaine and the kids home, and, upon his return, joined his mom in the chapel down the hall. His father was outside, puffing on his pipe and wondering how he was going to comfort Diane in the first few days and weeks after Eric passed.

Sheila and Mike sat by Eric's bedside listening to his wheezy, shallow breathing. They hoped the strong medications and stronger prayers would kick in to give him the few weeks they all thought he deserved.

Mike leaned towards Sheila and whispered, "I know these last couple of months have taken a toll on you. I want you to know I'm proud of you for making the decision to help Eric. I know how important your research and work are to you. You've done a fantastic job keeping Eric going to this point. He never complains of being in pain, so if things don't get better tonight, you can be proud you greatly reduced a dying man's suffering."

Sheila sighed, and her lower lip began to tremble. "Mike, if he doesn't make it, I almost feel like we failed him," she murmured. "I know we've done everything we could. But we were so close. We only had two more people to reach. I don't know. It doesn't seem fair. Here's the one guy who didn't squander the rest of his days fulfilling fantasies or trying to live longer merely for the sake of being around one more day. To see him get to a point where he knows his faith, and then have only a few more people to reach out to…well, it doesn't seem fair."

"I've been giving it a lot of thought since he started going downhill over these last few days," Mike replied. "Maybe *we* are supposed to reach out to the last few people on his list."

"But how will we get to these people? All we have are a few more names on the bottom of his list. We know they're in this area, but we don't know how Eric knew them or what he did to them. I'd hate to walk into a situation blind, not knowing what we're getting into. Who knows if it's worse than what he did to Roland Hughes or Jon Jansen."

"I'm sure the details are in his laptop and on those recordings he's been making over the last few weeks. The two of us could put it all together and figure out exactly what it was he wanted to say to those people. You know, as well as I do, that he's organized when it comes to the will and all. He'll mention something about them in there if he can't continue in person. Besides, worst-case scenario, we could get in contact with his former private investigator. I think I overheard him say his name was Rob. I'm sure the number is in his cell phone somewhere. He's bound to have an idea of where to find these people."

Just as Mike finished telling Sheila about his plans, Eric's wheezing stopped. He grunted and made a sound like his throat was being cleared. Groggy and hoarse, Eric turned to them and said, "You know, you should probably stop talking about me like I'm already dead."

⌘⌘⌘

Eric's fever finally broke in the early morning hours. He spent a total of three more days in the hospital until he was well enough to go back home. He was significantly weakened by his bout with pneumonia, but he was still able to walk and get around on his own. Only now, he spent more time resting and sitting than he did up and about. It was good to be home again, living out his days in the comfort and love in his home. Surrounded by the people he loved, celebrating life, enriching himself, and, in turn, enriching others through authentic and meaningful relationships.

Eric had left his phone on and unplugged, and it died while he was in the hospital. It sprung to life after being on the charger for only a few minutes. The familiar chime told him he had messages waiting for him. The first few were of no real importance, but the last two held an urgency that sent a chill down his spine. They were from Rob and were separated by a day. They were already a few days old. The first was a warning that Roland Hughes was the main person of interest in a murder that took place in western Pennsylvania. Rob had taken advantage of his numerous law enforcement connections (being an ex-cop himself) and found out the victim was the prosecuting attorney in the case that put Hughes away for six years.

The second message from Rob informed Eric that the body of Roland's accomplice from his last crime spree was found floating in a local river. This accomplice had turned against Roland in exchange for a lesser sentence. He was ultimately the person who testified and identified him as the mastermind of the attempted kidnapping/abduction that put Roland away for so long. The death was ruled as suspicious, and, once again, Roland was at the top of the list of suspects due to the connection of the case and similar geographic area where the attorney was killed.

Eric didn't need to hear anything else. It now appeared that Roland was working on a list of his own. But Roland's list was the opposite of Eric's. It was one of revenge and hatred. It seemed he was taking out the people who had wronged him in his past. Although Eric had tried to reach out to him, he was well aware that he, too, was probably on Roland's twisted list. Eric wondered how long it would be before Roland made it back to their hometown in order to cross him off.

Roland Hughes saw the flashing red and blue lights in his rearview mirror just after midnight. He'd been on Interstate 81 South for a few hours and had just taken the exit for the James Madison University campus in Harrisonburg, Virginia when he must have lost concentration and violated some minor traffic offense. The stolen car provided by his last victim might already be in the system. He figured the pistol he'd taken from his old partner (turned snitch) Frank was probably not yet reported. He pulled the 9mm Ruger semiautomatic pistol from under his waistband and held it to his side out of sight as the state trooper approached his vehicle.

"Good evening, Officer. Is there a problem tonight? I don't think I was speeding."

"License and registration please," the officer said without answering his question.

At that instant Roland came across with the pistol and fired three rounds quickly at the trooper without aiming. Fortunately, two of the bullets were absorbed by the trooper's ballistic vest. But the third struck soft flesh and then bone near his right shoulder. The trooper went down quickly and began screaming into the radio for help. Luckily for Roland, the officer couldn't get to his service weapon as the bullet struck him on the side where he carried his pistol. Unable to draw the gun and return fire, the officer began to roll away from the vehicle.

Roland sped off, happy to have avoided the close call. But as his adrenaline wore off, he became concerned that he'd have to replace his current stolen ride with another one.

It was that necessity that probably saved someone's life as it ruined his original plans for the night. Forced to search for clean transportation, Roland wouldn't have time to take advantage of the many young coeds he had planned to choose from the campus that night. But he knew time and reckless abandon were on his side, so his other activities would have to wait until he was safe in his final destination.

Nine

Less than one week ago
Reconciliation with Marcus Harrison

The first snow of the season hit the mountains of southwestern Virginia on the second day Eric was home from the hospital. Unusual for early December, the glistening flakes turned the lifeless fall view into a bright, snow-covered landscape. Eric sat on the back porch early in the morning, sipping a mug of hot tea. Another one of Sheila's "wonder cures," the warm liquid was as good for his soul as it supposedly was for his nourishment. Lady sat at his feet, and his laptop computer rested on his blanket as he soaked in the beauty of day. Thousands of snowflakes fell around him, making a quiet rushing sound like that of a distant waterfall.

Eric took a deep breath in through his nose. He held the cold air in his lungs and savored it for several seconds before letting it back out again. He hoped if he had to take his last breath looking at anything, it would be a view like this one. For now, he was merely thankful that he was actually able to take a full breath.

Although still weak, Eric decided he had to risk the snow and some discomfort in order to see the next person on the R&R list. As the rocker gently creaked beneath him, Eric waited for Sheila and Mike to join him on the porch.

In addition to the R&R list, he'd recently spent some time thinking about other people he'd wronged in a less serious manner than the others. With his health deteriorating, he knew he'd never have a chance to make time for everyone. Still, he wished he could go back and offer at least an in-person apology for some of the other wrongs he'd dished out over the last few years.

He thought of the time he stirred up dissension and negativity against the other bright young attorney who was in the running for partner several years earlier. Eric had spread vicious rumors and outright lies that were bought into by Simms, Miller. and Young about Jonathan Samuels. Samuels (as Eric always called him, mocking the fact that he had two first names) was the shoe-in for partner when Eric first started. He was the only obstacle Eric had to overcome in his early days with SMY in order to get to his coveted position.

As brilliant an attorney as he was, Samuels wasn't the wiser to Eric's scheming. He took Samuels and a few legal aides out for a night of drinking and unwinding and conveniently brought them to the place where Simms, Miller, and Young always went on their Friday evening outings. Since Samuels didn't know about the routine, Eric was able to manipulate him into bad-mouthing SMY by stirring the pot about him not being promoted earlier. Mr. Miller of SMY heard a lot of Samuels' drunken rant that night.

The plan worked perfectly. Samuels was sent packing with a "courtesy" letter of recommendation the following Monday. By the time Samuels knew he'd been set up, it was too late, and Eric was well on his way to the front-runner position for the future opening.

Thinking back on the situation, Eric still could not believe the depth of his former depravity and the lengths he would go to in order to fulfill his own desires. The numerous women he'd used and, in turn, been used by on occasion bothered him for the first time in his life. Some of them used sex to try to get his love. Others used him for some void they thought he filled for them.

But no matter what their reasons were, Eric was willing to use *any* of them for his own pleasure. There wasn't one woman he'd been with since Renee that he didn't treat like another trophy in his life: no better than the Mercedes he drove (although he treated a few of them worse than the car). Eric used his looks, charm, money, feigned feelings (including love), broken promises, and persuasive personality to make sure he always had someone, or a few someones on the side, in case he was in the mood for intimacy or companionship.

Next, he thought of the clients he milked for much more money than he ever should have collected. He couldn't count how many times over the years he'd taken simple cases and drawn them out or purposefully complicated them in order to collect above and beyond what was fair. At the end of the day, he still did his job, just at two or more times the rate he should have charged.

As Eric thought of those and other situations, he began to peck away at the laptop keyboard. In a few short minutes, he had a form letter typed out. He planned to use the letter to send a written apology (and maybe some compensation) for these situations. It wasn't the same as an in-person apology, but it would have to suffice, given his situation. After completing the letter, Eric made a list of as many names as he could think of and planned to leave the letters and special instructions for Rob to send off for him once he was able to track down those people.

⌘⌘⌘

By the time he was finished with his more minor offense list, Eric still wasn't ready to relive the painful memories tied to Marc Harrison yet. When they came outside, he easily distracted Sheila and Mike with another story and gladly sat and enjoyed their company before getting to Harrison. For some reason, the topic of relationships came up. It was one that Eric would have rather avoided until later on, but he enjoyed hearing more about the things his friends had learned and endured on their own journeys.

Sheila was amazingly transparent as she revisited her past and spoke of lost love and the regrets that haunted her. "I never really had time for a serious relationship because of my career, but I had tried to make it work on several occasions. I can't say that my problem was opening up to or getting close to people. But up to this point in my life, I have never really thought of myself as the committing type. Don't get me wrong, I do want to get married and have kids at some point. I've just formed a habit of removing myself before the other person's feelings got too deep, so as not to hurt them more. So far, I've been willing to deny myself the chance at romance for the sake of the other person's heart."

As Eric listened to Sheila continue about a few that got away, he found himself more and more drawn to this woman. He knew there was no chance at any type of relationship now. But what an irony his new friendship was. If he could have picked one person to spend the rest of his life with, it would have been Sheila. And other than being married and intimate, he realized how privileged he was that, ironically, he *was* spending the rest of his life with her.

Mike was also surprisingly comfortable talking about past relationships. Although he didn't give a lot of details, he clearly had no trouble sharing the things he'd learned. He was more guarded when it came to specific people or places (something he'd learned in order to protect the privacy of people who had confided in him as a pastor, he said). But he was not shy talking about the constant struggle. Eric never asked Mike's age, and should have known since they had spent a semester together in law school, but he guessed Mike was now in his early forties by the way he carried himself and the wisdom he displayed in regards to relationships and life in general. He was surprised to find out Mike was only two years his senior.

Mike was solid, poised, and controlled until he started talking about Lin. "She was the one that 'got away' in a sense for me," he lamented. "Looking back on what happened in China, I know there was nothing more I could have done without getting myself killed. But I often wish I could find her and take her away from that horrible fate. I pray for her every day and always ask for a miracle. I wouldn't be where I am today if it wasn't for her. I'd love to thank her and show her that I've been used to reach others because of the time she invested in me. I'd love to be able to show her the church, introduce her to my friends, and make up for lost time. And I would forsake a lot of things and maybe even give away my right arm just to hold her and protect her one more time. That, my friends, would be heaven.

"She is the reason I still haven't been married. I guess I just never got over her. I simply didn't know how to have closure. Grieving didn't work. I couldn't treat her like she was dead, knowing full well she was very much alive and suffering through God knows what. I put my prayers and tears into the situation, knowing the Lord hears me. And I know He watches over her. But it's still difficult, and there's not a day that goes by when I don't think about her."

Eric struggled with Mike's last statement. He believed it to be the truth but wondered how to make sense of it. The idea that God was somehow watching over her while she was confined to a miserable existence in a Chinese prison somewhere seemed odd. For that matter, if God was in control, why was *he* still suffering now that he'd turned his life around? Still new to the concept of accepting things on faith, Eric finally gathered up the nerve to ask the question.

"Okay, Jesus experts. I'm still new to this whole idea of looking at things from a spiritual perspective, not just a worldly one. Don't get me wrong. I'm grateful for my newfound faith and for the chance to continue to work on the R&R list. But I'm having a hard time dealing with the issue of suffering and pain, and, to go along with it, the whole cosmic 'good vs. evil' thing. Why is it that Lin and those good people in China have to suffer while evil people like Roland Hughes get to roam free? It doesn't seem fair sometimes. And on the topic of suffering, not to be selfish, but now that I've changed my ways and try to do the right thing, why won't He cure my cancer?"

"If you have a few hundred years, I'll try to start answering your questions," Mike said with a twinkle in his eye. "Seriously, those are questions that you, me, and six billion other people ask all the time. There are no easy answers. But they are valid questions."

"Well, I don't have a few hundred years, but I have all day, so please help me out with this one. It's something I'd like to try to grasp, well, you know, before I run out of time."

"Fair enough," Mike said. "First off, not being God, I can't give you all of the answers you're looking for. I'm not trying to shrug off the responsibility except to say that God doesn't need a spokesman like me—His Word does that for Him. But there are some things I've learned in my time as a believer that I think help to at least explain some of these issues. I think suffering and pain are results of a mixture of His design combined with our free will within that design. It's part of an ultimate plan and the 'rules' of His system. I'm not trying to give a churchy or cliché answer. Hear me out, and I'll try to explain it in the way I've come to understand and accept it.

"I don't know why humans only live for about a hundred years or so. But according to the Bible, death was not part of the original system. It was a result of our rebellion against God, which led to a broken relationship. The broken relationship caused us all to live under the curse of sin and death. So death is now a part of the world we live in. No matter how we try to avoid it or prolong our lives, one day we'll all physically die. The only difference is how it will come to us. Tossed into that reality is the fact that we have free will. You and I are allowed to make choices, even if it means those choices will harm ourselves and/or others. This is about to get really deep, so buckle up for this part.

"Think of the laws that govern our world. Not just the rules and regulations you're so familiar with. Also think of scientific laws like the law of gravity, thermodynamics, etc. These things are constants in the universe as we know it. No matter how much we'd love to be able to hover or fly, we're stuck walking or running in and of ourselves. But that doesn't mean we can't utilize things that can help us *overcome* the limitations imposed on us by those laws. We use our intellect to create vehicles that break the force of gravity and fly into the air and space. We use scuba gear to overcome our inability to breathe underwater. And we use complicated algorithms, formulas, and other technology to overcome and manipulate our world in order to explore and learn more about it through science.

Mike rose from his chair to stretch his legs and stared out at the snow as he continued. "Why do we do that? To work the system and gain knowledge about a world that came into existence long ago. We shouldn't blame the system for its limitations. We manipulate it for our knowledge and the greater good. Science makes its best guesses with the evidence that's already there in order to come up with ways to explain how the world works. So death and suffering, on one hand, are simply part of a complex system in the same way gravity is part of it. The system and the rules were put in place long before we were born, and they'll still be there long after we're dead.

"But that still isn't enough to answer your question! I can *explain* flight, underwater exploration, and the reasons behind volcanic eruptions to you all day long, but until you *experience* them, you won't fully understand and appreciate them for yourself. So to understand the pursuit of the knowledge of God and faith is the same type of pursuit as a scientific one. But there are different ways to go about it.

"The difference between the pursuit of the knowledge of God through faith and the pursuit of the knowledge of the world through science is the subject matter. God is a being. The only way you get to know or understand a being better is through an experience or a personal relationship. A personal spiritual relationship that, like the laws of science in our world, is part of a system. If you want to know why suffering is part of the system, you have to have a relationship with the one who made it.

"I think the best way to understand His relationship to us and how suffering and pain play into it is to look at an analogy that comes from one of the most important human relationships that exists: the one between parents and children. Take the quality of God's omniscience, for example. People have trouble acknowledging the fact that God is all-knowing because they say if He knows something bad is going to happen to a good person, He could stop it. Or He at least would not have created them in the first place, knowing they would suffer and die due to the broken relationship. But that is a misconception that can be explained by any parent on Earth.

Mike paused to take a sip of his coffee. "I don't have kids of my own. But through my family and others I'm close to who have children, I know parenting is a joy that is unmatched on this side of heaven. Every person making the decision to have children knows in advance that, theoretically, something bad could happen to their kids. Even before they're born, as we said before, their parents know they could be killed in a car accident, get cancer, or even worse, be assaulted by a despicable predator. Furthermore, no matter how careful they are, at some point every child will eventually die. Knowing this in advance, should parents just decide never to have children? Of course not. That would be the end of humanity.

"Knowing their decision to have children could lead to the beloved child's suffering does not stop them from having kids. Does that mean the parents are cruel or don't love them? No. In fact, it's the opposite. It's love that brings them together to have children in the first place. And it's their desire to express their love through a relationship with children that *leads* them to sacrifice all they are to become parents in the first place.

"So apply that principle to God. If we, as evil humans with the foreknowledge of possible pain and death, still allow children to be born in order to express our love for them, how much more does a just and loving God allow us to have lives in order to express His love for humanity? Furthermore, how much more meaningful is the sacrifice of *His* child in order to reconcile the broken relationship? We were the ones who rebelled and caused the rift and were powerless to do anything to reconcile the relationship. So God took it into His own hands and sent His only Son to die for us to be reconciled to Him.

"It's all part of that system again; these spiritual laws govern the way we live and what we can do (similar to the laws of science). You don't have to understand why they exist; you simply have to accept them and make your choices based on that acceptance. You, of all people, should now know the fullest extent of your decisions. Now that you know you have the free will to make choices that may harm someone, you'll carefully move forward so that instead of hurting them, you'll have a positive influence. Your head isn't spinning yet, so I take it I can continue?"

"It's not spinning, but man that's a lot to take in," Eric said.

"It is a lot, and it's something that has come through many hours of just trying to listen to what God is saying. The difficulty is that we're limited not only in our ability to understand, but also because, at some point, all of the analogies fall apart."

"I'm starting to get some of this stuff, although I don't think we'll ever get all of the answers on this side of things. Too bad I can't call you guys in a month or so and give them to you." Eric smiled. "So I get that there are some things we have to accept as part of the system. Suffering and pain are still things that will take me more time than I have to process."

Sheila finally chimed in. "Let me try to tackle this from a medical standpoint since it's my area of expertise. Like death, as Mike pointed out, physical and emotional pains are part of the system we now live under. They are consequences of our ability to experience love and pleasure. From a physiological standpoint, in order to feel pleasure, we have to have the sense of touch. How else would you know the feeling of a warm blanket, a cold drink, a hug from a loved one, or a passionate kiss?

"But in order for the system to work, there has to be the opposing sense to tell us when something is wrong. If you couldn't feel pain, you would have never known you had cancer. If people couldn't feel the heat of a fire, they wouldn't know not to get too close to prevent burns. You can't have one without the other. Because of the design, the human body has the potential to experience intense pleasure and horrible pain. But I don't know many people who would trade in the possibility of pain if they had to also give up the ability to feel pleasure.

"From a psychological standpoint, emotional suffering and grief are the consequence to love and attachment. In order to love something, you have to be able to put value on it. And if you value it, you have to be willing to accept that you could lose it at some point. Knowing that loving someone could someday mean they have to lose another person doesn't stop most people from daring to love. And most people would never trade in the risk of grief if it meant they could never experience love.

"I've seen so many people suffer pain and death in my short career, and I never get used to it. It's never easy, whether it's an elderly person who has led a full life or a young child with so many possibilities ahead of them. But I've never met *any* that would have asked not to be born just because their time had come. It's not necessarily the way they wanted to go, but most were grateful to have had some chance at life." Sheila paused for a moment to make eye contact with Eric.

Then she quickly continued. "There's a family that Mike and I both know from church who had a young son who suffered from a rare form of blood cancer."

"Oh yeah, the Stevensons," Mike interjected. "Wow, that was a difficult one for all of us."

"He was only five when he died," Sheila said. "I've seen people in pain before, but, in his case, the parents were just beside themselves with grief. Yet even in the midst of their horrible pain, I remember his mother saying if she had to choose between living with the pain in order to have the five years they did, they would not trade those five wonderful years of relationship in order to avoid the pain. That doesn't make scientific sense, but it makes perfect sense to anyone who has had children. No matter how many people question pain, suffering, and misfortune, very few would trade in those things if they had to give up pleasure, love, and genuine relationships."

After a short silence, Mike brought the subject to a close. "To bring it all full circle, free will is part of this system because what would love really be if you were forced to love a predetermined mate? It wouldn't be love then; it would be duty. If we didn't have free will, we couldn't choose vocation, where we would eat, what hobbies to partake in— everything would be part of the same boring system. And so we have the freedom to choose good things. However, with the freedom to choose good comes the freedom to choose evil. Unfortunately, in the exercise of free will, many people make choices that infringe on the free will of others. And that's where things break down into situations where evil gets a foothold and ruins lives. This is why the responsibility to live right and spread the good news falls to those of us who choose the path that leads to righteousness. It's not just for us. It's for everyone that falls into our spheres of influence."

For Eric, everything was starting to come together. Although he didn't fully understand everything Mike and Sheila had said, it all seemingly made sense. He had an otherworldly assurance that each word was absolute truth. As they sat in silence, Eric knew, beyond any doubt, that although Mike and Sheila were the mouthpieces, the message was God's. The deep truths slowly sank in, and the answers became a healing salve for Eric's hurting soul. He thanked Mike and Sheila for the explanation, and the trio sat in silence enjoying the snowy day for a few minutes to allow the conversation to fully sink in.

⌘⌘⌘

"So lemme tell you the details of the events that led up to the falling out of three best friends from high school: myself, Renee, and Marcus Harrison. The story of the way I wronged Marcus Harrison carries a theme as old as time. Well, human time, that is. It was a clear-cut case of betrayal involving a love triangle. Marcus was another friend of mine in high school."

"Man, you were a dangerous person to be friends with—or enemies with for that matter," Mike interjected.

"Yeah, tell me about it," Eric replied. "Marcus dated a girl named Renee Rutherford, who was another good friend of ours. I'm not sure how it happened, but after high school, the three of us ended up in college together. It worked out quite well. We picked up in our freshman year of college where we'd left off our senior year of high school. We studied together, partied together, and made the most of the time we had. Things were fine until Renee and Marcus got engaged. High school sweethearts from their sophomore year, Marcus knew he wanted to spend the rest of his life with Renee. At first it seemed like a good idea to Renee, too. But as time went on, the relationship became increasingly strained.

"I tried to be a good friend to both of them, while staying neutral through their difficulties. For Marcus, things just weren't moving ahead fast enough. He used to say that making wedding plans was like pulling teeth. For Renee, things were moving way too fast. She claimed to love Marcus. But in her own words, she couldn't decide on a major, let alone decide what to do with the rest of her life. Unfortunately, the more time I spent with Renee, the more my feelings changed. Neutrality morphed into attraction. I don't know if I was her escape, a potential rebound, or if she actually developed feelings for me at first. Regardless of the reason, I was able to steal her affection away from Marcus. We had been good friends, but I was willing to forsake that friendship in order to get my best friend's girlfriend.

"Similar to another situation where I got punched for my poor decisions, this one was no different. Marcus seemed obsessed for a while and even attacked me once. He was a little more successful than Mike here and was able to punch out a tooth."

"Lucky guy," Mike joked.

"He was definitely mad at me for betraying our friendship. But he was also infuriated with her for breaking off the engagement. The more he pushed, the more she ran to me. In the end, it didn't matter what the reason was. I won the battle, and Renee was the prize.

"I never spoke with Marcus again. I heard he transferred schools and ended up joining the military. But now I have to go to him and apologize for ruining his life—even if it was only ruined for that period."

After Eric finished his story, the trio returned inside to get bundled up. They climbed into the car to head out to Marcus' house.

"I'm not too worried about how things will go here," Eric said. "I'd like to think that, by now, this situation is long forgotten. But you never know. Just in case, I'll make sure my muscle, Pastor Mike, is close by if needed."

⌘⌘⌘

When they were only a few minutes away from Marcus' home, Eric told Sheila and Mike of his plans to send letters out to some of the people he would not be able to reach in person. They promised to ensure all of the letters would get out if Eric didn't have time to send them himself. He also expressed his desire to move quickly after meeting with Marcus, since the last person he needed to see on the R&R list would be the most complicated. The results of his last meeting could cause changes in the way he would spend the last few weeks of his life.

Mike's SUV did well on the snow-covered roads, even though there were at least two to four inches of snow accumulated on the grass, sidewalks, and areas on the road that were not as heavily traveled. As they pulled into Marcus' driveway, movement behind the home caught Eric's attention. Several people were sledding down the small hill to the north of the house.

The trio exited the vehicle as someone dressed in snow gear waved them towards the hill. Eric opened the gate on the side of the property and led Mike and Sheila into the backyard. They approached the snow-covered people who were laughing and playing at the bottom of the hill.

"I'm looking for Marcus Harrison," Eric said.

"Well, you found him," a tall man replied. He pulled down the hood that covered his face and revealed a bearded man who looked slightly older and a little heavier than the last time they had seen each other.

As Eric got closer and removed his own hat and sunglasses, Marcus recognized Eric. "Wow. Now there's a blast from the past," Marcus said.

"Hello, Marcus. I know it's been a long time, and I know the last time we spoke was not under the best circumstances."

"That's the understatement of the century," Marcus replied.

"I'm sorry to interrupt your fun, but I was wondering if I could borrow a few minutes of your time. These are my friends, Mike and Sheila."

"Nice to meet you both. This is my wife, Tammy, and the kings of the hill over there are Jenna, Chase, and little Marcus." Marcus excused himself from his family and pulled Eric aside. "Listen, Eric, I don't mean to be rude, but let's not kid ourselves and pretend that we parted as friends. I don't really have much to say to you, so why don't we just say good-bye and call it a day."

Eric was disappointed. Desperate to speak his peace, Eric asked if it would change things if Marcus knew that he was dying. Marcus shook his head. "I'm sorry to hear that regardless of our past. Okay, I'll give you five minutes. Let's go inside and talk by the fire while the kids play."

Everyone removed his or her boots and coats at the door before heading into the large suburban house that belonged to Marcus.

"So what in the world brings you to my neck of the woods? Here to steal my wife from me?" Marcus asked as they settled in.

"Ha, now that's a good one," Eric said. "No, not here for that." Eric looked around at some of the decorations and pictures on the walls. "Marcus, it looks like you've done pretty well for yourself. You have a beautiful family and a lot to be thankful for."

"Thanks, Eric. But you didn't come here to talk about the house and the family, so why don't we cut to the chase about why you've tracked me down after all these years. I'm giving you the courtesy of my time because of your condition. But don't mistake that compassion for friendship."

"Sure, Marcus, I don't want to take up too much of your time. Sheila here is my doctor, and Mike is my pastor. I'm here because I don't have a whole lot of time left, and there are some things I wanted to say to you. People sometimes use stupid clichés like 'all is fair in love and war' and 'to the winner go the spoils' to justify doing the wrong thing when it comes to relationships. I was one of those people. What happened between us back in college was wrong. It was wrong on so many levels. I was your friend, and I should have protected your trust instead of exploiting it. I can't speak for Renee and can't apologize for her decisions during that time. But I came out here to take responsibility for my actions and say I'm sorry for the things I did to you back then. I'm sorry for betraying your friendship and causing you a lot of pain. There's nothing I can do to make up for those things. You deserved better than the way we treated you. And I deserved to have my tooth punched out."

At first, Marcus was speechless. Then his countenance seemed to change. "Thank you for coming here to say that, Eric. At the time, I hated you for what you did. It changed who I was for a while. I was bitter and resentful towards you both. But it's actually been a long time since I thought of it. You see, I look at my life now, and I can't imagine it without Tammy and the kids. I couldn't see it at the time, but if Renee hadn't broken my heart and you hadn't betrayed my friendship the way you did, I never would have transferred out and met Tammy. She is the love of my life and the perfect woman for me, Eric. So yeah, what you did was a horrible thing. But I wouldn't be where I am today if it wasn't for that situation. So I'm not sure if I should thank you or knock out another tooth...."

"Well, you don't owe me any thanks," Eric said, relieved that he'd been able to apologize. "I've had to do this five times now so I've prepared myself for most reactions I've encountered. You don't owe it to me, but what I'd love to ask is that you'll try to find it in your heart to forgive me."

"Well, considering how things worked out...I will give it some thought. It took some courage for you to come here and say these things today, so I'll at least give you the courtesy of thinking about it. And in spite of our past, I'm sorry for what you're going through now."

"Thanks, and it's okay. I still struggle with the questions and doubts, but I've come to accept that there is a reason behind all this. I'm just not sure what it is yet. But one thing I have realized with this news was the revelation that I've been a pretty selfish and mean person through the years. Earlier, when I said that I've had to do this five other times, I meant I've also had to go to other people I wronged in my past. I went to them to apologize, ask for forgiveness, and offer any restitution appropriate for those situations. Luckily I have my two friends here with me to help get to everyone on the list. And now I'm down to the last entry on the list. And that's Renee."

"How is she?" Marcus asked.

"I don't know. That's why I have to go see her. We broke up during our senior year. I left for law school and haven't heard from or talked to her since then."

"Yeah, I saw her once at the county fair a few years ago. She had a daughter that looked, oh, I don't know, eight or nine years old. She looked great, but I think she was divorced or something."

"Yeah, I had heard she had a daughter," Eric said as he stared at the fire, which was slowly burning out. He was clearly hoping someone would quickly change the subject.

⌘⌘⌘

Sheila caught Eric's reaction and did the math in her head. She looked over at Mike ,who must have been thinking the same thing because he was counting on his fingers. They both made eye contact, and their furrowed brows showed they had put the pieces together.

⌘⌘⌘

After returning from Marcus' house early in the afternoon, both Sheila and Mike wanted to ask Eric about Renee. They hoped to find out if their hunches about his reaction and their math were both right. They discussed back and forth who should bring it up but didn't get up enough nerve until they were sitting around the fire after dinner.

Jarvis and Diane had already gone to bed. Randy was on duty but taking calls for service from his parents' house due to the weather. The four of them talked about the weather and other trivial matters.

But when the conversation afforded an opportunity for the question, Sheila brought it up without skipping a beat. "So, Eric…Mike and I found one detail of the story about your ex-girlfriend Renee fascinating."

"And which one is that?" Eric asked, knowing it was a leading question.

"Oh, that would be the part where Marcus told us about seeing Renee with a daughter at the fair a few years ago. You know, you haven't told us much about the reason you need to see Renee. Care to enlighten us before our big trip tomorrow? Enquiring minds want to know."

"Well guys, technically there are two people left on the list. One of them is Renee. The other one is our daughter, Emily."

"Your what, who?" Randy asked.

"Yes, my daughter, Emily. This is a long one, so you all might want to get comfortable. I'm not proud of the things I'm about to tell you all," Eric said. "In fact, this story contains two of my life's biggest regrets."

"Come on, Eric." Mike spread his arms wide. "By now, nothing you could possibly say could surprise us or make us more disappointed in you."

Eric gazed intently at both of them. "We'll see. Seriously, working up the courage to go back and face the rest of my past holds nothing to the tale I'm about to tell you." Eric took a deep breath and shook his head as he stared into the fire. "I believe on faith that I'm forgiven for the things I've done. But sometimes I can't understand how God could forgive me for the deliberate sins I've committed when it comes to this last situation. Maybe I shouldn't have waited until the end to get to this one. But to be honest, I haven't been ready. I think part of me was hoping my death sentence would have happened before I had to face this one.

"But that would have been the easy way out. To be honest, I'm scared both she and my daughter will be so disappointed that they won't even give me the time of day. The other part of me thinks that this meeting will be the culmination of my life here on Earth. Ideally, I'll be able to talk first with Renee and then get permission to spend some quality time trying to build a relationship with a daughter that I've forsaken for nearly thirteen years."

Eric stood up to add a log to the fire. The flames reflected in his eyes as he continued with the story. Sheila, Mike and Randy sat captivated.

"The story pretty much picks up where the one with Marcus left off. After he was out of the picture, Renee and I grew close really fast. I fought so hard to win her affection, and once I did I felt as if I needed to make up for lost time. It wasn't as easy for her at first. She was happy to have been able to end things with Marcus. But she was sad for what she put him through, especially since she and Marcus' mother had already begun to make wedding plans. But after a few weeks, most of that was forgotten. We moved on with our lives and focused on getting to know each other all over again.

"It's clear to me now that I didn't know what true love looked like in a relationship. But I thought I was in love. I now realize it was more a combination of lust, immature infatuation, some caring, and hormones. But it felt so right. I actually got to the point where I didn't feel complete without her beside me. Don't get me wrong; we had our share of fights just like everyone else. But for the most part, we enjoyed each other's company while studying for our future. I'd say our future was the biggest point of contention for us.

"Renee didn't care what profession she ended up having as long as we were able to be together. I, on the other hand, *had* to become an attorney. And as much as I thought I loved her, she knew she shouldn't do anything to get in the way of that dream for fear I'd choose it over her if push came to shove. Ironically, she didn't need to worry about being the one that came between me and my dream. Something, well, some*one* else, was about to do that for us.

"Before I continue, I have to say that I'm really embarrassed and ashamed about the next part of the story. The decisions I made after finding out Renee was pregnant probably shaped me into the selfish and apathetic person I became for most of my adult life. I can't believe it took this death sentence to make me realize it. If only I hadn't been so stupid."

"Eric, there's nothing you're going to say that will change the fact that we all love and support you. You have become a different person. That's what happens when God gets a hold of your life," Sheila said.

"She's right, Eric. Think of those horrible things as being as far away as the east is from the west," Mike added. "The debt is paid, and the sin is forgiven. In God's eyes you're as pure as the snow that is piling up outside your doors and windows."

"Thanks. Renee came to me one night in the last semester of my undergraduate studies with what she called 'exciting and scary news.' She began to cry and said she was scared to tell me, not knowing how I would react. Thinking it was something simple like a job opportunity or a desire to change her major, I put my arms around her and told her there was nothing she could say that would change anything between us. I finally broke through her reluctance and found out she was ten weeks pregnant.

"A flash of emotions overcame me, but neither joy nor happiness was in the mix. I was scared, in denial, angry, and unprepared to take responsibility for another human. As upset as Renee was, I didn't want to worry her anymore, so I told her everything was going to be okay. She fell asleep in my arms, and I sat up all night wondering what I was going to do.

"When she woke up the next morning, she could tell I was distant. I told her I stayed up all night and had come up with a viable solution to our problem. I told Renee I wanted her to get an abortion. Expecting her to resist at first and then give in after I reasoned with her, Renee did the opposite. She flipped out. And I mean *flipped*. I'd never seen her like that. She said she'd forgive me for the mere suggestion that we 'kill' our baby, but I had better never bring it up again. She was not even going to entertain the thought.

"Then my old survival mechanism kicked in, and I flipped out in return. After about a half hour of screaming, the only thing we were able to accomplish was breaking some dishes, pictures, and furniture. I ended up leaving and didn't go back for a whole day.

160

"When I finally returned to our apartment, Renee was still cleaning up. When I walked in, I scared her, and she cut her hand pretty badly on some broken glass. On the way to the hospital, we didn't speak much, but I reached out and began to stroke her hair. She said she was sorry, to which I responded, 'Me, too.'

"As I waited for her to get ten stitches in her hand, I contemplated my next move. I thought I loved her and wanted to be with her. But I wasn't going to budge on our options—whether it was murder or not. I didn't care back then. I didn't want to have to worry about a baby, and she needed to know it, no matter what the outcome.

"On the way home from the hospital, I took a deliberate detour straight to the clinic I'd looked up the day before. I pulled into the lot and told her that I was sorry for the fight, the broken items, her injury, and her broken heart. I told her I truly loved her and wanted to be with her. But I didn't know what love was. The only thing I loved other than myself was my future as an attorney. I told her I wished it could be different, but if she wanted to be with me, she'd have to choose me over the baby. I also told her if she chose the baby, that I would have nothing to do with its upbringing and would not be supporting it financially.

"Looking back, I realize I never did call the baby 'he' or 'she.' I always called our child 'it,' because that way, I could ignore the fact there was a real human inside her. Renee began to cry and, to my surprise, called my bluff. She chose the baby. As she opened the door and stepped out into the rain, she said, 'You're not sorry, Eric. You're the only person you'll ever love.' Then she slammed the door, and I never saw or heard from her again.

"I heard updates about her and the baby from time to time when I'd go home, or from friends that we had in common. That's how I found out she named our daughter Emily. But other than those sporadic updates, I was left completely out of the loop on the direction of their lives.

"That's the sad story of how Eric Stratton made the worst decision of his entire life. Some of the other stuff I've done was bad. This one topped them all. I crushed the heart and spirit of the one woman I stayed with for more than a few nights on end. Keep in mind this was the woman I stole from my best friend. In the end, I chose my stupid career over love for her. And I abandoned and forsook my own flesh and blood. I continued the pattern of selfishness and self-preservation right up until about two months ago, when I received my death sentence.

Eric exhaled loudly. "You know, looking back on this whole thing, I realize I may be dying physically right now, but I started dying inside a long time ago. I guess my body finally caught up with my rotten soul. It must truly be an amazing grace in order to save a filthy wretch like me."

Ten

Yesterday
Reconciliation with Renee and Emily Rutherford

Snow continued to fall as Roland Hughes stared out the window from the home of his elderly grandparents. It had been about a week since he stole the latest car in order to make his way back home. Once he was safely tucked away inside the house, he spent the week enjoying the benefits of being a free man. He watched TV as much as he wanted to, ate home-cooked meals, and slept for many hours of the day—all luxuries that were rare in the confines of prison.

For Roland, this would be his only opportunity to do all of these things in relative safety from being recaptured. He had a loose plan for his celebration of freedom. Roland had no intentions of turning himself in or getting caught. He planned to do whatever it was that he wanted to until he ran out of resources or someone was able to physically restrain him. He decided that in order to do that, someone would have to stop the beating of his heart in his chest.

When Roland first arrived back home in the stolen car, he had missed the local deputies by only a few hours. They came to carry out an "attempt to locate" call for him at his grandparents' house as a normal part of the investigation into the double murder in Pennsylvania. By the time he arrived and stowed the stolen car in the garage, his grandparents became his prisoners. He pressed them for all pertinent information, and they told him about the visit by the deputies.

Roland figured it would be another couple of weeks or so before they bothered to check back. One way or another, he planned to be gone by then. It was just a matter of working down the list he had prepared during his last few days in prison.

Roland's grandparents were locked away safely in their bedroom so they couldn't contact anyone. He had ripped the phone jack out from the wall and used a large wardrobe to block access to the only window. Even if they put their feeble bodies together, they would not be able to move the heavy oak chest. He finished off their home prison by tying off the bedroom door from the outside. He checked on them often enough to make sure they were okay, but he ignored their pleas for release. He would let them go eventually, but for the time being, he needed to be free to carry out this agenda and take care of the business at hand in his old hometown.

As much as he hated many and would kill almost anyone to preserve himself, he would never hurt the people who raised him. They were the only people on Earth who ever really cared for him. So he allowed them to live under his terms. Roland only allowed them out of the room when it was time for them to cook or to make controlled appearances outside (so they would not arouse the suspicions of nosy neighbors).

In order to keep them in line, Roland always kept one of them inside and threatened to kill the other if they tried to run away for help or tell anyone what was really going on. Not knowing if he would ever follow through with his threats, his grandparents obeyed his every command with no hope of obtaining help from someone outside.

Roland was proud of how much he had been able to accomplish since his release. He was able to get vengeance on his old partner and the prosecutor in Pennsylvania. The state trooper was merely a bonus victory he could claim for being able to do what was necessary in order to survive on his terms. Although news reports said the trooper would survive his injuries, he was still proud to have been able to get away from a trained law enforcement officer. For all of his life, others had determined how he would live, what he would do, and how successful he would be. Now, with a newfound boldness, Roland felt unstoppable.

He was free to relax for a while and plan his next moves. He took a long drag off a cigarette as he watched the snow pile higher outside. And then it hit him. He decided this would be as good a day as any to pick up where he left off before he was arrested six years before. Only this time, he would be successful because he had three advantages. The first was the home field. No one knew the back roads and cut-throughs better than he did. The second was the fact that he was working alone, and there was no one to mess things up or turn him in. The third was the snow.

Roland knew that not as many people would be out in the bad weather. With the snow falling, visibility would be worse even if there were witnesses around. He could even pack snow around his license plate to cover the numbers to be even more difficult to track. He also had a four-wheel drive, which eliminated many of the typical cruisers that would be able to give pursuit, should it come down to that. He'd have to put a kit together quickly, and then it would be time to go out on a hunt.

Gathering rope, duct tape, a knife, a mask, a backpack, and his stolen Ruger pistol, Roland headed out to look for his next victim. Since school was out due to the weather, he knew it wouldn't take long to find someone. It was just a matter of being at the right place at the right time. If fortune shined upon him, he might even have time to go see his old friend, Eric Stratton, and return the favor for his recent prison visit.

⌘⌘⌘

Eric awoke to the pale light coming in from outside and wondered if the snow was still coming down. It had stopped for a few hours after the trio left Marcus' house, only to pick up again during the evening. He wanted to look out the window to see how much snow had accumulated. But his body wasn't ready to respond. Eric's physical condition was quickly deteriorating, and he needed much more time to get around. His midsection ached as if pummeled by a boxer. His back and neck were stiff, and his head was now throbbing. The only things that didn't hurt were his legs. He lay there for a minute trying to get up enough motivation to roll out of bed to begin the day. The day he would hopefully see his daughter.

The thought of having a daughter was still odd to him. By now, she would be about twelve or thirteen. So many thoughts had gone into his last encounter. Although he would be completing the list, this would be the most difficult reconciliation for several reasons. First was the dynamic of having to meet with Renee. And second was the difficulty of trying to explain to Emily (if Renee would even let him) the reason for his abandonment and lack of contact for so many years. And last, if he was able to build a relationship with her in the time he had, he'd then have to break the bad news to her that he was dying. He practiced the meeting in his head many times but could never see it being a positive one. He thought back to the conversation he had with Sheila, Mike, and Randy the night before and tried to use their encouragement to push the negativity aside. Still, he was nervous.

Eric's first thoughts centered on the best way to approach Renee. He had broken her heart, abandoned her and their unborn child, and clearly chosen his profession over his love for her. Short of cheating on her, there wasn't much more he could have done to wrong her. He tried to put himself in her shoes and then tried to find the words that would speak as compassionately but urgently as possible. He decided he would start with an apology, tell her about the death sentence, and let her reaction determine where things would go from there. And as difficult as it would be to break the ice with Renee, the task of doing the same with Emily was much harder.

How would he explain his decisions to a young girl? Did she even have the capacity to understand what was going on? Would she be able to comprehend his death sentence (or should he even tell her about that at all)? The questions and hypotheses ran through Eric's mind again and again. In the end he decided it was going to end up going one of two ways: either he would be invited to be a part of their lives again, or he would be turned away to live with the horrible choices he made years earlier. Either way, he couldn't afford to spend any more time thinking about it. It was time to move.

Eric crawled out from under the warm blankets. When his feet hit the hardwood floor, he grimaced in place as they got used to the sting of the temperature difference. He grabbed the blanket off the bed, wrapped himself back up, then shuffled over to the window. The snow was still untouched in the backyard except for a small trail where Lady had gone out to make her first patch of yellow snow.

It looked like there were about six to eight inches on the ground already. Forecasters were calling for the snow to slow down and for the clouds to break by noon. The previous night, the trio decided to head out after they had a chance to eat breakfast and quickly dig out the sidewalk, driveway, and cars.

Eric headed downstairs to find that his mother was the only one awake. Pots and pans were clanging together in the kitchen, so he easily sneaked past her into the living room. He quietly walked around the house, looking at all the pictures hanging on the walls. The photos held so many memories. Some of the older shots captured his parents' lives before they had Eric and Randy. The latter ones painted a visual catalog of the boys from infants all the way through their college and career years. Every time they came together, a new picture was added to the wall. The ones taken at Thanksgiving were the newest addition to the family record. Eric smiled as he relived the ones depicting him wrestling on the ground with his niece and nephew. He hoped Emily would be added to the pictures in due time.

Eric grabbed one of the albums from the shelf and found a warm corner of the sofa near the fireplace. The album he chose contained older pictures he hadn't seen in years. As he turned the pages, he smiled at the old haircuts, out-of-date clothing styles, and good times from his childhood and teenage years. He was thankful to be able to look back and say that all of the hard times and bad choices were over. He knew the child and adolescent he had been in the pictures could finally be proud of the man he'd become.

Ironically, he was no longer proud of his life due to the vocation and material things he'd acquired. It was because he was a new man. He was glad the new man wasn't tossed to and fro like a boat in an open sea storm. He had a purpose to fulfill and lives to enrich in the last few weeks of his life.

As he flipped through the remainder of the photo album, he realized his regrets were waning. He had been successful in his attempts to reconcile with his past and the people he had once hurt. But the one that lingered the most were the two people he'd see today.

He shook his head as he once again thought of the mindset he used to live in. He was a selfish young man who was willing to forsake true love and murder an innocent so he could live the life he wanted to. He was so ashamed of those horrible decisions and so thankful to God that Renee was willing to walk away from him no matter how much it hurt. True love sometimes involves sacrifice, and Renee gave up her own happiness and future with Eric in order to protect the daughter who couldn't stand up and protect herself. If nothing else, Eric hoped he'd be able to convey that thankfulness to Renee later in the day.

As he finished looking through the old pictures, Eric found one from his college days that depicted him and Renee together. Eric had his arm around her, and they were both smiling at whoever was holding the camera. The picture brought back a flood of memories. Eric smiled as he remembered the feelings of being young and carefree. It was a time before he had made all of the horrible choices that hardened his heart. Eric pulled the picture from the album and tucked it into his pocket. He hoped that if things weren't going the way he hoped with Renee, that he could take the picture out to remind her of better times. Eric closed the album, and prayed once more for the meeting with his ex-girlfriend and long-lost daughter.

⌘⌘⌘

When Eric walked back into the kitchen, Diane was making a hearty breakfast of eggs, French toast, bacon, and fresh fruit. He walked over to the stove and put his arms around her. Diane breathed deeply and put her utensils down. She turned to hug Eric, realizing this would be one of the last times she'd have to spend alone with her son. As they stood, locked in the embrace, Diane allowed her thoughts to drift back in time.

How many times had she held her son over the years and tried to protect him from the dangers in the world? How many prayers had she lifted up for his future, his health, and a return to his faith? And now, standing in the kitchen, she realized that some prayers had to be answered with a "no" in order for others to be a "yes." That was okay with her because "no" was still an answer to prayer. And the most important "yes" she ever heard came when Eric made his profession of faith.

Finally, she had to break the silence. "Even though there were many years I longed to see you more often and had hopes you would come to your senses on some issues, I never stopped being proud of you, Eric. Sometimes I wish I could have done a little more. I love you so much!"

Diane began to quiver, and Eric squeezed her tighter. The horrible cries of sadness that flowed like a rushing spring stream made Eric long to take the pain away from his mother. But he could no more do that for her than she would be able to take away his death sentence.

"Mom, I love you, too. There has never been a time in my entire life when I didn't know you loved me and would do anything for me. I could not have asked for a more perfect mom. So don't go blaming yourself for any of the decisions I've made. I had to find my own way, even if that meant I had to come to faith the long way."

Diane turned away quickly and flipped the bacon before it burned. "I know, Son. It's just that—well, there are some things that need to be said between a parent and their child. It's something I know you will never experience, but know it's the way things are."

"Mom, don't be so sure it's something I'll never experience."

Perplexed, Diane turned to face Eric....

⌘⌘⌘

Eric knew it was time. He told his mom everything about Renee and Emily, repeating the story he had shared the night before with Mike, Sheila, and Randy. He still wasn't proud to hear the description of what he'd done coming out of his own mouth again but felt just that much "lighter," knowing he wasn't trying to hide the skeletons anymore.

"And before everyone else comes down, Mom, I want you to know something else. I want you to know that even though I've made a lot of mistakes in the last few years, I feel like God still has a plan for me. Before my time is up, He's going to use me in some mighty way, whatever that turns out to be. So just keep praying until I breathe my last breath. It's weird. I have a feeling that this is all happening for a reason; that I'll be able to serve a greater purpose before all is said and done. Who knows? Maybe I'll experience a miracle, and God will take my cancer away."

Diane smiled. "Of course He could do that," she replied. "But even if He doesn't, He's still God, and I'm proud of the man you have become. He's already brought you back to us, which makes this a little more bearable in the long run."

Just as they were finishing up, Mike, Sheila, and Jarvis emerged almost simultaneously. Jarvis reached for a slice of bacon, only to be thwarted by a quick hand-slap that caused him to withdraw his attempt. "Okay, Mama, I get the picture!"

"Are you ready for the big day?" Mike asked.

Eric nodded. "I am. I didn't think the day would come where I'd actually be ready to face up to this part of my past. Truth is, I have no pride left. No part of me is lying or putting up a front anymore. All these years, I've been justifying my horrible decisions, thinking my past would disappear with time somehow. It never did. So now I get the privilege of facing up to that and seeing two people I love face to face. So yeah, I'm ready and have been waiting for this day for nine weeks. Nine weeks or, my whole life, depending on how you look at it."

Sheila began checking Eric over, asking him about his discomfort and force-feeding him more medicine. He stared at Sheila until she turned and looked him in the eye. "Sheila, you've been so good to a dying man. Thanks for taking care of me as if I were your own husb— well, like I was family. I couldn't have done this without you." Sheila seemed embarrassed, but put down her equipment and hugged him.

"You're welcome, Eric. And you don't need to say it again. Seeing you come to the place you are today and the people whose lives you're trying to touch, well, that's a reward in and of itself. The full payoff comes today. I know you want to start this one on your own. But as soon as it's comfortable enough, I want to meet the woman who stood up to you and the daughter you've never met. Do you try to imagine what she looks like in your mind?"

"I didn't for a long time. I tried to block out the guilt by pushing away the thoughts of how old she was, where she'd be, and what she might look like. The more time that went by, the easier it was to suppress those questions with apathy. But in the last nine weeks or so, that's all I've thought about. I've worried I wouldn't have enough time to get to her. In a way, maybe it's helped me to survive this long. And here we are on the day I've been waiting for and the moment that will change my life yet again. I just hope Renee lets me see her. Isn't it ironic that her name is Emily?"

"Yes," Sheila said. "I've thought of that several times."

"I'll be proud of her no matter who she is, what she looks like, or how she reacts to me. But if she's anything like the Emily that meant so much to you, I'll be a very happy man."

"I know, Eric. Okay, before we leave, I want to make sure there's nothing else I need to know about your condition and that we have everything we need. We definitely don't want a repeat of what happened at Eddie Crowley's house."

"Oddly enough, Sheila, I feel great. I'm sure it's just adrenaline, and I'm sure I'll crash if there is a disappointment for me today. But for a dying man, I think I feel pretty good. How do I look?"

"Beautiful, Romeo," Mike said. "Well, why are we sitting around here talking this wonderful thing to death? Let's go clean off some snow and make this dream a reality!"

⌘ ⌘ ⌘

A large accident on Interstate 81 tied up many of the emergency resources in the area for quite a while. This caused Randy to come back on duty around two o'clock in the afternoon instead of having his normal 3:30 shift change.

The night before, he'd been up until the end of his shift at 2:30 a.m. listening to his brother tell stories of lost love, abandoned children, and the hope of reuniting with them both. Working on about five hours of sleep, he was exhausted, and his eyelids became heavy. Randy was slow in his patrol and finally had to pull over to stretch his legs for a few minutes. He stepped out onto the snow-covered ground and was glad to see the sun for the first time in about a week. It had been cloudy or snowing on and off for most of the week, and even with his sunglasses on, it took him a minute to adjust to the brightness.

Randy stood outside by his cruiser for several minutes, soaking in the weak winter sun and hoping people would stay inside so he wouldn't have more accidents to work. On days where there were any types of storms, criminals usually stayed inside. But there were always bad drivers on the roads. Schools were closed, allowing traffic to be kept to a minimum. His radio occasionally beeped with non-emergency calls as he drifted off into his thoughts, trying to process the last few weeks.

Randy had really enjoyed seeing the change in his brother. He witnessed a side of Eric that hadn't come out since they were much younger. He wasn't sure what happened to change him for the worse, but what Eric called his "death sentence" had put him back on the right path. That ironic fact saddened Randy a little, and he wished Eric could enjoy more time with his daughter.

Randy was thankful for his family and the perspective that caused him to cherish every moment with them. He wanted Eric to know the joy of seeing your children grow, and he hoped Eric would have a few more weeks or months to get to know her. Randy wanted to meet the niece he'd just found out existed in the last twenty-four hours and hoped someday she and his kids would meet and be able to play together.

No matter what, Randy was thankful for the time he'd been able to spend with his brother before the end. In addition to the story about Renee and Emily, he and Eric had talked the night before. They were able to apologize and forgive each other for things that had built up over the years. And now that he had his little brother back in his life, it was such an odd thought to imagine how things would be without Eric around anymore. Even though Randy hadn't seen much of him in the last few years, he knew he was still somewhere out there practicing law or whatever it was he did with his time.

But soon he wouldn't be able to pick up the phone and call Eric...ever again. The thought hit Randy hard, and he had to clear his throat in order to push the tears away. He got back in the cruiser and drove towards the interstate to take his mind off the impending sadness welling up inside him.

⌘ ⌘ ⌘

What was supposed to be an after-breakfast departure time turned into a late-afternoon adventure, as the snow took much longer to clear than expected. What was supposed to be a twenty-minute drive was stretched by the snow and a pit stop. Eric didn't want to go meet his daughter empty handed so they stopped at the local Wal-Mart. Sheila and Mike did some grocery shopping while Eric looked in the jewelry and toy sections for a few things. He settled on a soft stuffed animal and a small locket. He hoped Renee would allow him or the family to pass on a tiny picture of him for Emily to put in one side of the locket. He also picked up a card for Renee and a bouquet of flowers for each of them.

⌘ ⌘ ⌘

Roland Hughes made a sharp right turn onto a quiet suburban street and knew he'd found his victim the moment he turned the corner. On his first pass, he stared long and hard. She was an attractive young girl, between fourteen and sixteen years old, he guessed. Standing near the side of the road, she was cleaning snow off of a car. Roland smiled. Since she was petite, she could easily be overpowered if she didn't buy into the ruse he came up with on the way over. He was more careful now and checked the area for others. He noticed a man walking towards the houses nearby. There was also an SUV sitting idle on the side of the road about a block away from his intended target. He'd have to wait for them to leave.

Roland's heart pounded from the excitement of the hunt, and the reward success would bring. No one had the power to stop him, and he was finally poised to fulfill a dream that was over six years in the making. He continued down the street, then turned around and parked a few blocks away. He sat like a hawk waiting to pounce on prey from above. The man who had headed towards the houses was no longer in sight. Then he saw the reflection of brake lights on the snow, and the other vehicle passed him as it left the neighborhood.

Roland pushed on the gas and came to an abrupt stop several feet away from the teenager. He rolled the passenger window down and called out to her. "Excuse me, young lady. I was wondering if I could bother you for just a second."

⌘ ⌘ ⌘

Eric walked toward the houses in the quiet neighborhood. It seemed like a nice place to grow up, and Eric was glad that Renee had been able to find a decent place to raise their daughter. As he rounded a corner, he saw the address he thought he was looking for, although in his excitement he had left the paper on the back seat of Mike's SUV. He looked at the numbers on the house one more time and was sure he was headed to the right door. His heart was pounding, and despite the chill in the air, he was sure he was sweating under his jacket. He felt a little woozy and somewhat nauseated but wasn't sure if the cause was his health or his anxiousness over what was about to happen.

He stepped toward the door and whispered a quick prayer before knocking. After he knocked, he heard shifting on the other side of the door. He took a deep breath when he heard a lock release and then saw the handle turn. He took a step back, hoping it was Emily who would answer. To his surprise, a man opened the door, and for the first time, the thought of another male raising his daughter bothered him a little. But that thought was quickly suppressed since he'd given up his chance to be her father long before.

"Hi there, my name is Eric Stratton." Eric offered his gloved hand, which the man grabbed and shook. "I'm looking for Renee Rutherford."

"Renee who?" the man asked.

"Rutherford. She's supposed to live here."

"I don't know if she's supposed to live here, but she doesn't anymore. I moved in about two weeks ago and don't know of anyone who goes by that name."

Eric hadn't even prepared himself for the possibility that he could make it this far and have a small hiccup postpone his meeting. Thoughts began racing through his mind. What if they had moved away to some far-off state? What if they had left on early Christmas vacation and wouldn't be able to be located? What if something terrible had happened, and he was too late to meet them?

"Well, did you know the previous owner?" Eric asked.

"Yes, it was an older lady whose husband passed away. She went to go live with her family in Kentucky."

"Okay. Thanks. Sorry to bother you." Eric turned away and headed back towards the street. He reached into his pocket to call Sheila but his phone wasn't there. He realized he had left that on the seat as well.

⌘⌘⌘

Sheila and Mike had dropped Eric off near the Rutherfords' house and had driven back towards town to do a little more shopping and sightseeing. When the time was right, Eric had planned to call them back, and they would hopefully join him in meeting and speaking with Renee and Emily. As the temperature rose outside, the windshield had some sort of haze on it that the defrost would not clear up for some reason.

"Hey, can you reach into the back seat and hand me that roll of paper towels?" Mike said.

As Sheila turned to get the paper towels, she noticed Eric's cell phone and the paper with the Rutherfords' address sitting on the seat next to the seat belt latch. "Turn around, Mike. Our little genius forgot to bring his phone with him. And I think he went to the wrong address—he said he was headed for 1730 Charter Oak Place, but this paper looks like it should be 1739. He must have read it wrong in his excitement."

Mike wiped the windshield off and spun a U-turn at the next intersection.

⌘⌘⌘

Roland had to switch to plan B since the girl wouldn't buy his fake story about being lost. She seemed leery and would not take a step closer to the car. Not wanting to scare her off too quickly, Roland thanked her anyway and drove back to the corner. Now that he'd have to get out of the car, he donned his mask just in case anyone saw him.

He spun around two blocks down and floored the engine. He came to a stop one car down from where the girl was standing and jumped out. He pointed the gun at her, yelled curses, and ordered her to do what he said if she didn't want to get hurt.

⌘ ⌘ ⌘

Eric had no idea how long it would be before Sheila and Mike returned. He kicked himself for leaving the cell phone and the paper with the address in the car. But at the same time, he didn't want to go knocking on everyone's door just yet. If he had to wait for them to return, the least he could have done was call Rob to see if he could get a new or better address. But he didn't have the phone, and he'd have to spend more time waiting. It was the one thing he now despised, as it always felt like he was wasting precious time.

Just as he was about to turn the corner to head back to the spot where they dropped him off, Eric was startled by a loud, bloodcurdling scream that echoed off the buildings behind him. He ran to see what was wrong, and as soon as he walked past the house, a surreal and horrific scene stopped him in his tracks. His first thought was that it looked like a scene from some horrible slasher movie unfolding before him. Time seemed to move forward in super slow motion.

Back on the street close to the spot where he'd been dropped off, a man wearing a black ski mask was struggling with a young girl, trying to drag her into a vehicle. She continued to scream for help and got away from the attacker once, only to be chased down and overcome. The attacker continued to try dragging her to the vehicle parked nearby.

Eric's legs finally overcame the temporary paralysis, responded to his commands, and carried him towards the girl. He dropped some of his gifts along the way. Despite the snow, his health, and his subconscious desire to head away from danger instead of towards it, Eric began to run. Like an Olympic sprinter, he covered the distance between him and the insanity that unfolded before him in a few seconds. The masked man almost had the girl at the driver's door when Eric leaped off his feet and tackled him to the ground.

The masked man had no idea what hit him at first. He landed near the left front side of the car, and Eric came to rest in front of the engine. Eric made it to his feet half a second after the masked man and prepared himself to fight. That's when he finally realized the masked man was holding a gun. They both paused for a second, staring at each other as if they were about to engage in an old Western-style shootout.

But Eric was woefully unprepared for such a standoff. Adrenaline furiously pumped through his veins as the masked man raised his pistol.

Just before pulling the trigger, the masked man said, "Eric Stratton, you can't help but ruin my fun! Oh well. I guess I can cross you off my list." The masked man tilted his head to the side as his mouth twisted into a crazy smile.

In that instant Eric realized who the masked man was just before he reached up and lifted the mask enough for Eric to see his face. Roland stared at Eric for a few seconds, then pulled the mask back down. Eric couldn't think of any words that would be appropriate for that moment. They wouldn't have been heard anyway over the report of the gun firing shot after shot into Eric's chest.

⌘⌘⌘

The young girl Roland attempted to abduct wasn't able to process the situation quickly enough. But then her survival instincts and adrenaline kicked in and got her to her feet in order to run away to safety.

The man who appeared out of nowhere and tackled the attacker had given her the time she needed to escape the man in the mask. She was running towards her house when she heard a loud bang from behind. Instead of continuing to safety, she froze in her tracks. Not sure if the shot was meant for her or for the man who helped her, she foolishly turned just in time to see the second shot fired at the man who saved her.

The young girl's mother was locking the door to the house at 1739 Charter Oak Place when she heard two loud bangs and then a scream. She dropped her bags, ran towards her car, and saw her daughter standing on a small hill beside the road.

Calling out her child's name, she ran toward her…and got to her just in time to get a slight idea of the situation and the people involved. She wrapped her hands around her daughter from behind, instinctively clasping one hand over the child's eyes since she seemed unable to turn from the horror. She should have taken her daughter to safety, but she, too, had a hard time turning away. The shock of the event kept her eyes glued to it. The masked man looked like he was preparing to fire a third shot into the other man who was still standing.

Focused intently at the surreal scene on the street, she didn't see the SUV speeding towards the masked man.

⌘⌘⌘

Roland planned to fire every remaining bullet from the Ruger pistol's magazine into Eric's body. He paused slightly between shots as he tried to savor his revenge. His wicked smile grew with each shot, and he thought back to the horrible things Eric and his friends had done to him all those years ago. If revenge was truly a dish best served cold, this was the best meal of Roland's life. After he had fired two rounds from the 9mm pistol, Roland was surprised that Eric was still standing and staring into his eyes. Just before he fired the third bullet, Roland watched as Eric's lips moved, but no words came from them. He went to squeeze the trigger again, but instead of hearing the explosion of gunfire, he heard the crunching of his bones as the SUV he'd seen earlier slammed into him from the side.

⌘⌘⌘

Eric's brain was working so quickly that he was surprised by the first shot. Ironically, he wasn't thinking about how bad the bullet would hurt as it tore through his body. The first thought that crossed his mind was the irony of how small the world was. Talk about being at the wrong place at the wrong time.

Or maybe, for the first time in his life, making the right choices allowed him to be at the right place at the right time. The second bullet that exploded into him interrupted that thought. There was some pain, but the pain was overshadowed with the realization that it was not the cancer that was going to kill him. For some reason, that thought brought a smile to his face. In some strange way, it was his way of beating the cancer and making the most of his last days.

Not knowing when the next bullet would come, an odd thankfulness washed over him. He whispered a prayer, thanking God for answering his early request and allowing him to go out in a blaze of glory. He watched as Roland was about to deliver the next shot, and then strangely, Roland disappeared from his line of sight in a quick blur.

Eric fell first to his knees once Roland was gone. His focus shifted from the spot where Roland had been standing to the girl he saved. She was standing on the hill across the street from him being held by another woman. Just before he fell onto his back, Eric tried to focus on the other woman's face. He was amazed at how much the woman resembled Renee Rutherford.

Eleven

Mike slammed on the brakes and the SUV slid to a stop in the deep snow. They both quickly exited the SUV, completely ignoring the man they had just run over. As Sheila ran to help Eric, Mike ran to the top of the small hill toward the woman and the girl, both of whom seemed frozen in place.

Mike introduced himself as a pastor and ushered them away from the view of the carnage on the street. He wasn't even thinking of the possible legal ramifications of his actions. He'd have to deal with that later on. For the moment, he knew he did what he needed to in order to try to save Eric's life. He was most concerned about these two strangers and Eric.

Mike attempted to calm the young girl and her mother and asked them if they needed to go home or if they could stay and talk to the authorities who were bound to arrive any minute. They agreed to stay once some of their neighbors came out.

"That's good," Mike said. "I know this is a difficult situation, but we need your help. I'm going to go help that man down there, and then I'll be right back. What are your names?"

"M-My name is Renee. And this is my daughter, Emily," the woman answered nervously.

"Rutherford?" Mike asked.

"Yes, how did you know that?"

"My friends and I came here to see you today. Renee, you're going to have to quickly prepare your daughter for this. The man who was just shot is Eric Stratton."

All color left Renee's face as Mike ran to help Sheila with Eric.

180

Sheila had already called 9-1-1 and gave directions and a quick situation report until she had to put her phone down to help. She left the phone on speaker as she leaned over Eric to care for him. His eyes were open, and he had a pulse, but he was not responsive as she attempted to treat him. She would have moved him to a warmer place, but there was nothing close enough, and the damage was extensive. She had already removed her wool gloves and was using them to plug and put pressure on the small wounds in the front.

When Mike arrived, she had him hold the gloves in place as she lifted him to feel Eric's back. The exit wounds were much more devastating. Sheila related her findings into the open cell phone, hoping the paramedics would be better prepared when they arrived. Mike kept hard pressure on the front wounds, and they hoped his weight would help with the ones in the rear.

Miraculously, Eric was still breathing rapidly, which ruled out the possibility of a sucking chest wound. But his pulse began to weaken as his blood stained the snow beneath him.

Randy was dispatched to the area of Cedar Terrace in the Crescent Heights subdivision for several reports of shots fired, one report of a car accident, and another report from a doctor on the scene of a shooting. Randy activated his lights and sirens and despite the snow and slick roads, he arrived on the scene within three minutes. He jumped out of the cruiser and headed for the crowd gathered on the side of the road. As the first responder on the scene, people rushed to him and started yelling things left and right.

The first person Randy was able to get through to in the commotion yelled, "An armed man was hit by a car, and he crawled away!" The man pointed to some bushes across the street where the gunman was last seen. He saw that people were already helping the man on the ground. Oddly, Sheila and Mike were part of the group of people helping the man. Sheila looked up, caught Randy's gaze, and yelled, "Find the other man! He has a gun!"

Randy radioed in the splotchy information and asked for a unit to get on scene to help with the crowd while rescue arrived to take care of the man Sheila and Mike were helping. He also gave a description of the shooter and started following the blood-soaked snow between two cars and into the bushes nearby.

⌘⌘⌘

Roland was badly injured. He couldn't move one leg, and it was getting harder and more painful to see straight, breathe, and stay conscious. He realized the leg he couldn't move was missing the shoe that had been on it. He heard the approaching siren and then the commotion and shouts of what sounded like police and the rescue squad.

Roland knew it was only a matter of time before they found him. He didn't know how many rounds he had left, but he wasn't going to go down without a fight. He moved a few branches aside and got a clear view of some people in a crowd, including the girl who would have been his victim. Once again, some stupid girl had ruined it all for him. And once again, Roland blamed his actions and misfortune on someone else. If she hadn't resisted his attempts to get her in the car, he knew he would have been long gone by now. Instead there he lay, broken and bleeding, with only a few rounds of ammunition left in his pistol.

Roland was in a lot of pain, but he had just enough strength and focus left to raise his gun and take aim at the girl. He closed one eye and, although his hand was shaking, moved his finger to the trigger.

Right before he took the shot, a uniformed police officer burst through the bushes.

"Drop the gun!" the policeman shouted, as he closed in on the bloody man leaning against the fence. Instead of dropping it, the bloody man turned the weapon towards the policeman, who quickly fired shot after shot from his duty weapon until the man dropped the gun.

Roland Hughes breathed his last breath, satisfied that he kept his promise to never go back to jail.

⌘⌘⌘

Eric must not have been finished with his work just yet. He thought the beautiful sunset and the face of the angel above him were the last things he'd ever see. But five loud bangs in the distance brought him out of a dream-like state back to the chaos and pain of the present. The voice he'd mistaken to be God-like turned out to be Mike shouting directions at him. As the voice became clearer, Eric could hear the urgency in his voice.

The sights and other sounds around him also came back into focus, and the scene started to make sense again. The familiar-faced angel with the beautiful eyes turned out to be the girl he saved from the attacker. She now stood over him with a confused expression. Eric tried in vain to speak out loud to the girl, but he could only muster a faint whisper. They were about to roll him over in preparation for transport, but Eric motioned to Sheila and whispered for her to lean over him.

Eric knew that he was dying, and he didn't want to spend his last few minutes riding in an ambulance, only to die separated from the loved ones that now surrounded him. Except for his parents, they were all present, including Randy, who had appeared on the scene. Save the waning pain and slight discomfort, it was exactly the way Eric wanted things to end.

Sheila told the paramedics that she was his doctor and asked for a few minutes before they rolled him away. The paramedics, whose faces revealed the truth that there was no hope, allowed Mike, Randy, Renee, and Emily to gather around him on the ground so they could be close enough to hear him. Mike propped him up, allowing Eric to lean against him so he could breathe a little easier.

Eric whispered that he wished he had a little more time to see his daughter.

Sheila, now crying, looked across and said, "Eric, you did it. You completed your list, and you saved your daughter! This is Emily!"

Puzzled, Eric turned and realized that the woman he had seen across the street was, in fact, Renee. And the girl he'd saved from the attacker, the one who stared at him with the angelic eyes and familiar face, was also the daughter he'd abandoned so long ago.

Eric reached up to touch the young girl's face. "Wow, Emily, you're beautiful just like your mother. I'm sorry I was late, Emily, but it looks like I made it after all. I'm sorry I didn't come sooner. You deserved to have your daddy around. Please forgive me. Please forgive me."

Emily leaned over and hugged him. Saddened by the moment and trying to process the chaotic situation, Emily started to cry.

Eric reached into his pocket and pulled out the locket. He put it in Emily's hand, and she grasped it to her heart.

"Thank you, Dad." It sounded as weird to Eric coming from her mouth as it was for her to say it. "Thanks for finally making it."

Eric turned to Renee and reiterated his apologies. "I'm so sorry for what I put you through. I'm so sorry I wasn't there. Please understand that I'm a different person now, and if I had the chance to take it all back somehow, I would."

Hot tears streaked down Renee's face. She also had trouble grasping the totality of the situation. "I forgive you," she said. "I forgive you, and I'm so glad you came back. It's almost like you were supposed to be here the moment we needed you the most. Thank you, Eric, for listening to whoever it is that brought you back to us today."

Eric looked up at Randy, whose eyes welled up when they made contact. "Take care of Mom and Dad, Bro."

Randy nodded and squeezed his hand.

He then turned to Sheila and tapped on Mike's arm. "Thanks again, friends," Eric said to them. "I won't have to guess what God looks like, because in a few minutes I'll get there. You've already showed me a picture of his love through your lives. If it hadn't been for you two, I wouldn't have been able to be here. You helped me save my little girl. And I wouldn't be ready for what's about to happen. Now I'm ready."

Randy looked down and saw that Eric was holding the list in his right hand. He pulled out a pen from the pocket of his uniform and crossed off the last names from the R&R list for Eric. He made eye contact with Eric one more time, and they shook heads together, as if in agreement of a job well done.

Eric stared as the tear-stained faces of his loved ones blended in with the stars that suddenly appeared in the night sky. Just before he died, Eric thanked God for allowing him to have such a moment. He thanked Him for being able to make it just in time. And he thanked Him again for being able to end his journey in a blaze of glory. The reconciliation was over, and having completed his task, Eric was fully able to forgive himself.

It was the perfect ending to the last fall Eric Stratton would ever spend on Earth. He was barely able to utter his last words.

But a chill ran up Sheila's spine as he said, "Are you here to carry me home to Jesus? Good, because I have a few questions I'd like to ask Him."

⌘⌘⌘

Four days later, Mike stepped up to the podium and cleared his throat before he began to speak. He looked over at Eric's parents, Randy, Elaine, and the kids. His eyes then turned to Sheila, Renee, and Emily up front. Finally, before speaking, he looked lovingly at his friend, Eric. Although cancer had spread from his pancreas and ravaged his entire body, and he had sustained two bullet wounds to the chest, Mike was amazed at how good he actually looked there, surrounded by his friends and loved ones.

It wasn't a big funeral, but the people who mattered most to him were there to say good-bye. In addition to those closest to Eric, there were other people Rob had been able to reach who showed up in order to hear what it was Eric wanted to say to them. Mike and Sheila were given strict instructions to ensure they were treated well and heard the message Mike preached at the funeral. Per Eric's wishes, that message frankly spoke of Eric's realization of his imperfection, the things he learned on his journey over the last nine or ten weeks, and the importance of relationships. It also conveyed, again, his sincerest apologies for the person that he allowed himself to become (prior to his death sentence), and his thankfulness for the one he ended up learning to be. He also had thanks for the people who loved and cared for him, especially during his last fall.

Finally, Mike concluded with two requests. The first was a plea from Eric for everyone to evaluate their lives to see if they were making the most of their time, not merely pining away in selfish pursuits like he had been. And his final plea to those in attendance was a warning not to put off reconciling the most important relationships in life—the relationship with friends, loved ones, and most importantly, with God.

⌘⌘⌘

After everyone else had gone home, Mike and Sheila stood together at the gravesite of their friend Eric as the late fall sun began to set over the Green Hill cemetery in western Virginia. There Eric's body lay beside his grandfather and grandmother on the hill where Eric made his peace with himself and the Immortal and Invisible God.

"So what do we do now that we have all this time on our hands?" Sheila asked.

"Hah, good question. I have to say I've definitely learned a thing or two from our friend here. I'm sure the Lord can pass that message on to him for us. Because if I've learned one thing from him, it's that I don't want to have any regrets when my journey finally comes to an end. The first thing I'm going to do when I get back to the church is sit down with the board and discuss a few things with them. They seem to be running smoothly over there, so I think I'm going to extend my sabbatical. Call me crazy, but I'm going to China to find Lin, if it's the last thing I ever do."

"Well, I'd say that's probably the second noblest thing I've heard in the last six months. You know, coincidentally, I've been thinking about doing some medical missionary work in the great country of China."

"You don't say?" Mike said as he put his arm around Sheila. They both bowed their heads and prayed as the twilight shimmered through the wind-blown branches on Green Hill.

⌘ ⌘ ⌘

Eric Stratton and Dr. Sheila Redmond stepped off a China Eastern Airlines flight just after midnight local time at the Xianyang Airport in China. They were headed for a small village outside of Yulin to the north. Eric and Sheila followed the long line of people through the security stations until it stopped at the table marked in four languages, including English, with the sign *Customs.*

The chiseled and stern young Chinese officer had a crisp uniform and a serious look in his eye. "So Docta Redmond," he said with a heavy accent, "what is da pahpose of ya veesit to da People's Republic?"

"I'm here with permission from the Chinese government to perform medical relief work near the city of Yulin." Sheila was nervous but controlled her feelings, knowing the mission and high stakes involved with their visit. She handed her passport and official papers over to the young officer. "My team will meet me there. And this gentleman is one of my volunteers, as well as a patient. His name is Mr. Eric Stratton."

Mike passed his late friend's doctored passport to the officer. The officer squinted while glancing at the photo. Then he turned his attention to Mike. Mike smiled a cheesy smile back, which the officer returned with a scowl. Mike prayed their ruse would work. Thankfully Robert Jenkins' connection had done an excellent job with the passport, and it looked real enough to fool the officer.

And so Mike Davenport, posing as Eric Stratton, was welcomed to the People's Republic of China. The search for Mike's long-lost love, Lin, began only one month after the death of the real Eric Stratton.

Epilogue

Eric's last words

Eric Stratton had been gifted at several things before receiving his "death sentence." The first was arguing in court. The second was managing his money. When he died, Eric was worth a little over three million dollars. Many people benefited when he passed away.

Among the more notable things Eric accomplished was making sure that certain people were taken care of. The beneficiaries included not only family, but also close friends, as well as a few surprises. His daughter, Emily, and her mother, Renee, his parents, and his brother Randy were among those in his family who would not have to worry about things for a long time. He also left some money to his aunt Mary in order to take care of taxes on the family home for a few years.

Some of the surprises included people like Eddie Crowley and his parents (for his long-term care). There was also a generous grant of money designated to the Officers' defense fund in the Fraternal Order of Police given in the name of Officer Jon Jansen (as well as a few thousand dollars to more than make up for his lost time from work). A large donation also went to the New Hope Church's general fund. Sheila got a grant for her groundbreaking cancer research. Additionally, Mike would not have to worry about paying for his trip to China in order to look for his long-lost love, Lin.

Finally, Eric left a large sum of money to be used for advertisements in major newspapers like *The Washington Post, Washington Times, Wall Street Journal,* and *The New York Times.* He took out full-page advertisements that ran for two weekdays and on the weekend. Eric prayed that his story would reach a few others with a message of hope and redemption. The following is the message Eric Stratton left to the world after his last fall on Earth (the latter portions were added by his loved ones in honor of his memory):

Dear Friend,

If you're reading this letter, that means I've passed on to the other side and can't speak to you face to face. But I'm writing you a few short lines to share some things I learned in my last fall here on Earth.

So many people (including myself) say we're living for the minute and getting the most out of life. We go from job to job, party to party, or relationship to relationship seeking to fill a void that exists at the center of almost every one of us. I tried to fill that void with a career, material things, partying, and short flings. I have to tell you that lifestyle never got me anywhere. I acted like I was content. I may have been happy from time to time, but I was far from content—far from satisfied.

When I was diagnosed with terminal pancreatic cancer, and my doctor told me I only had a few months to live, I began to reevaluate my life. As I lay there in my lonely hospital room, that void at the center of my being was fully exposed. It made me realize that all of the things I pretended had value did not. I was merely existing and covering the void with things that would not fit. The void was only meant to be filled with one thing: meaningful relationships.

In my last days on Earth, I came to fully understand and appreciate the fact that we're not meant to live on this Earth alone. We were made for two very important relationships; one is with each other; the other is with our Creator.

I never really understood the power we yield to enrich or destroy the lives around us until I embarked on a journey to right the wrongs I'd committed in my past. Some of you have read about one of those wrongs in a highly publicized situation where I framed an innocent man in order to try to benefit for myself. I was wrong in that situation and many others. How I wish I could go back and change those destructive choices. They had negative effects on so many.

I wish I could have gone back in order to give that time over to a positive influence on others through meaningful relationships and a little more giving of my time. Sadly, I cannot change my past. But I'm writing this to you in hopes that you'll let this message sink in just a little, to make the world I've now left a better place one relationship at a time.

Friends, one day you'll all be where I am now. I urge you to live your lives in such a way that you won't have the same regrets I did when I found out my time was almost up. Instead of spending all my time with loved ones, I had to chase down those I had wronged in order to make amends.

And so I have this advice for you to take or leave (though I hope you'll take it) as you continue your journey. There are four things I hope and pray you'll remember from this letter:

First, cherish your loved ones. Never take them for granted, and don't let a minute go by without letting them know through words and deeds what they mean to you. Don't let true love slip away because of selfish ambition or passing desires. And treat everyone as you want to be treated; this sums up so much.

Second, be thankful for your blessings. Make the most of good fortune and your God-given talents, and enjoy life a little. But also use these blessings to enrich the lives of others. When my time came, I didn't wish I'd spent more time at work. I wished I'd spent more time in relationships. That said, if you haven't been blessed with material things, work hard, and you'll find contentment in little gains.

Third, seize the day. Your time will come to an end at some point. Spend your days not only working to live but also doing something that is meaningful to you. Live your life in such a way that you will not have regrets when your time comes.

And fourth, be reconciled to God. Take it from me; there ARE NO atheists in foxholes, convalescent wards, or on death row. Some might not have the wherewithal to acknowledge Him verbally, but in those circumstances, we all knew He was there. As I said before, we were made for two important relationships—the second happens to be with our Heavenly

Father. The pursuit of the knowledge of God has nothing to do with religion. It has everything to do with a relationship. It is possible to find God in this life and to have a relationship with the Lord and His son Jesus Christ—and it's not that difficult. All you have to do is turn to Him and accept His free gift of salvation by grace through faith. It costs you nothing, but you gain everything. Don't put this one off too long…you never know when your last day will come.

Friends, take the time today to reflect on your life. Be glad if you're already living this way. If not, ask yourself what you can do to make these important changes. Don't wait until you get a "death sentence" like I did…you may not get a few months' notice.

And remember, no matter how the setbacks and trials of life might try to say otherwise, each and every one of you was put on this Earth for a purpose. Find that purpose, and follow that course until you breathe your last breath.

Eric Stratton wrote this letter several weeks before he died. He was a native of Virginia and an attorney by trade. He was a beloved father, son, brother, and friend. Eric died protecting his only daughter from suffering and death at the hands of a deranged predator.

For more about Eric Stratton and his life and death, go to **www.thelastfallbook.com** for a copy of his story.

About the Author

JASON "JAY" BLEVINS is a husband and father of three amazing young children. He has been published in *Celebrate Life Magazine* (May-June 2007), *Calvary Chapel Magazine* (Fall 2008), and *Reader's Digest* (Short Humor March 2007). He was a contributing writer for the new *Holy Bible: Mosaic* (Tyndale, 2009).

Professionally, Jason spent five years as a defense contractor involved in the War on Terrorism. His other experiences include time spent working for the Federal Government as an Intel officer and deputy sheriff in the Washington, D.C., metro area. He has a degree in Christian Ministries and spent over five years working in youth and young adult ministries.

When he's not writing or spending time with his loved ones, Jason loves hiking, camping, fishing, canoeing, and doing anything that will keep him from growing up.

www.thelastfallbook.com
www.oaktara.com

Breinigsville, PA USA
29 November 2010
250231BV00001B/24/P